The Deputy
Gracie Island Book One
Leigh Fenty

Copyright © 2023 by Leigh Fenty

All rights reserved.

No portion of this book may be reproduced in any form without written permission from the publisher or author, except as permitted by U.S. copyright law.

Chapter One

The Deputy

P oppie watched her brother Lewis wade through the marsh toward the partially submerged car. The water reached almost to the top of his knee-high boots, and he walked slowly through the thick grass and reeds. She'd been on the front porch twenty minutes ago when the dark blue sedan swerved off the gravel road and traveled another fifty feet through the foot-deep water of the high tide.

Lewis' house sat on pilings, leaving three feet between the floorboards and the sandy ground below. It was located five hundred feet from the low-tide line on a berm, and during high tide, water surrounded it on three sides. When they got an exceptionally high tide, the berm would be underwater. He usually had warning of such an event, but he kept a rowboat tied to the porch in case he got caught off-guard.

In the waning light of sunset, Lewis reached the car and shone a flashlight through the window, then took a step back. Poppie watched him take another look at whoever was inside, then make his way to her. This time, he seemed to move faster through the water.

When he got within shouting distance, he yelled, "Call nine-one-one."

Poppie headed for the house, but as she picked up the phone, Lewis was behind her and took the receiver out of her hand. He was winded and appeared to be freaked out, which was rare for him. Of the two siblings, she was the one more likely to overreact to things. Not him.

"What's wrong?"

Lewis just shook his head as he dialed the phone. There was no cell phone service on Gracie Island. The residents were connected by underground landlines, and if you lived more than three miles from town, you needed to use a shortwave radio to get in touch with the dispatch office in the sheriff's department.

Emergencies on the island were few and far between and usually involved a medical situation, so there was only a single dispatcher working the phones and manning the radio. One worked the day shift, and one covered the night shift. Between the hours of eleven p.m. and seven a.m., the calls were routed to the chief's home number. On the weekends, the shifts were covered by several men from the volunteer fire department on a rotating schedule.

"Stan? This is Lewis Jensen. I need Chief Goodspeed right away. There's a car in the marsh next to my house." He listened for a moment. "Yeah. It's an emergency." Another pause. "Thank you. I'll be waiting for him." He set the receiver into its cradle.

"The chief's on the way."

Poppie frowned at him. "You know the nine-one-one operator?"

"Of course. Stan works the night shift. And he's probably pissed as hell to have his usual night of doing nothing interrupted."

Poppie followed Lewis to the kitchen. "So, who was in the car, and why aren't we helping them?"

"He's beyond help."

"Are you sure?"

"Pretty damn sure, yeah." He went to the sink and splashed some water on his face, then filled his cupped hand and took a drink.

"Are you okay?"

"Sure. Yeah."

Twenty minutes later, Poppie and Lewis were watching Chief Deputy Sheriff James Goodspeed wade toward the car. The tide was going back out by this time, and the water was now only ankle-deep. By the light of the chief's flashlight, they watched him open the door and examine the driver. He then circled the car, looked in all the windows, and opened the trunk. After checking the license plate, he jotted a few notes on a small tablet he pulled from his pocket before he made his way back to them.

James stomped the mud off his boots, then went up the steps onto the porch. "Tell me exactly what happened."

Lewis nodded toward Poppie. "She saw it. I was in the house."

The chief turned to Poppie. "And you are?"

"Poppie Jensen. I'm his sister. I'm visiting."

"What did you see and hear?"

Poppie took a moment to get the facts straight in her head. "I was on the porch, and I saw the lights coming down the road. I heard a loud noise I didn't quite recognize, but when the car swerved, I figured it must've been a tire blowing or the car backfiring."

"And then what happened?"

"The car went off the road."

"Did you go check on the driver?"

She looked at Lewis. "He did."

The chief took Lewis aside. "Did you see the driver?

"Yeah."

"I want you to keep what you saw to yourself. If it shows up in the Lighthouse Courier, I'll know where it came from."

Lewis shook his head. It seemed he wanted to forget what he saw and wasn't about to go tell anyone. "I won't say anything."

James put a hand on Lewis' shoulder. "I need you to go track down my deputy."

"It's the fifth, sir."

"I know what damn day it is. Just find him, sober him up, and bring him back here."

"Yes, sir. I'll go get him."

Lewis and Poppie drove into the town of Gracie, which was two streets of businesses, each a couple blocks long, surrounded by a few blocks of houses on three sides, and a wharf on the fourth. Gracie was a fishing village that had long since served its purpose. It sat on the northwestern side of Gracie Island, which was ten square miles of sand, marsh grass, and rocks. As the fishing industry changed and the once bountiful fishing areas dried up, the serious fishermen moved on. Gracie Island was now home to three hundred people, give or take, who were either unwilling or unable to leave their homes.

Every so often, a few families would move to the island. But with the unpredictable weather and the lack of jobs, most left within a year or two. Lewis came to Gracie Island six years ago to work a summer job on one of the few remaining fishing boats. He fell in love with the island and stayed on. Though he went home to Boston to visit the family a couple times a year, it'd taken the entire six years to talk his sister into coming to visit him.

Lewis and Poppie drove to a bar named The Rusty Pelican and parked out front. It was between Steadman's Groceries and the movie theater, which looked like it'd been closed for some time. All the buildings in town were built on pilings, leaving a foot between them and the ground below. Instead of sidewalks, there were raised wooden walkways. When Poppie asked about the architecture, Lewis told her, like his house, it was to protect them from occasional excessive high tides and the flooding they got a couple times each winter. The buildings were all painted in bright colors of yellows, blues, greens, and reds, which was charming despite the often gloomy weather. Poppie wondered if they did it on purpose.

She looked at the sign in front of the bar. Underneath the words "The Rusty Pelican" was a picture of a seagull.

Poppie cocked her head. "I'm no expert on sea birds, but I don't think that's a pelican."

Lewis laughed. "It's a long story."

"Do tell."

"The original owner of the bar Willy Ross, painted the sign himself. He was so proud of it, and no one in town wanted to point out his mistake. It took him a month to realize what he'd done."

"But he didn't change it?"

"He wanted to. But the town held a meeting and voted to keep the seagull. They even gave him a name." Lewis glanced at her. "Seamus."

"Willy had no say in fixing the sign in front of his own business?"

"You can't go against the town."

"That's...kind of stupid. But also charming...in a way."

"Well, look at him. He's adorable. You can't paint over that. Seamus has become a Gracie Island celebrity of sorts. He even gets his own float during the fourth of July parade."

"Your town is weird." She opened her door. "So, the deputy's a drunk?"

"No. Not really." Lewis got out of the truck. "Come on."

"He's a friend of yours?"

"Yeah." Lewis waited for Poppie to come around the front end before going up the steps to the porch. It seemed every structure had a porch. Even the movie theater. Poppie didn't ask why. She assumed it had something to do with the floods or the rain or any number of other severe weather-related phenomena.

They went inside the dark, musty bar to find only a few patrons occupying two of the dozen tables. There were three men at the bar, which had a mural of a mermaid painted on the wall behind it. The mermaid theme was carried throughout the rest of the bar, along with old fishing nets hanging on the walls, filled with plastic fish, seashells, and crustaceans.

Lewis headed for a man seated at the end of the bar by himself. As they approached his back, Poppie noted the man's broad shoulders and strong neck, as well as a head covered by a mop of brown wavy hair.

Lewis put a hand on the deputy's back. "Jasper?"

The deputy turned, and his deep brown eyes surprised Poppie. His facial hair was short and on the scraggly side, and she couldn't tell if he hadn't shaved in a few days or if he had trimmed it short to appear that way. She imagined if he smiled, he'd be quite pleasant to look at.

But instead of smiling, Jasper frowned at her, then looked at Lewis. "Hey."

"The chief needs you."

Jasper held up the drink in his hand. "It's my night off."

"Not anymore."

Jasper turned back to the bar. "Tell him to go screw himself."

"I'd rather not. But I assume if I go back without you, you'll be able to tell him yourself."

Jasper squinted at his drink, then set it down and waved at the bartender.

The bartender, with a name tag that read Mellie, walked over to him. She appeared to be in her late twenties or early thirties, with bright red hair, a nose ring, and several tattoos on her bare arms. She wore a tank top and tight jeans, and Poppie imagined she probably made very good tips.

Mellie nodded at Lewis, then turned her attention to Jasper. "You're not empty, hon."

He pushed the glass toward her. "I know. I need a coffee. Large. To go."

Jasper turned back to Lewis, then glanced at Poppie before saying, "You shouldn't have to deal with the chief on my account."

Mellie returned with a large paper cup in one hand and a glass in the other. She set them both on the counter. "The coffee won't do much. But if you want to get rid of the last few shots of bourbon, drink this."

Jasper picked up the glass and looked at it. "By 'get rid of,' you mean...?

"It's the fastest way I know of to sober up."

He sighed, eyed the brown liquid in the bottom of the glass, then downed it. He gasped, then coughed and made a face. "Shit. What the hell is it?"

Mellie smiled. "You don't want to know."

Jasper sat for a moment. "I don't feel anything."

"Just give it a minute."

He tapped his fingers on the bar, then grew pale, got to his feet, pushed his way between Poppie and Lewis, and made a dash for the men's room, which was at the end of a dark hall. Poppie watched him pull open the door as another man was leaving the bathroom. She assumed the exchange of words they had was frustration from the man and an apology from Jasper.

Mellie smiled at Lewis. "Works every time."

"How long's he going to be in there?"

"I'd give it about five."

Lewis looked at Poppie, and she mumbled, "Gross."

Mellie laughed. "Whatever works."

A few minutes later, Jasper came out of the men's room and shambled down the narrow hallway. He had his hands on the walls for support, and when he got to the end, she could see he'd gone from pale to green. Though he was hunched over, Poppie put his height a few inches over six feet. He wore jeans and a blue denim shirt that was only partially buttoned. His t-shirt underneath had writing and a logo, but she couldn't quite make it out.

A moment later, the deputy straightened, and it looked like he was about to go back to the restroom, but then he took a deep breath and nodded at Lewis. "Okay. Let's go."

Lewis studied him for a moment. "Are you sure?"

Jasper nodded, then walked unsteadily toward the door with Lewis and Poppie following. Before going out, he stopped and ran his hands through his hair. "My coffee."

Poppie sighed. "Go ahead. I'll get it."

He frowned at her again, then opened the door and followed Lewis out into the brisk night air.

Poppie retrieved the coffee cup from the bar, then hurried outside, where she found her brother standing next to his truck while Jasper got rid of a few more drinks in the high grass next to the building.

Lewis laughed at her disgust. "Fresh sea air."

"Can we make him sit in the back?"

"No. Come on. Get in."

She sighed and got into the truck, then slid to the middle of the seat. Lewis got in behind the wheel, and they waited for Jasper while he turned on the outdoor spigot and splashed some water on his face, then ran his wet hands through his hair. He straightened, took a moment to get his balance, then went to the open truck door.

He peered in at Poppie. "Who *are* you?"

"Poppie. Lewis' sister."

"Poppie? That's a weird name."

"Okay, *Jasper.*"

He climbed into the truck and sat next to her. "Mine's a family name. What's your excuse?"

Lewis started the engine. "Okay, you two. Play nice."

When they got back to the house, Jasper saw the ambulance parked next to the chief's Bronco. James was talking to Bruce Kellerman, who came over from the mainland three days a week to man the one ambulance in town. He mostly sat at the café or on a bench in the park when the weather was good and worked on a screenplay he was writing. Bruce was sure when he finished it, it'd be a blockbuster and would be his ticket to a better life.

When Lewis pulled in next to them, the chief left Bruce and approached the truck as Jasper was getting out.

James looked Jasper up and down. "Can you function?"

Jasper nodded. "Yes, sir." He glanced at his shirt and secured two of the buttons.

James looked at Lewis and Poppie. "Okay, you two. Go on inside and leave us to it. Remember what I said about keeping this to yourself."

Lewis nodded. "Got it."

James waited for them to go inside the house, then turned to Jasper. "Go take a look and tell me what you think." Jasper nodded, then took his coffee cup from the truck and drank from it before setting it on the roof.

The water was only a few inches deep now, and the marsh grass and sandy soil kept it from being too muddy, but Jasper was still reluctant to wade toward the truck. If you stepped in the wrong spot, the sand would suck your foot down, often resulting in losing your footwear while trying to pull it out. He didn't have his vehicle, in which he carried a pair of rubber boots for such an occasion. He looked at his leather lace-up boots. They'd be wet for days after this.

James gave him a little shove. "It's just water, kid."

Jasper sighed. "Right." The chief handed him a flashlight, and they headed for the vehicle.

When they got to it, Jasper looked through the window, then opened the driver's door. The man behind the wheel had a bullet wound in his left temple. Jasper's stomach lurched, and he swallowed the saliva that suddenly filled his mouth.

He glanced at the chief. "Okay. Don't see that every day. Or, in my case, ever." He shone his flashlight behind the vehicle to see the path it'd taken from the road, then at the windshield, which was intact. "Was the window rolled down?"

James nodded.

Jasper looked toward the road, which ran along a stand of red oaks and holly. "The shooter was in the trees." He glanced at the chief. "You figure someone from the mainland?"

"Can't rule anyone out at this point. But the plates are from Massachusetts."

As they headed for the Bronco, Jasper asked, "The ferry?"

"I already called Jake. Told him to cancel the morning run."

"That's going to piss some people off."

"Can't be helped. We've got a murderer loose on the island."

Jasper nodded. "Unless he has a boat."

James opened the door to his Bronco and picked up the radio. "Stan? Patch me through to O'Conner."

After a few moments, Duke O'Conner, the harbor master, came on the radio. If there was a strange boat on the island, he'd know about it. "What's up, Chief?"

"Any new boats come in over the last day or two? Or leave in the last hour?"

"No, nothing in or out for the past two days aside from the ferry."

"Okay. Thanks."

James hung up the radio receiver, then closed the Bronco door. "He'd have to be crazy to take anything small across the open water."

Jasper retrieved his cup and took another sip. "Well, we're talking about someone who just shot a man in the head." His coffee had already gotten cold in the cool night air, so he poured it out into the grass next to the gravel drive.

"Maybe he'll wash up on the beach and save us the trouble of hunting him down."

Jasper squeezed the back of his neck and tried to ignore the pain above his eyes. "But more than likely, he's still here." He dropped the empty coffee cup into the bed of the truck. "So what's next?"

"I want you to photograph the scene. Don't miss anything. Once we move the body and tow the vehicle out, we won't get a second chance."

It was pretty much the last thing he wanted to do, but Jasper nodded. The wind had picked up, and the smell of rain was in the air. On Gracie Island, the weather could turn on a dime.

James started back toward the vehicles. "Better get started before the rain hits."

The rain arrived before Jasper finished with the photos, but he'd started on the outside, so he finished documenting the inside of the car and the body. This was his first gunshot victim, and he tried not to let it affect his already queasy stomach. He'd been alright until he had to photograph the back of the man's head and what the exit wound had left on the headrest. He put down the camera and went out into the rain to get rid of what was left in his stomach.

When he finished photographing the scene, he tucked the camera inside his jacket and made a dash for Bruce, who was still waiting in the ambulance, though the wet grass made dashing more of a fast walk. Jasper got into the passenger seat to get out of the rain.

Bruce appeared to be unhappy with Jasper for getting his seat and the floor wet but didn't say anything about it. Instead, he asked, "You done?"

"He's all yours."

"Do you need a lift back to town?"

Jasper sighed. "No. I need to stay with the vehicle. Henderson won't be able to haul it out until low tide." He looked through the windshield at the pouring rain. "Hopefully, the rain will stop by then." He opened the door. "Do you need help loading him up?"

"No. I got it."

Jasper left the ambulance and headed for Lewis' porch. Under the shelter, he took a moment to figure out his next move. He checked his watch. Low tide was an hour away. The house was dark. Lewis and his sister—*What the hell was her name?*—appeared to be asleep.

There was an old couch along the wall, but Lewis' dog Hank was asleep on it. Hank was possibly the most laid-back dog that ever lived. He hadn't made a sound during the night's activities. Jasper didn't want to bother him, so he sat in a wicker chair and put his feet on the railing. He'd only gotten halfway to where he wanted to be at the bar, but he was still feeling the effects, even with the half cup of coffee and Mellie's magic potion. He tried to stay awake but realized he'd dozed off when he heard the tow truck arrive. He stood and waved at Willis Henderson, then yawned and rubbed his eyes. The fogginess in his head was almost gone. But the pain above his eyes was still there.

Willis rolled down his window and yelled across the yard. "I've got it from here."

Jasper acknowledged him with a thumbs up, then watched Willis drive slowly through the marsh to approach the vehicle. Fifteen minutes later, Willis drove out with the car loaded on his truck.

When Willis gave him a wave and kept going. Jasper said, "Oh shit," and stepped off the porch as he tried to flag Willis, who couldn't see him in the rain.

Jasper went back onto the porch. "There goes my ride."

The chief had left him there without a vehicle or a radio, leaving him no way to call the truck back. He glanced at the house and considered going inside to use the phone but decided against it.

He frowned at Hank on the old couch. "Sorry, buddy." He shook the dog awake. "Get down." The dog cocked his head, then yawned and closed his eyes. "Hey. Get down."

When the dog still didn't respond, Jasper picked up the forty-pound animal and set him on the ground. "Sorry. But I need to borrow your bed."

He picked up the blanket the dog was sleeping on and shook it out, then smelled it. The dank, musty smell was something he was used to. Everything on the island smelled musty.

With a sigh, he stripped out of his wet clothes, took a cushion from the wicker chair, and laid down on the couch. It was more comfortable than it looked, and Jasper fell asleep to the sound of the rain falling a few feet away.

Chapter Two

"You don't like me very much."

J asper woke to the sound of Poppie's gasp when she came out the front door and spotted him on the couch. He opened his eyes and pulled the blanket a little higher over his bare chest. Hank was curled up at his feet. The rain had stopped sometime during the early hours of the morning, and the fog that rolled in every day was thick, blocking the sun somewhere overhead.

Poppie glanced at his clothes in a pile next to the couch. "What are you doing here?"

"Sleeping. Or at least I was." He stretched and got a groan from Hank when his foot nudged him. "What time is it?"

"Eight."

He rolled onto his side and covered his head with his arm. "Go away, please."

"Me go away? You're the one loitering on my brother's porch."

Jasper peeked at her from under his elbow. "Loitering?"

"Or whatever."

He moved his arm and looked at her. "I didn't want to wake him up to drive me home. And I didn't want to walk home in the rain."

"The chief left you?"

"It's not the first time."

She studied the pile of clothes and then the blanket. "I hope you're not naked under there."

He almost smiled. "What's it to you?"

"Well, it's highly…inappropriate."

"More inappropriate than borrowing underwear from Lewis?"

She frowned and shook her head. "You can't wear those clothes home. They're still wet."

He peered over the edge of the couch at his damp clothing. "Around here, nothing is ever truly dry. You'll get used to it."

"Still. I'll throw them in the washer for you."

"You don't need to do that."

She picked them up. "It'll take an hour and a half. So get some more sleep. I won't bother you again."

"Can you bother me one more time with some pain relievers?"

"I'll see what I can find."

He watched her go inside. She was on the short side and petite, with straight blonde hair and fire in her blue eyes. He had at least six inches and sixty pounds on her. In a wrestling match, he could probably take her. But in a battle of words, he'd have his hands full. Lewis had mentioned his sister was feisty. His assessment wasn't wrong.

Jasper looked at Hank. "Don't mess with her."

The dog thumped his tail, then rolled onto his side and rested his head on Jasper's feet.

Poppie returned a few minutes later with a bottle of Tylenol and a glass of water.

When she handed him two pills, he shook his head. "Keep them coming."

She gave him two more and the water.

He swallowed the pills, then handed the glass back to her. "Do you ever smile?"

"I could ask you the same question."

He laid back down. "Wake me when my clothes are done."

His pile of clothing consisted only of jeans, a t-shirt, and a flannel button-up. He was still wearing underwear unless, of course, he'd gone commando. Poppie shivered. "I don't want to know." She held up the t-shirt to see the design on the front of it. It was a jaunty shark wearing a baseball cap with the words *The Gracie Island Sharks*. She threw the clothes in the washer and turned it on.

While she waited for the laundry, she scrambled some eggs and fried some bacon, and the smell brought Lewis out of his bedroom. He came into the kitchen and poured himself a cup of coffee, then looked over her shoulder at the stove.

"That's a lot of food."

"Deputy's still here."

Lewis looked toward the couch in the living room. "He is?"

"He slept on the porch. Apparently, the chief left him here last night."

"Yeah. It's not the first time." Lewis went to the table and sat.

Poppie poured herself some orange juice and joined him.

"So what's with his drinking? You say he's not a drunk, but last night tells another story."

Lewis sighed. "It's not my story to tell."

"I'm your sister. I'm not going to run to him and tell him you told me."

Lewis took a sip of coffee, then set the cup down. "And Jasper's my friend." He fingered his cup for a moment, then looked at her. "Every month on the fifth, he gets wasted. Takes a day off, then goes back to work."

"Why on the fifth?"

"On December fifth, eighteen months ago, his wife died in a boating accident. It's his way of coping."

"Oh my gosh."

"Yeah."

"Well, now I feel like a jerk."

"You should."

She got up to stir the eggs and flip the bacon. "What happened?"

Lewis shrugged. "I don't know. All I know is he was there and tried to save her."

"That's traumatizing."

"Yeah. He hasn't been on the water since. He won't even take the ferry to the mainland."

"He hasn't been off the island in a year and a half?"

Lewis shook his head and then stood. "I'll go see if he wants to eat." He poured another cup of coffee and went out the front door.

When Lewis didn't return, Poppie filled three plates and brought them to the porch. Jasper was sitting on the couch with the blanket wrapped around his shoulders and down to his knees, with Hank's head on his thigh. The deputy was cradling the coffee cup in his hands and looked like he could use another couple of hours of sleep. He also looked like he could use a comb.

Jasper frowned at her again and ran a hand through his hair as though he could read what she was thinking.

Lewis was sitting in the only other chair, so she set the plates on a table and dragged it in between them, making a loud squeal against the wooden planks of the deck. Jasper grimaced at the pain it seemed to cause and watched her pick up a plate and lean against the railing.

Jasper slid to the end of the couch, getting a sigh from Hank. "You can sit. I won't bite."

She had her doubts, but she went to the couch and sat at the other end, leaving Hank and two feet of space between them.

Jasper freed his arms and tucked the blanket around his waist, then picked up a plate. Poppie glanced at him and momentarily lost her train of thought before returning her attention to her breakfast. The man obviously worked out, but she wasn't about to let him know she noticed. Something else she noticed was that his crazy, and probably unmanageable hair, was somehow adorable.

She shook her head to clear away the thoughts of the deputy, who'd been barely civil to her. No matter how attractive he may or may not be—it was really hard to tell since he'd been drunk and hungover since she met him—he'd been grumpy and not very friendly. She'd reserve judgment until she spent time with him under normal circumstances. And when he was dressed. His not being dressed was definitely messing with her perspective.

He studied his plate for a moment before taking a bite. He glanced at her as he chewed. "Did you make this?"

"Yes."

"Not bad."

"Wow."

Lewis laughed. "I think you two got off on the wrong foot."

Neither one of them responded as they continued to eat.

After a few minutes, Jasper said, "The chief wants you guys to come into the office today and give a written statement."

Lewis set his fork down. "We told him what we saw."

"I know. We just need it on paper."

Lewis shrugged. "Okay. We can take you to town and do it then."

Jasper took his last bite of food. "Can you run me by my house first? I need to change into my uniform."

"Sure. No problem."

When they'd finished eating, Poppie took their empty plates, then glanced at Jasper.

"Your clothes are done."

He nodded, then got to his feet, holding onto the blanket. He followed her into the kitchen, then stopped when she turned and glared at him.

"Stay there. I'll get them." He mumbled something she couldn't quite hear. "What?"

He shook his head. "Nothing."

She took his clothes out of the dryer and handed them to him. "You can change in Lewis' room or the bathroom if you need to...you know."

"Pee?"

"Just go get dressed."

He didn't move. "You don't like me very much, do you?"

"I don't know you. So I can't say one way or the other. But I'm leaning towards the negative."

"Why?"

"Um. It's kind of obvious."

"Not to me."

She took a breath. "You're... Just go get dressed, please. I can't have a conversation with you...like that."

"Naked?"

"Are you?"

He turned and started heading for the bathroom. "I guess you'll never know for sure."

Poppie studied Jasper's house after he went inside to change into his uniform. It was small and fairly well maintained. The paint was a faded blue, but the white trim looked like it was recently re-painted. Like every other building in town, it had a big front porch with two wicker chairs on it. The flower boxes hanging from the porch railing were empty. And she concluded it was because his wife was no longer there to plant flowers in them.

Poppie had always appreciated the sight of a man in uniform, so when Jasper came out of his house in his khaki shirt and olive cargo pants, she tried not to react. There was a sheriff's department patch on his shoulder and the top button was undone showing the collar of a white t-shirt underneath. He hadn't shaved, but it seemed he'd tried to tame his hair a bit by combing it straight back off his forehead. His vehicle was at the sheriff's station, so when he got back into the truck, she noticed he smelled...clean. During the ten minutes they waited for him, he must've taken a quick shower.

As he pinned his badge under his nameplate, she noted his last name.

"Goodspeed? You're related to the chief?"

"He's my father."

That explained a few things. While the chief was pleasant enough to her and Lewis, he'd treated Jasper like an employee, not his son.

"So, sheriffing is the family business?"

"I guess."

Lewis looked past Poppie to Jasper. "Third generation, right?"

"Fourth. My great-grandfather, the original Jasper Goodspeed, was the first Chief Deputy Sheriff of Gracie Island."

Poppie glanced at him. "That's quite a legacy."

Jasper shrugged as a response.

When they walked through the door of the sheriff's office into the reception area, Maisy, the daytime dispatcher, came out from behind the desk and gave Jasper a hug. "How you doing, sweetheart?"

Jasper glanced at Poppie, who raised an eyebrow, then he stepped away. "Fine. Is the chief in?"

"Not yet. He's at the marina. Seems there are a lot of unhappy people wondering why the ferry isn't running."

"Does he need help?"

"He'll call if he does." She glanced at Lewis and Poppie.

"Can you get a couple of witness statement forms for Lewis and…" He looked at Poppie. "His sister."

Jasper left them in a small office to fill out their statements while he went to his office and poured himself a cup of coffee. He set the camera on the desk and turned on his computer.

His office was basic and impersonal, with an oak desk and chair, a bookshelf with procedural manuals, and a plant in a basket on the floor.

If it wasn't for Maisy, the plant would've died years ago. But with her daily watering and monthly fertilizing, it had grown to five feet.

Maisy was much more than a dispatcher. She was the glue holding the sheriff's department together. She was the first line of defense for anyone walking through the door. She handled all the paperwork, filing, mailing, and making sure it got done in the first place. Jasper didn't know how much she got paid. But whatever it was, it wasn't enough. She'd worked for the chief for twenty-five years, and Jasper had known her all his life.

Internet service was barely adequate on the island. City Hall was the only building in town that had it via a satellite dish on the roof. There was a room on the first floor with six computers available to the public. But they didn't get much use. The citizens of Gracie Island didn't much care what was going on in the rest of the world.

But for the sheriff's office, it was a necessary evil, and Jasper needed it to download the pictures he took. He connected the camera to the computer and started the process. If the signal was clear, it'd only take a few minutes.

He watched the loading circle for a moment, knowing that today, it might take a little longer. As he sat in his chair, James came through the door looking frustrated.

Jasper gave him a small smile. "How'd it go?"

"Well, considering most of the folks complaining, had no plans to go to the mainland today, it was damn pointless. You tell them they can't do something and all hell breaks loose."

"So you didn't tell them why the ferry wasn't running?"

"No. Too soon. Did you get the photos downloaded?"

Jasper nodded toward the computer. "Working on it."

James went around the desk and grumbled at the computer. "Let me know when it's done. Probably won't happen until the fog lifts."

"Will do."

He studied Jasper for a moment. "You look better today."

No thanks to you. "What's next?"

"The ferry's closed until further notice. No boats have gone out. No leads."

"Okay."

"I want you to do a thorough search through town. Check every building. Every house. He's here somewhere."

Jasper thought about the enormity of the task. "I might need help with that."

James sat on the edge of Jasper's desk. "I don't want word to get out. Might cause a panic."

"Don't the people have a right to know there might be a killer wandering around the island?"

James got to his feet. "Not yet. Get a couple of the guys from the fire department to help you. Guys you can trust not to say anything."

Jasper knew when not to argue with the chief, even when he thought the man was wrong. James had been protecting the citizens of Gracie Island for thirty years. First as a deputy, then as chief. The man had his faults, for sure. But he was good at his job.

"I'll get right on it."

"Until we have more information, keep the circle small."

"Yes, sir."

Jasper leaned back in his chair and watched the third picture slowly load on the screen, then called two of his friends in the volunteer fire department. Since fires were few and far between on an island where nothing ever thoroughly dried out, the men were anxious to help with Jasper's unspecified mission.

When Lewis and Poppie appeared at his door, he stood and took the statements from them. He glanced at them, then looked at Lewis.

"You saw him?"

"Yeah. That was a first for me."

Jasper put a hand on Lewis' shoulder. "Me too." He looked at Poppie, who shrugged.

"I didn't see whatever it is everyone's trying to keep from me."

"Trust me. It's better that way." She didn't seem convinced, but she refrained from commenting further.

Lewis nodded toward the guitar sitting in the corner of the room. "You going to be at The Loft tonight?"

"Friday night. Of course."

"Poppie might like to see what Gracie Island is all about."

"See you there." Jasper went back to his desk. "And bring your harmonica."

Poppie waited until they were in the truck before she said, "Please don't tell me you play the harmonica now."

"You're going to love it."

"Any music with a harmonica in it is…"

"Just wait and see. Jasper's one hell of a guitar player. And he sings, too."

She shook her head. "Of course he does. What kind of music is this?"

"I'll let you be surprised."

As they drove by the wharf with the empty ferry tied to it, Poppie asked, "So, how long are they keeping us prisoners on this island?"

"Prisoners? Come on. It's not that bad. You aren't scheduled to leave until Wednesday."

"I know. But when I know I can't leave, it makes me feel…trapped."

"Wow. I like you, too."

She put a hand on his arm. "I love visiting you. I'm just not so sure about your island."

"You'll miss it when you're gone."

"Hmm. Doubtful. Will the ferry be running by Wednesday?"

"There will be a lot of pissed-off people if it isn't."

Chapter Three

The Sailor's Loft

Despite her protestations, Poppie was looking forward to going out with Lewis. She was interested and a little excited to see what the nightlife on the sleepy island looked like. And how could she not be a bit curious to see grumpy Jasper singing and playing the guitar? He was probably really good, which would make it harder for her to continue to dislike him.

When they pulled up to The Sailor's Loft, she was surprised by the turnout. The parking lot was full, and more cars lined the street. "Is everyone in town here?"

"No. Only about a quarter of them." He stopped behind a car pulling out, then parallel parked across the street from the restaurant.

The restaurant was in a huge clapboard building that looked like it'd been there a while. It was painted a light blue with white doors and shutters. There was a huge wooden flagpole out front that resembled a ship's mast, with the American flag flying from the top of it. The big front porch had a few tables, all occupied, and the front doors were open. Below the flashing neon "The Sailor's Loft" sign was a smaller one that read, "A family-owned restaurant since 1975."

"Who owns this?"

"Kat Goodspeed."

"You're kidding."

"Jasper's mom."

"So, does the chief hang out here?"

"No. They've been divorced since Jasper was in high school."

When Poppie opened the car door, she could hear the music coming through the front doors, and she looked at Lewis.

He smiled. "It's cool, right?"

"What is it?"

"Sea shanties. Songs passed down for generations."

"Okay. That's interesting." And not at all what she was expecting.

"Come on."

As they passed the mast, Poppie noticed a large bell mounted on it with a braided line hanging from the clapper. Above it was a sign that read,

Twilight and evening bell

And after that the dark!

And may there be no sadness of farewell.

When I embark.

"What's that for?"

"The words are from a Tennyson poem called, 'Crossing the Bar.' Every time you go past the bell, you ring it once for everyone you've lost to the sea."

"Sailors? Fishermen?"

"Anyone."

Poppie took a moment. "So does Jasper—"

"Yeah. Every time. Actually twice. His great uncle went down in a storm in the eighties. Twenty men on his boat all lost their lives. It was a major loss for the town. And it was the beginning of the end to the fishing trade."

"My goodness. How sad."

The interior of the building was divided into two areas. There was a large dining room with patrons at several tables who seemed to want to hear the music from a less frantic environment. Through a large archway with swinging doors was the packed bar. The music coming from the stage at the end of the room was loud and lively, and everyone was enjoying it and singing along. Every table was full, and it was standing room only along the back wall.

Poppie leaned into Lewis' ear. "There's nowhere to sit."

He took her arm. "I called Deidre. She saved us a couple of seats at the bar."

"Deidre?"

"Bartender." At Poppie's raised eyebrow, he added, "She's just a friend. Pretty sure she has her eyes on Jasper."

They made their way through the tables, and Lewis made eye contact with Deidre, who pointed at two seats with used glasses on napkins in front of them. They sat and pushed the drinkware toward the back of the bar. Once Poppie sat down, she checked out the three musicians onstage. Along with Jasper on the guitar, there was a man playing banjo and a woman on the piano. Poppie watched Jasper. He was thoroughly enjoying himself, and she finally got to see him smile. She'd guessed right. He was quite pleasant to look at. She listened to him singing. *Well, aren't you just full of surprises?*

Lewis nudged her. "Don't go there. You'll only get your heart broken."

She turned to him. "I have no aspirations about Deputy Goodspeed."

"Mm-hmm. I know you, sis."

"He's surly. Annoying at best." *But look how cute he is up there playing his guitar.*

"Just how you like them. The more annoying, the better. And don't think I didn't see you checking him out on the porch this morning."

She shook her head. "I certainly was *not* checking him out."

"Whatever. But as long as he's still getting drunk every month on the fifth, he's not ready to move on."

"I don't care."

When Jasper noticed them, he gave her a nod and waved Lewis to the stage.

Lewis got to his feet and called Deidre over. She was tall and pretty in an over-made-up sort of way, with shoulder-length hair highlighted with varying shades of blonde. Poppie was instantly jealous.

Deidre smiled at Lewis. "What'll you have?"

"Can you get Poppie a rum and coke? And I'll take a beer. But hold on to it until I get back." She started to leave but stopped when he said, "And Deidre, keep an eye on my sis. Make sure none of these barnacle rats bother her."

She nodded. "Sure thing."

Lewis patted Poppie on the arm. "Save my seat." He headed for the stage to join the others. After shaking hands with Jasper and waving at the crowd, he took out his harmonica and began playing.

Once again, Poppie was impressed. "Son of a B."

Deidre returned with Poppie's drink and leaned toward her over the bar. "They're good, right?"

"Fantastic. I had no idea my brother was in a band, or whatever that is."

"I keep telling Jasper they need to name themselves and make it official."

Poppie nodded and smiled. She wasn't sure why she was jealous of a woman she didn't know over a man she didn't even like.

The musicians continued playing for another half-hour before a woman, who Poppie knew had to be Jasper's mother, stepped onto the stage. She had the same deep brown eyes, and brown wavy hair pulled up into a loose bun with just a few strands of gray. The band finished their song, and she went to the microphone next to Jasper. She was several inches shorter than her son, which surprised Poppie. The chief wasn't all that tall, either. Their son had passed them both by several inches.

Kat put an arm around Jasper and kissed him on the cheek, then spoke into the mic. "Sorry to interrupt the music, but last call for food. The kitchen closes in thirty minutes. Of course, the bar is open until one."

The crowd, who apparently was more interested in the bar, cheered.

Jasper put his hand on the microphone. "Before we take a break, who wants to hear our favorite Gracie Island restaurateur sing a ballad?"

The crowd erupted again, and Kat waited until they quieted down. "Only if my son accompanies me."

After another favorable response from the crowd, Jasper started playing, and when Kat started singing, he came in with the harmony. It was beautiful, and Poppie was beyond impressed.

When Lewis returned to the bar and sat next to her, he said, "Uh oh."

She glanced at him. "What?"

"That did it. You're in love."

She punched him in the arm. "Shut up. It's beautiful. Don't ruin it."

When the song was over, the musicians left the stage, and Poppie watched Jasper greet half the people in the bar before making his way to her and Lewis.

He leaned toward Lewis' ear. "Sarah was asking about you."

Lewis glanced at the stage toward the piano player, who was looking through some sheet music. "Really? We've only talked about music. I thought maybe there was something there, but I wasn't sure."

Jasper nodded toward the stage. "Go find out."

Lewis took a couple of swallows of beer. "Okay." He looked at Poppie. "You going to be okay?"

"Between your bartender friend and the deputy, I think I'll be safe."

Jasper watched Lewis until he approached Sarah, then smiled at Poppie. "What did you think of the music?"

"It's very cool. I loved it. And your mom... Awesome."

"She is pretty awesome."

"Deputy Goodspeed, your little island is starting to grow on me."

"It does have its charms."

When a dark-haired woman came up to Jasper, Poppie noticed an instant change in his demeanor as he lost his smile. She was a few inches taller than Poppie, a little overweight and didn't appear to be related to him. But he definitely knew who she was.

The woman put a hand on his arm. "Great set tonight, Jasper."

"Thanks."

"Are we going to see you for Sunday brunch?"

He sighed. "Not sure. I'm working on something for the chief."

"Okay. If you can, we'd love to have you. The kids miss you."

"Yeah. I miss them, too. I'll try."

The woman left, and Poppie asked, "Family?"

"My sister-in-law."

It didn't seem as though he was going to volunteer any more information, and she knew better than to let on she knew anything, so she decided to change the subject.

"How's the case going? Any leads?"

He looked at her for a moment. "I can't really talk to you about it."

"Hmm. I guess I get that. Even though I'm the one who saw it all go down."

He gave her a small smile. "I guess you've earned the right to some information. Unfortunately, I don't have any to give you. I spent the day canvassing the town. Talking to people. Looking in every nook and cranny."

"Didn't find anything?"

"Zilch."

"So what now? Do you think he's still on the island?"

"No one has left. Unless he took a small boat or swam, he's still here."

Deidre came up to them and smiled at Jasper. "Lewis told me to keep an eye on his sister."

Jasper raised his hands. "Just talking shop."

She laughed. "What can I get you?"

"I'll take a Coke." He looked at Poppie. "You want another?"

"Sure. Rum and Coke." Poppie recognized flirtation when she saw it. But it was all one-sided. Jasper seemed oblivious to Deidre's affection for him.

Deidre left to get their drinks, and Poppie looked at Jasper. "That's unsettling. The fact he could still be here."

"I truly don't believe it was a random act. Don't let it keep you up at night. If he's here, we'll find him."

She finished her first drink. "How many murder cases have you worked?"

"Um, one."

"This one?"

"Yeah."

Deidre delivered their drinks, and Poppie tapped her glass to Jasper's. "To getting the bad guy."

"Hear, hear."

She watched him take a sip of his Coke. "Still recovering from last night?"

"Despite your first impression of me, I'm not that much of a drinker."

"I guess it might affect your job performance."

He shrugged. "The chief manages."

"The chief is a...drinker?"

He leaned in close and lowered his voice. "The chief is a high-functioning alcoholic."

"Goodness."

"We keep it on the down-low. Not too many people know. Although it's hard to keep something like that quiet around here."

"I'm sorry."

"He made the choice."

Between sets, the music came from a jukebox near the bar. When Deidre came up to Jasper with a smile, he looked at her.

"What's up?"

"I taught you to dance to this song."

He listened for a moment. "Nah."

"I most certainly did." She walked around the end of the bar. "Come dance with me. For old time's sake."

He shook his head. "I don't think—"

"Come on. It's one dance." She pulled him to his feet.

"Don't you have a bar to run?" Jasper glanced at Poppie, then allowed Deidre to pull him to the small dance floor with three other couples on it.

As Poppie watched them dance, Lewis came up beside her. "What's going on there?"

"She said it was the song he learned to dance to. With her."

Lewis watched Jasper and Deidre for a moment. "I think he needs rescuing."

"He looks pretty happy to me."

Lewis nudged her. "Go cut in. Trust me, the last person he wants to dance with is Deidre."

Poppie stood. "Fine. But if he gets mad at me for interrupting, I'm blaming you." She went to the dance floor and tapped Deidre on the shoulder. "Can I get in on this, please?"

Deidre gave her a curt smile. "Sure." She patted Jasper's chest. "Thanks."

Jasper watched Deidre go, then looked at Poppie.

She sighed. "It was Lewis' idea. He said—"

"Thank you." Jasper put his arm around her waist and took her hand.

"Really?"

"Yes. Deidre's the last person in the world I want to dance with."

"Hmm. I would've thought that was me."

He smiled. "You're the *second* last person I want to dance with."

"So, does this mean you don't hate me?"

"Hate you? Who said I hated you?"

"Maybe hate is too strong of a word. How about you find me annoying?"

"Well, yeah. That's true." The song ended, and he took a step back from her. "Thanks for rescuing me."

"You're welcome. You owe me one."

"I'll remember that."

He walked away, and Poppie remained standing in the middle of the dance floor until she felt a hand on her arm. She turned to see Sarah.

"The song's over, honey."

"Oh, right." She headed for the bar, and Sarah followed her.

"You know our deputy is…off the market, right?"

"Yes. I know." Poppie noticed Sarah watching Lewis across the room. "However, the harmonica player is quite available."

Sarah smiled at her. "I'm Sarah."

"Poppie."

"Your brother is very—"

"Cute? Please, just say cute."

"Adorable."

She left to join the others on the stage, and they played another set, shorter than the last but just as good. When they finished, both Lewis and Jasper returned to Poppie at the bar.

Deidre handed them both a fresh beer, and Jasper took a sip before asking, "So, how did it go with Sarah?"

"We're going to brunch Sunday after church."

Poppie shook her head. "Does everyone do brunch on Sundays?"

Lewis laughed. "It's a Gracie Island thing. You go to church. You do brunch. If you've got family, you do it at home. If you don't, you come here or go to the Cove Café."

"Wait a minute. Since when do you go to church?"

"I don't. It's not a prerequisite to go to brunch."

She looked at Jasper. "Do you go to church?"

He shook his head. "I don't go to brunch, either."

"And what happens after brunch?"

Lewis smiled at Jasper. "Softball!"

"You guys play softball?"

Jasper took a sip of his Coke. "Every Sunday, rain or shine."

"Year-round?"

Lewis shook his head. "No. We take a few months off in the winter. When the winds blowing sideways, it's kind of hard to pitch the ball."

"You guys are crazy."

Jasper looked at her for a moment. "There are a lot of hard-working guys here. It gives them a chance to blow off some steam."

"Okay. I look forward to watching you guys in action." She looked at Lewis. "You still pitching?"

Jasper put a hand on Lewis' shoulder. "Lewis is our ringer. Best ball player in town."

Lewis played varsity baseball in high school for three years, and several colleges tried to recruit him. But Lewis had chosen not to go to college.

Poppie smiled at her brother. "He's the best, all right."

Lewis took a few steps back from them. "Okay. Enough ass-kissing."

Chapter Four

The Lighthouse

Every Saturday, Jasper took the road that took him across the island. There were three residences along the route occupied by people who valued their privacy and rarely got into town. Jasper was their link to civilization. He brought them supplies, any current local news, and some much-needed conversation.

Today, however, he had a second agenda. If the shooter wasn't hiding in town, maybe he was in the wilds, which is what the islanders called the unpopulated areas. There weren't many places to hide, though. It was mostly grass with a few stands of white oak. The terrain was flat, with the elevation varying less than fifty feet over the entire island.

This made the island susceptible to the storms that came off the open water at the east end. They'd been hit by two hurricanes over the last fifty years. Both were glancing blows, which the town survived, but the damage had been severe. The hardy citizens of Gracie Island rebuilt, and the last big storm was thirty years ago. Some in town said they were due for another.

Jasper took the road from town to Harper's Fork. If you turned left, you went to the small cluster of homes where Lewis lived. To the right was Lighthouse Road. It divided the island in half and ended at the lighthouse on the east side.

He turned right and headed down the rough road. A quarter-mile past the fork, he spotted a truck up to its axles in the mud along the side of the road. He recognized the truck, and he pulled over and got out of his Jeep.

"Lewis, you in there?" When a blonde head appeared in the window, Jasper grinned. "What are you doing there, Poppie?"

"What's it look like I'm doing?"

He rubbed his chin. "Looks like you're stuck in the mud up to your ass."

"Can you pull me out?"

He shook his head. "Not with this. I can call Willis, though."

She rolled the window the rest of the way down and rested her arms on the door. "Willis?"

Jasper moved to the front of the Jeep. "Tow truck driver."

"How long will that take?"

He folded his arms across his chest. "Well, I guess it depends on how busy he is."

"How busy could he be?"

"Again, depends on how many tourists take a wrong turn and end up in the mud."

She glared at him. "I'm not a tourist."

He returned to the Jeep and opened the door.

She leaned out the window. "Where are you going?"

"Just calling Willis on the radio."

Jasper left a message with the weekend dispatcher, then got out of the Jeep again. "Might be awhile."

"Will you stay here with me?"

Jasper checked his watch. "I've got things to do. I'm on the clock."

She frowned, then seemed to change tactics. "Please don't leave me."

He smiled. "Hold on." He went to the back of the Jeep, removed his lace-up boots and, put on a pair of knee-high rubber ones, then walked to the edge of the road.

"What are you doing?"

"I'm rescuing you. I owe you one, remember? I can't wait here for Willis. But I can take you with me."

"Where are you going?"

"You're not really in a position to complain."

She looked at the mud. "Fine."

Jasper stepped into the mud and sunk several inches. He made his way to her, then opened the truck door.

"Okay. Come on." He held his arms out.

"What do you mean?"

"I'll carry you to the road."

She laid her head on the back of the seat and bounced it a couple of times.

He backed up. "If you'd rather walk…"

She sat up. "No." She frowned at him. "Fine."

He moved to the door, and she put her arm around his neck as he put his arms around her shoulders and under her knees.

He lifted her with a grunt. "Whoa. You're heavier than you look."

"What?"

He started laughing. "Just kidding. You're actually surprisingly light. What are you? One-ten? One-twenty?"

"I'm not telling you that."

He carried her to the road but didn't set her down.

She kicked her feet. "What are you waiting for? Put me down."

He took a moment. "It seems I should be able to take advantage of the situation somehow."

"Take advantage? Really Deputy Goodspeed?"

He set her down. "You're lucky I'm friends with your brother."

She moved a few feet away from him as she tugged on her t-shirt and straightened her jacket. "You're not very nice."

"I just rescued you." He hadn't noticed until now, in the light of day, how blue her eyes were.

"In retrospect, I think I would've preferred to wait for What's His Name, the tow truck driver."

He stepped toward her with his arms out. "I can put you back."

She held up a hand. "Don't come near me."

He laughed. "You're in no danger, Miss Jensen."

"I wasn't worried." She looked at his boots. "Are those standard island wear?"

"If you're going to spend any time here, you need to invest in a good pair of Wellies."

"I'm not planning on staying around too much longer."

He removed his rubber boots, banged some of the excess mud off, then put them into the Jeep. While he put his leather boots back on, he looked up at her.

"Where were you going?"

"Into town."

"You took the wrong fork."

"I know that now. Can you take me back to town before you go on your secret mission?"

"No. Like I said, I'm on the clock. You're welcome to come along. Or you can wait here for Willis to show up." He pulled his pant legs down over the top of his boots and stood.

She glanced at the truck. "We can't just leave it here."

"Of course we can. Not a lot of vehicle theft on the island. Especially seeing as everyone knows what everyone drives. Besides, Willis is the only one who can pull it out of there."

"So, where are we going?"

He opened the passenger door for her. "To the lighthouse."

"There's a lighthouse?"

He closed her door and got in behind the wheel. "I make this drive every Saturday to check on the residents who live out here."

"People live out here?"

"A few. Town's too crowded for them."

"Crazy."

"Most of the people on the island would say you're the crazy one living in Boston."

She shrugged. "To each his own."

He laughed but didn't respond as he started driving.

"So, if you're on the clock, why aren't you in uniform?"

He put his hand on his gun between the seats. "I'm partially in uniform."

She frowned at the gun. "How many times have you shot that thing?"

"I go to the range a couple of times a month."

"How about in the real world?"

He sighed. "Never. I've pointed it a few times. But not here."

"Where then?"

"I had to go to the police academy in Augusta, then spent six months working with the PD there before I applied to work for the sheriff's department."

"Hmm. I thought you got the job because your father was the chief."

"Fifty years ago, maybe. I got the job in spite of my father. Or perhaps it was *to* spite my father. Not really sure."

Poppie buckled her seatbelt as she watched Jasper expertly maneuver the Jeep along the rough road. He handled the manual transmission like a pro, and she couldn't help but be impressed. Lewis had tried to teach her to drive a stick shift a few years ago, but she hated it and gave up trying after the first lesson.

"So, who's first?"

"Sam Jeffers. He lives by himself and is pretty cranky to anyone who bothers him."

"Even you?"

"No. I bring him whiskey and cigarettes."

He turned onto a smaller road, even rougher than the main one, and bounced along for a half-mile through the trees. When they reached a clearing, Poppie saw a rundown house and a couple of outbuildings. There was also a pen with four goats and a chicken coop with a dozen chickens pecking in the grass.

Jasper pulled up to the house and turned off the motor. "Stay here."

"Seriously?"

"Yeah. Like I said, Sam doesn't like visitors." He got out of the Jeep and retrieved a bottle of Wild Turkey and a case of cigarettes from the backseat. "I'll be right back."

Poppie watched him go up the rickety steps and knock on the door. A few moments later, a man with a full beard and long scraggly hair opened it. He nodded at Jasper, then looked beyond him to the Jeep.

Poppie gave him a small smile.

She couldn't hear what he was saying, but he seemed to be unhappy Jasper had brought her with him. After a moment, Jasper calmed him down and handed him his whiskey and smokes. After a few more minutes of conversation, Jasper returned to the car.

She looked at him. "Is everything okay?"

"Yeah."

"He didn't look happy."

"Sam's never happy." He turned around and headed for the main road. "The Redfords are gone for the summer, but I want to check their property before we head to the lighthouse."

"For a man with a gun?"

"Hopefully not."

Two miles down the road, they took a second turn and went another mile to a clearing. The Redford's house was small but in better shape than Sam's. They also had goats and chickens, along with three horses.

Poppie got out of the car. "Who's feeding the animals?"

"Sam takes care of them. He *likes* animals."

She took a cloth band from her wrist and pulled her hair into a ponytail, then went to the horses. A big bay came to the fence, nodded his head at her, and she patted his nose.

Jasper came up behind her as he clipped his holstered revolver to his belt. "You like horses?"

"Everyone likes horses."

"Not really."

She turned to him. "You don't?"

"I don't *not* like them. I'm just not going to go out of my way to spend time with one."

"Just pet his nose. He's lonely."

Jasper sighed, then ran a hand down the horse's muzzle. "There. I'm going to go check the house."

She kissed the horse on the nose, then followed him. "I'm coming with."

He took a flashlight out of his pocket, then opened the door.

Poppie looked at the dark house. "No electricity?"

"Just a generator." He stepped inside and switched on his flashlight. "Lewis' neighborhood is at the end of the electrical grid. No electricity, phone service, or radio signal a mile past the fork."

The living room was small and sparsely furnished, and they went from there to the kitchen, which had basic amenities and a table in the corner.

She looked at the empty counters. "Are you sure they actually live here?"

"Pretty minimalistic, for sure." He headed for the closed bedroom door. When he opened it, a black blur jumped through the door, then charged across the floor and out the front door. "Holy shit!"

Poppie laughed. "Is the big bad deputy afraid of the little puddy tat?"

"That was a feral puddy tat, who'd just as soon scratch your eyes out as look at you."

She watched the cat through the open front door as it ran for the brush. "How'd he get inside?"

"Probably through an open window." Jasper shone his light around the room. Like the rest of the house, it had very little furniture.

He went back to the living room. "Looks clean and unbothered."

"No bad guy?"

"Not here."

They went outside, and Jasper closed the door. "Go say goodbye to the horses. Time to move on."

Poppie went to the corral and gave the horse a final pat, then joined Jasper in the car.

"Now, the lighthouse?"

"Yes. The Andersons are gone, too, though not on purpose. They're stuck on the mainland until the ferry starts up again."

"So, this is more of a checking property than checking residents trip."

"Yeah. Along with making sure there haven't been any outside visitors."

"Right. So if no one is expecting you, you could've taken me back to town."

"I suppose. But it wouldn't have been nearly as fun."

They continued down the road for another three miles, and as they cleared some trees and came over a small rise, the lighthouse became visible, appearing to be another half-mile away.

Jasper slowed down. "There it is."

"Wow, that's beautiful."

The road got worse, and Jasper continued slowly as he avoided potholes and muddy spots.

Poppie leaned forward to see the fifty-foot-tall stone structure through the windshield.

"How old is it?"

"It was built around the turn of the century. 1910, I think. Lost several ships out there in the shoals before they put it up. One of the old stories is before the lighthouse was built, they'd send a man out to the edge of the rocks with a lantern during the big storms."

"Seems a little inadequate."

"Probably lost a few guys, too. Even if they didn't get swept off by a wave, they probably later died of pneumonia."

"Nice story."

Jasper pulled in front of the stone house a few hundred feet from the lighthouse.

"The original lighthouse was made of wood, but it was partially destroyed during the last hurricane. My grandfather was a stonemason, and he helped rebuild it. This time out of stones and mortar. He also built the Andersons' house." They got out of the Jeep. "They do lock their doors, so we can't go inside. But I'll check to make sure no one has broken in."

He went to the front door and tried the knob. Finding it still secure, he moved to the big window at the front of the house.

Poppie came up next to him, pulling the long strap of a cloth purse over her head, hanging it from one shoulder.

Jasper watched her adjust it. "You can leave that in the Jeep."

"My phone's in here."

"Your phone is useless anywhere on the island."

"I know. Which is pretty…third world country. But I can still take pictures."

"And you say you're not a tourist."

She peered through the window. "Oh my gosh. It's like a museum in there."

"It's quite impressive."

"Is that a…whale's—"

"Jaw? Yes. Jack has found some crazy things washed up on the beach."

"He made a couch out of it?"

"Jack has a lot of time on his hands."

They continued around the house, and Poppie peered into another window.

"So Jack's the lighthouse keeper?"

Jasper tried the back door. "In a manner of speaking. He gets to stay in the house and earns a small stipend from the county to keep an eye on it. It's automated. But Jack makes sure it keeps working. Keeps the batteries charged. Washes the windows."

Poppie looked at the top of the lighthouse, which had windows all around it. "That's a full-time job. What does Mrs. Anderson do?"

"She's an author. Pretty well-known, actually. Bindi Anderson. She writes romantic adventures set in nineteen-century New England."

"Well, she's practically living in the nineteenth century, so that's appropriate."

Jasper looked at her. "You don't like our island very much, do you?"

"I like it fine. I just wouldn't want to live here."

Chapter Five

"Why does he smell like cookies?"

After checking the house and finding everything secure and untouched, Jasper and Poppie walked to the lighthouse. They followed a gravel path through rocks made round and smooth by centuries of waves breaking on them. The lighthouse itself was built on a house-sized boulder jutting twenty feet into the ocean. An occasional large wave would break over the rock foundation, leaving small pools of water in the depressions along the surface. Poppie and Jasper took the four steps carved into the rock, then walked along the top of it to the lighthouse door.

Poppie took a few pictures of the lighthouse with her phone, then turned toward Jasper.

He held up his hand. "Don't even."

"Are you afraid I'll take your soul?"

"I just don't like my picture taken."

"Well, that's a shame. Don't you want to have something to show your children someday?" As soon as she said it, she wanted to take it back. She glanced at him, but he didn't seem to react how she thought he might.

"Not planning on having any kids."

She thought it best to let the subject end. So she dropped the phone into her purse, then tried the door. When she found it locked, she said, "Oh darn. I wanted to go inside."

Jasper dug into his pocket and pulled out a key. "This, I have a key for."

Poppie looked at the key ring with two keys on it.

"What's the other one for?"

Without answering her, he unlocked the door and opened it. Poppie went inside, and he followed.

"Why do you have a key to the lighthouse?"

"It's county property. And if something happens to Jack, someone has to come and make sure the light keeps working."

"Like getting marooned on the mainland?"

"Yeah. Like that. And I don't want to be the guy holding the lantern on the rocks if the lighthouse goes out."

A motion-activated bulb came on and lit the circular space with only a spiral metal staircase in the middle of it. They had plastered the inside of the stone walls to make them fairly flat and painted them white, making it brighter inside. A built-in wooden bench ran along the wall, starting on one side of the door and ending on the other. Above it was a mural running the length of it, depicting seafaring life a few decades ago.

Poppie looked around. "This is so cool. Who painted the mural?"

"I have no idea."

She smirked. "I thought you knew everything about this island."

He shrugged. "No one knows. It's a mystery."

She wasn't sure she really believed him but didn't question him further. Instead, she went to the staircase and looked up. "Can we go up there?"

"Are you sure you can handle it?"

"Of course. I go to the gym once in a while." The stairs that seemed to go on forever intimidated her, but her curiosity won out. "Can *you* handle it?"

Jasper started up the stairs, and Poppie followed him. Halfway up, she stopped to catch her breath, then frowned at Jasper when he turned and grinned at her. The fact he didn't appear to be tired at all was annoying, and she tried to slow down her breathing.

She smiled. "Mr. Anderson must be in great shape."

"Do you need to sit down? Take a nap?"

"Shut up." She pushed past him and continued up the stairs. Despite her burning leg muscles and her pounding heart, she didn't stop until she reached the top. The view was worth the effort. From the top of the lighthouse was a three-hundred-sixty-degree view of the ocean and Gracie Island. "Son of a B. This is incredible." She tried to catch her breath without letting on that she felt like her heart was going to jump out of her chest.

Jasper smiled. "So, I take it you're not a cusser."

She ignored him and went to the window facing the ocean. There was a dark bank of clouds directly in front of them but out several miles. Every few seconds, a bolt of lightning flashed through the clouds.

"Goodness. That's beautiful. And a bit scary."

"It's headed this way."

To Poppie, it seemed too far away to be of much concern. "So, anything else out there?"

"France is only three thousand miles away."

"Have you ever been?"

"Nope."

She turned to him. "How can you spend your whole life on this tiny island?"

"Easily. I've no desire to go anywhere else."

She turned back to the window. "You don't know what you're missing."

He stepped up next to her to take in the view. "Maybe *you* don't know what you're missing."

She circled the light in the middle of the space and looked at the endless ocean and then the island. She stopped and studied the land below, trying to figure out where everything was. Jasper came up behind her and stood close enough to make her feel uncomfortable. He smelled good, but she couldn't quite figure out what it was she was smelling. Was it…cookies? *No, that can't be right.*

She glanced back at him. "So, where is town?"

He pointed slightly to the left. "Town is there." He put his hands on her shoulders and moved her to the left. "If you move over a foot, you can see the marina through the trees."

Why does he smell like cookies? And why is that so appealing? She cleared her throat. "So then, Lewis' house is…" She pointed to the right of the marina. "That way?"

"Yes." He put a hand on her arm and moved it a few inches. "Right about there." He let go of her arm and took a step back, which relieved and disappointed her at the same time.

"The island isn't very big, is it?"

"About twelve square miles."

She turned and looked at him. "And you're happy here?"

He nodded. "The two years I spent in Augusta were the worst two years of my life."

She started walking again toward the ocean side of the lighthouse. "Maybe because you had to point guns at people."

He laughed as he followed her. "That could've been part of it." He stopped and leaned toward the window, peering down at the Anderson's house below. "Son of a bitch."

It took a moment for Poppie to spot what had caught his eye. "Who's that?"

Without answering, Jasper headed for the stairs. "Stay here."

Poppie ignored him and followed him down. It took her longer to get there since he was taking two steps at a time. She was sure he was going to fall and break his neck. But he seemed to make it as she heard him go through the door before she got to the bottom.

When she went outside, Jasper was sprinting toward the dock with two small motor boats tied to it. The man they spotted from the window had started the engine in one of them and was pulling away.

Jasper stopped at the end of the dock and watched him go. Poppie came up beside him and bent over to rest her hands on her knees. She took a couple of breaths, then watched Jasper look at the other boat.

Lewis had told her Jasper hadn't been on the water since his wife's death, and she could see the struggle he was having. He glared at the boat, then watched the man get farther away from them.

Jasper sighed and stepped into the boat.

Poppie knelt on the dock. "Just let him go."

He looked at her. "I can't."

She stood and watched the man, now further from the shore.

Jasper started pulling on the motor, then stopped when he saw the direction the man was heading. "He's going to hit the rocks in front of the lighthouse."

"Well, that would solve the problem, wouldn't it?"

Jasper glanced at her, then watched the man. He'd apparently spotted the rocks underwater and swerved sharply to avoid them. The maneuver didn't work, however, and with a bang and a crack they heard from the shore, the boat stopped abruptly. It spun around, causing the motor to hit the rocks and grind to a halt with a screech and a puff of blue smoke.

The abrupt stop caused the man to fall into the water. He disappeared beneath it for a few moments, then came up sputtering. He started flailing and calling for help as he tried to get to the quickly sinking boat.

"Shit." Jasper turned back to the motor and got it started, then looked at Poppie. "This time, please listen to me. Stay here."

She nodded as he untied the line holding the boat to the dock and headed toward the man in the water.

As he got close, Jasper turned off the motor and drifted toward the rocks. The panicking man reached for the side of the boat and pulled the edge of it below the surface of the water. Jasper leaned back to try to counteract the move.

"Take it easy!"

The man lost his grip on the boat, and it bounced back up as he started batting at the water with his arms. "Get me out of here!"

"I will. Just calm the hell down." Jasper moved to the side of the boat and grabbed the man by the collar and the belt, and hauled him in. The man fell onto the bottom of the boat and remained still for several moments while he caught his breath. When he sat up, he glared at Jasper.

Jasper rolled up his wet sleeves as he sat on the bench in front of the motor. "I just want to talk to you."

The man moved to the other seat near the middle of the boat, putting him a few feet away from Jasper. He wiped the water from his eyes and pushed wet hair from his forehead. "The hell you do."

"What are you doing out here? Why did you run? There's nowhere to go."

The man folded his arms defiantly and stared out at the water.

Jasper shook his head. "Okay. Suit yourself. Maybe you'll feel more like talking down at the station."

The man turned back toward Jasper, then suddenly lunged at him and the gun on his hip. Jasper turned his body to avoid the blow but was struck hard on the shoulder as the man flew past and landed in the water again. Jasper felt a pop, then searing pain, but before he could react, the man tried to get back into the boat and, this time, successfully pulled the edge of it below the water. Jasper went overboard, landing a few feet from the man as the boat flipped onto its side and slid below the surface.

As Jasper started treading water, he realized his right arm was useless, and the pain in his shoulder was more acute in the frigid seawater. Watching the second boat sink, the man panicked again and grabbed for Jasper, sending them both underwater.

Jasper surfaced and did his best to fight the man off while partially incapacitated and knowing the man would surely drown them both. He needed to take control of the situation, but the freezing water and the pain in his shoulder made it hard to think. He took a deep breath to clear his head as he tried to avoid the man's flailing arms. He needed to render his captive unconscious. It was their only chance of getting to shore. Jasper reached across his body and wrestled his gun out of its holster, then hit the man on the head. The first blow stunned him. The second did the job.

They were about five hundred feet from shore. Under normal circumstances, Jasper would have no trouble swimming the distance. But he had an injured shoulder and an unconscious man to drag with him. He wrapped his damaged arm around the man's chest, not sure he'd actually be able to hold on to him, and started swimming on his side, using his good arm and his legs to propel the two of them through the water.

Chapter Six

A tiny bottle of rum.

Poppie watched helplessly from the dock as the two men battled. When she saw Jasper head for shore, dragging the unconscious man along with him, she left the dock and went to the shoreline. When Jasper reached the water's edge, he crawled out of the water, hauled the lifeless man onto the rocky shore, then laid on his back and closed his eyes as he tried to catch his breath.

Poppie dropped onto her knees next to Jasper. "Is he alive?"

Jasper turned his head and looked at the man's chest moving up and down. "Still breathing."

"Are you okay?"

"Not sure." He closed his eyes again. "Give me a minute." He got his breathing under control, then opened his eyes and looked at her. "I need help getting up."

"You're hurt?"

He held out his left hand. "Help me up."

She took a moment. He was a big guy, and she wasn't sure she'd be of much use.

He groaned. "What's the problem?"

"Nothing." She took his hand in both of hers.

"Just pull." He squinted at her. "Gently."

She tugged on his arm and got him to a sitting position.

He retrieved his hand and rubbed his right arm.

"Is it broken?"

Without answering her, he struggled to his knees, took another moment, then got to his feet. "We need to secure him before he wakes up." He looked toward the dock. "Get the rope, there on the piling."

Poppie went to get the rope and brought it to Jasper, but he didn't take it from her.

"Put his arms behind his back and tie his wrists."

She frowned at him. "You want *me* to tie him up?"

"I can't. Not with one good arm. You know how to tie a knot, right?"

She looked down at the man, who seemed like he was coming out of his stupor. "My grandmother taught me how to macrame."

"Okay, then macrame the hell out of him before he comes to."

Having never tied anyone before, Poppie had no idea what she was doing. But she'd seen it done in the movies, so she did the best she could and only made one correction when Jasper told her to. In the end, both she and Jasper were satisfied the man was secure.

Poppie studied Jasper for a moment. "You must be freezing."

"Too mad to be cold." He looked at the bank of dark clouds that were now a lot closer. "We need to get inside before the rain starts."

"How long do we have?"

"About five minutes."

She frowned at him. "You can't possibly know that."

"You really want to argue with me about it? We need to get to the lighthouse."

"Why not go to the Jeep and drive to town?"

"Not until the rain passes. We'll end up in the ditch just like Lewis' truck."

She frowned again. "I didn't run it off the road."

Jasper shoved the man with his foot and got a groan in response. "Get the hell up."

The man opened his eyes and peered at Jasper. "You cracked my skull, man."

Jasper reached for the man's arm with his left hand and hauled him to his feet, then looked at Poppie. "Take his other arm."

"Seriously?" Before Jasper could yell at her, which she was sure he wanted to do, she took the man's arm, and the three of them headed for the lighthouse. By the time they got to the door, the rain had started.

Poppie put her hand on the doorknob and found it locked. She glanced at Jasper.

"I didn't lock it."

"It locks automatically. Get the key out of my pocket."

She frowned. "Why don't I hold the guy, and you get the key out of your pocket?"

"Poppie, just do it."

She sighed as she let go of the man and went behind Jasper to reach into the wet pocket of his jeans. When she couldn't feel it right away, he looked down at her.

"Having fun?"

"Shut up." She felt the key and pulled it out, then unlocked the door.

They went inside, and Jasper dragged the man to the metal stair railing. "Use the excess rope to tie him to the rail." He knelt in front of the man. "Don't move." The man grinned, and Jasper pulled his revolver.

"Fine, I won't move. I'll let your girlfriend tie me to the rail."

Poppie came up beside Jasper. "I think you're putting way too much confidence in my abilities to restrain the bad guy."

"You're doing fine. Tie him to the support beam under the steps."

Jasper stood but didn't put his gun back until Poppie was through. He then holstered the weapon and checked the knots before sitting on the bench and leaning against the wall.

Poppie sat next to him.

"Is your arm broken?"

"I believe my shoulder is dislocated."

"Oh my gosh. Can we pop it back in?"

Jasper frowned at her. "I don't think it really works like that. And I'm certainly not going to trust you to do it. No offense."

"None taken. I wasn't volunteering."

Jasper took his gun back out and pointed it at the ground before releasing the cylinder and removing the bullets. "Do you have a handkerchief or anything?"

"I have a pack of Kleenex. It's what us modern girls use."

"Can I have them, please? And a pen if you have one."

She dug in her purse and pulled out both items, and set them next to him. He propped the gun between his knees, and she held up a Kleenex.

"Can you wrap that around the pen?"

She did as he asked, then handed it to him. Several tissues later, it seemed he was satisfied the gun was as dry as he was going to get it, and he left it open to dry completely. He then dried the bullets and set them next to the gun.

The man laughed. "It's not going to work after being in the saltwater."

"I can test it on you if you want."

The man stopped laughing. "What do you want from me? And what gives you the authority to hold me here?"

Jasper took his badge from his shirt pocket and held it up. "Cumberland County."

"I've got nothing to say to you."

"Fine. Then keep your mouth shut." Jasper leaned against the wall and rubbed his arm.

Poppie watched him for a moment. "We should immobilize it."

"Okay, Dr. Poppie."

"Seriously. It might help."

"Do you have a sling in your purse?"

"No." She thought for a moment. "But we could use your flannel."

He looked at his flannel button-up. "I suppose that might work." He leaned forward. "You'll need to help me."

He clipped his badge to his belt, then unbuttoned the shirt. Poppie pulled the sleeve off his left arm, then carefully removed it from his shoulders. Before taking it the rest of the way off his hurt arm, she took a moment. "You ready?"

"Just do it."

She removed the shirt, causing only a small groan, then wrung it out before rolling it up to form a sling. He was wearing a t-shirt which was wet and clung to his chest and she hesitated a moment.

He glanced at her. "What's wrong?"

"Nothing." She rested his arm in the loop, then tied it behind his neck. "How's that?"

"It's good. Thanks." He leaned against the wall again. "I don't suppose you have any narcotic pain reliever in your purse."

She picked it up. "I have extra-strength Tylenol."

"Insufficient, but better than nothing."

She took out the bottle and handed him two pills. When he frowned at her, she gave him another.

He looked at the pills, then put one in his mouth and swallowed it. It seemed to go down hard, which caused him to cough, and he winced at the pain it created in his shoulder.

"Do you have a bottle of water in there?"

She dug around. "I have a tiny bottle of rum." She held it up.

He took it from her. "I'm not even going to ask." He swallowed the last two pills with the rum, then finished the bottle. He made a face and handed it to her. "I hate rum."

"Sorry I didn't have whiskey for you."

"Next time." He leaned his head back and closed his eyes. Then opened them and sat straighter.

"You're exhausted."

"I'm fine." He stood and took a walk around the staircase, then opened the door and breathed in the cold, wet air. He filled his cupped hand with rain and drank it, then returned to the bench. "Talk to me, Poppie."

"About what?"

"Anything."

"Um…what's your favorite food?"

He looked at her. "That's what you're going with? Everything."

"You can't like everything."

"Okay. Most everything. When your mother and your aunt own a restaurant and are excellent cooks, it all tastes good."

"That's totally cheating. There has to be one thing you prefer."

"Why?"

"Fine. Whatever. Don't tell me."

"Why would I keep it from you?"

The man looked at them and grumbled. "Good God, you two argue like an old married couple. Much more of this, and I'll be begging you to shoot me."

Poppie and Jasper said, "Shut up," simultaneously, then Jasper got to his feet and circled the room again. When he walked by the prisoner, the man lunged at Jasper and knocked him to the ground. He'd gotten free from the stairs, but his hands were still tied. He straddled Jasper's back and put a knee into his injured shoulder. Jasper yelped as the man looked at Poppie.

"Untie me."

She looked at Jasper, who shook his head and said, "Don't do it."

The man pushed down harder on Jasper's shoulder and looked at Poppie. "Now, please."

Poppie got up and knelt beside him, then untied his hands. She stood and backed away from him. "Just go. Don't hurt him anymore."

The man got to his feet and looked down at Jasper. "I'm just going to slow him down a little." He kicked Jasper in the head, then went to the door. After smiling at Poppie, he went through it.

Poppie ran to Jasper and knelt beside him. He was out cold. "Jasper?" She took his hand and brushed the hair out of his face. "Please wake up."

Jasper groaned and opened his eyes. "I'm awake. I think."

"Can I help you up?"

"Not yet." He closed his eyes again.

"Jasper?"

He squeezed her hand. "Just give me a minute. Is he gone?"

"Yes. I'm sorry. I didn't want him to hurt you anymore."

"It's okay." He pushed himself up to his knees. "And thank you."

She took his arm and pulled him to his feet, then helped him to the bench.

"How's your head?"

"My head?"

"Yes. He kicked you in the head. You passed out."

Jasper leaned against the wall. "My shoulder hurts so much, I can't feel anything else." He ran his hands through his hair and felt his head. "Oh, ouch. There it is."

Poppie touched the spot. "There's a bump."

"It's not the first or the last. I'll live." He looked at her. "It's not your fault."

"Of course it's my fault. I tied him with macrame knots." She brushed a tear off her cheek.

Jasper couldn't help but laugh. "It's okay, really." He took her hand and squeezed it before letting go. "It wasn't your responsibility. It's mine."

She sighed. "You're not super mad?"

"I'm mad, but not at you." He stood slowly and stretched, then went to the door. "How long was I out?"

"A minute or two."

He opened the door. The rain had slowed. "We'll never be able to track him in the rain."

"So, are we going back to town?"

"Yeah. We should be able to drive now. But the roads will be a mess."

"We can take it slow, right?"

"Yeah. Just one problem." He looked at his arm. "I can't shift. You're going to have to drive."

She stood. "I can't. I don't know how to drive a stick. We'll crash."

"Poppie. You can do it."

She sat back down. "I hate this whole day."

"Me too. But we did accomplish one thing."

"What?"

"The bad guy is still on the island."

"And on the loose, thanks to me."

"We'll get him again. He doesn't have many places to hide."

She looked up at him. "Are you still having fun?"

Chapter Seven

"I'm sure the horse already has a name."

Poppie was behind the wheel, and Jasper turned in the passenger seat to watch her.

"Just relax. You can do this." He tried to sound calm for her, but he had his doubts as to whether she'd actually be able to drive them back to town.

"What do I need to do? I remember something about a clutch and gears." She put her hands on the steering wheel. "Maybe you could shift with your left hand."

"Push in the clutch with your left foot. Put your right foot on the brake, then turn the key."

She sighed, then followed his instructions. The Jeep started, and she glanced at him.

"Okay. Now, since the road is so bad, you probably won't need to leave first gear. Maybe second as we get closer to town."

"Where's first?"

"Straight up."

She studied the diagram on the shifter nob. "So, now?"

"Yes. Keep the clutch depressed."

She put it into gear. "Now what?"

"Slowly release the clutch as you press on the accelerator."

"It's going to stall."

She'd been overconfident to the point of being an annoyance since he met her. So her lack of it now was surprising. "No, it's not. Just use a little finesse."

She did as she was told, and the car lurched forward.

He braced himself with a hand on the dash. "Good, keep going. But look at the road. Watch that massive—"

She hit a deep pothole, then bounced out the other side, causing him a great deal of pain, and he mumbled a few choice swear words.

"Slow down. But not too slow, or you'll kill the engine." He glanced at her. "Not permanently. We'll just have to start over. Just a little bit of gas. Slow and steady."

She continued down the rough road, avoiding most of the larger holes and muddy spots. She glanced at him. "I'm doing it."

"Yes. You are. Keep your eye on the road." Every bounce and bump sent pain through his shoulder, but he tried not to let her see it. At the speed they were going, it'd probably take them an hour to go the ten miles to town. It was going to be a long and painful hour.

They'd gone about a quarter of a mile when Poppie said, "Uh oh."

"What?"

"There's not much gas left."

Jasper leaned over to check the gas gauge. "Son of a bitch bastard. I filled up this morning."

"Did he siphon the gas?"

Jasper shook his head and settled into his seat. "That'd be the polite way to do it. And it would've taken too long. More likely, he punched a hole in my gas tank or cut the fuel line."

"How far can we go?"

"Just pick up the speed, and we'll go as far as we can. You'll need to put her into second."

"Okay. Clutch and then straight down?"

"Yep. Do it."

Poppie successfully shifted into second, then made it another quarter mile before the gas light came on. "The light just came on."

"Keep going."

They got another eighth of a mile out of the Jeep before it sputtered to a stop.

"I should've shot him in the leg when I had the chance."

"Or hit him a little harder on the head." She took the keys out of the ignition and handed them to Jasper. "What now?"

He stuck the key back in the ignition. "Willis will need the key when he comes to pick it up." He opened his door. "Now we walk."

"How much further is it?"

He looked around to get his bearings. "Nine miles to Lewis' place."

She laid her head on the seat and closed her eyes for a moment, then sat up straight and opened the door. "Okay. Let's do it."

Jasper got out of the Jeep. "If we're lucky, we'll make it before dark."

"How long is it going to take?"

"About two hours. Depends on how fast you can walk with those tiny little legs of yours."

"Excuse me. My legs may be short compared to your long ones, but they're in proportion to my body."

That, he had noticed. "I didn't say they weren't."

They started walking along the muddy road, running through knee-high grass and brush, broken up by stands of trees.

After about five minutes, Poppie mumbled, "Stupid A-hole."

Jasper started laughing, then stopped and rubbed his arm. "Please, for me. Just say the word."

"What word?"

"Ass. Just say ass."

"No."

"It's not a bad word. Jesus rode through Jerusalem on an ass."

"When it pertains to an animal, it's not a bad word. When you pair it with hole, it is."

"What do you think is going to happen? Do you think the sky is going to open up and strike you down with a bolt of lightning?"

"Of course not. I just choose not to swear."

He stopped walking. "Please, for me. Just this once, say it."

She stopped too. "Fine." She took a moment, kicked a stone with the toe of her shoe, then said, "Ass."

"Now say, asshole."

"No."

"Say it. Say it. *Say it.*"

"No. Oh my gosh. You're such an—"

"Asshole?"

"Yes." She sped up and got ahead of him.

He let her go until she got too far away, then called out to her. "Hey. Slow down. It's dangerous."

"Are there wild animals out here?"

"Only human ones."

She slowed down and let him catch up to her, then they continued down the road. After a few moments, she asked, "Do you have any pets?"

"Where did that come from?"

"Just making conversation."

He sighed. "Yes. I have a dog and a cat."

"Wow." She glanced at him. "Let me guess. You have a German Shepard."

"No."

She thought for a moment. "Pit Bull."

"No."

She stopped and put her hands on her hips. "What then? A Chihuahua?"

He walked a few steps beyond her, then stopped and turned to face her. "Actually, yes."

She started laughing. "That's just perfect. Is it a tiny little one?"

"Five pounds soaking wet."

"Aww. What's his name?"

He started walking again. "I'm not telling you."

She caught up to him and took his arm. "Come on, Deputy. What's his name?"

"*Her* name is Penny."

"Just Penny?"

"Princess Penny."

She laughed again. "Princess Penny Goodspeed. Even more perfect. How about the cat?"

"Pure black male named…Sargent Pepper."

She let go of his arm as they continued walking. "I'd love to meet them."

"Sorry. That's not going to happen."

She frowned at him. "Why?"

"I don't like visitors."

"Like none at all? Or just the ones you find annoying?"

He smiled. "None at all."

"Not even your mother?"

"Of course, my mother comes over. She brings me food."

"Do you have any siblings?"

"No." He looked at her. "No more personal questions."

"Fine. We'll just walk for nine miles in silence."

"Sounds good to me."

She stopped walking. "Why didn't we use the radio in the Jeep to call for help?"

"Oh, man. I'm an idiot. Why didn't I think of that?" He frowned at her. "The radio stops working about a mile past where you ran Lewis' truck off the road."

"I didn't run it off the road. It slid off the road."

"I thought we weren't talking."

They continued walking in silence. She lasted for thirty minutes until they came to a fork in the road. She stopped and looked around. "Is this the road to the Redfords?"

"Yes."

"They have horses."

"So?"

"Horses would get us to town a lot quicker."

"Not necessarily. By the time we walk to the house, saddle them up… Might save a half hour."

"Great. Let's go." She started down the road to the Redfords' house. He stayed where he was. "Hold on. I didn't agree with this."

She glanced back at him and frowned. "Why is it your decision?"

"Because I'm—"

"A man? A deputy sheriff? Smarter? Prettier? What?"

He walked up to her. "All of the above. I also happen to live on the island."

She turned and started walking again. "You do what you want. I'm riding a horse the rest of the way."

"That's horse theft."

She turned back to him but continued walking backward. "What do you do to horse thieves on Gracie Island?"

"We string them up on the mast in front of The Sailor's Loft."

"Well, I'm not stealing it. I'm borrowing it. I'll return it tomorrow." She turned around and kept walking.

Jasper sighed. Groaned. Then followed her. "I'm not coming with you because it's a good idea. I'm only coming because if something happened to you, your brother would blame me."

"You're just mad because you didn't think of it."

They reached the house without any further conversation, and Poppie went to the corral and pet the horse who came to greet her. She looked at the other two.

"We should bring the third one, so he doesn't get lonely."

"We're not bringing the third one."

She took two lead lines and went into the corral. "Which one do you want?"

"I really don't care."

She connected a rope to the brown and white paint. "You can ride this one and give it a cute little name."

"I'm sure the horse already has a name."

She handed him the rope. "Hold him. I'm going to take the bay." She brought the second horse to Jasper. "I'll go get the saddles, seeing as you're…injured."

He squinted at her. "You were going to say useless."

She headed for the shed and returned a few moments later with a saddle, a halter, and a blanket.

Jasper watched her put the blanket on the bay's back and then the saddle. "Do you know what you're doing?"

"Yes. I've ridden quite a bit."

"Where in Boston do you ride horses?"

"I spent every summer at camp in the Minute Man National Park."

"And how long ago was that?"

"Until I was sixteen."

"*And*...how long ago was that?"

"Ten years. But I've ridden since. Besides, it's like riding a bike. Once you know how you never forget."

"Okay."

She finished saddling the bay, then fetched the gear for the paint and saddled it. She looked at Jasper's right arm in the sling. "Can you get on by yourself?"

"Are you going to lift me up?" He led the horse to a bale of hay and stood on it before throwing his leg over the saddle and mounting the horse. It hurt, but again, he didn't let her see it. He gathered the reins and walked the horse away from the corral.

She mounted her horse and moved up beside him. "Are you okay? We'll take it slow."

He clicked his tongue and urged the horse into a trot.

In a few moments, she came up beside him. "Hey. You said you didn't know how to ride."

"I said I don't go out of my way to spend time with horses."

"No. You inferred... Whatever. Where did you learn to ride?"

"As a kid on this island, you need to entertain yourself. My friends and I rode all over. On the beach. Into the wilds."

"Wow. You had friends?"

He broke into a lope. But when they came to an area with deep mud, he stopped.

Poppie came up beside him. "You're a show-off."

"We need to walk them through here. Stay behind me." He glanced at her. "Please."

"Okay."

He took the horse to the side of the road, and they walked along the very edge where the grass kept the mud from getting too deep.

He looked over his shoulder at her. "So. What's Poppie short for?"

"Who says it's short for anything?"

He looked straight ahead again.

She sighed. "Okay. Fine. My name is Penelope." When he didn't say anything, she said, "I know you're grinning right now."

He shook his head. "Penelope's a great name."

"It's horrendous."

He glanced back at her again. "You've just got to own it. Why Poppie? It doesn't really translate from Penelope."

"Lewis started calling me Poppie when I was a baby because he couldn't say Penelope."

"Aww."

"Shut up."

"No. Seriously. That's cute."

"So, what kind of name is Goodspeed? Where's your family from?"

"Its origins are British and were derived from Godspeed. It was given to someone who was kind and helpful. Performed good deeds and such."

"Hmm."

He stopped and turned in his saddle. "You don't think it fits?"

"Too soon to tell."

Chapter Eight

"What happened to three?"

When Jasper and Poppie rode up to the house, Lewis came off the porch and met them in the driveway.

"What the hell?"

Poppie got off her horse and tied it to a tree, then went to Lewis and hugged him.

"What's going on? Where have you been? And where's my truck?"

Jasper cleared his throat. "Can I get some help getting off this damn horse?"

Lewis went to him. "What happened to your arm?"

"Just help me down, please."

Poppie held the horse's head while Lewis pulled Jasper off the horse.

He landed with a grunt and a wince. "Thank you." He headed for the house. "I need to use your phone?"

"Fine. But where's my truck?"

Jasper glanced over his shoulder. "Your sister will tell you all about it." He went into the house and dialed the sheriff's office.

James answered the call. "Chief Goodspeed."

"This is Jasper."

"Where the hell have you been?"

I'm fine, dad, thanks. How are you? "The guy's still on the island."

"You saw him?"

Jasper sat on a chair next to the phone, figuring he could more easily handle the chief's wrath from a sitting position. "I had him in custody."

After a pause, James said, "Had?"

"He got away. But at least we know he's still here."

"How'd you let him get away?"

Jasper ran his hands through his hair, then got to his feet. "It's a long story. And I'll fill you in. But right now, I need a ride into town. Can you send someone?"

"What happened to your Jeep?"

"Can you save the questions for later?"

"Sure. I want you to come straight here."

"Right after I go to the clinic."

"Are you hurt?"

"I'll be fine. I'll see you soon." Jasper hung up, then called Willis.

"This is Willis."

"Hey. Why is Lewis' truck still in the mud?"

"The storm, man. I'm going out now."

"After you get it back to Lewis, you need to go pick up my Jeep."

"Where's it at?"

"About a mile inland on Lighthouse Road."

"What happened to it?"

"Ran out of gas. Sort of. I'll explain later. But I'd like you to bring it to the shop tonight, so you can get to work on it in the morning."

"Okay. Will do. You sound tired."

That was a slight understatement. "It's been a really long day."

Willis laughed. "Go have yourself a beer or two."

"It'll probably take three or four."

Jasper went back outside, and Lewis walked over to him. "She has to be exaggerating."

Jasper shook his head. "If anything, she probably left some things out. It was a hell of a day."

Lewis nodded toward Jasper's arm. "Your shoulder's dislocated?"

"I believe so."

"Shit. Is someone coming to get you?"

"Yeah."

"Well, come sit down. You look exhausted."

"I'm fine." He frowned at the horses, then turned to Lewis. "Can you take these guys to the Redfords' in the morning?"

"Am I going to have my truck by then?"

"Willis is heading out now."

"Okay. Sure, we'll get them back. I'll put them in the backyard for the night."

"Thanks."

At the sound of a vehicle on the road, they all looked to see who it was. Jasper was surprised to see the chief's Bronco.

"Son of a bitch."

Lewis put a hand on Jasper's good shoulder. "He came himself."

"Only so he can yell at me."

James pulled up to them and got out of the vehicle. After studying the horses for a moment, he looked at Jasper. "Are those Bo's horses?"

"Yes."

"Where's your Jeep?"

"Can we talk on the way to the clinic, please?"

"Sure." He seemed to just notice Poppie, who looked almost as bad as Jasper did. "Were you with him on this little adventure?"

"Yes, I was." She looked at Jasper. "Let us know how you are after you see a doctor."

Jasper nodded. "Okay. Go shower and eat. You look like hell."

She smiled at him. "Right back at you."

As he headed down the road, James glanced at Jasper. "So, what happened to your arm?"

"The guy jumped me. Tried to take my gun. Hit me in the shoulder and knocked me into the water."

"Water?"

"We were on a boat at the time, below the lighthouse. The town also owes Jack two new boats."

James knew Jasper hadn't been on a boat since his wife's death. He glanced at Jasper. "What happened to his boats?"

"One hit the rocks, and the other was capsized. It might actually be salvageable unless the storm pushed it into the rocks."

"You were on two different boats?"

Jasper sighed. "Yes. He took off in one, and I followed him. When he hit the rocks, I pulled him into my boat. Can we just...save all this until tomorrow?"

James grumbled to himself for a moment. "Maybe if you weren't chasing around with that girl, we'd still have our man in custody."

Jasper rubbed his neck and leaned his head against the seat. "If you knew me at all, you'd know the last thing I was doing was *chasing* around with Poppie."

"It's been...what? Two years? It wouldn't be inappropriate, other than the fact you were on the job."

Jasper sighed. "It's been eighteen months, two weeks, and three days. I've no desire to chase any woman around, especially Poppie Jensen."

"Of course. Sorry, I misread the situation."

Jasper tried to remember the last time his father had apologized to him. "I'll tell you the whole story later. But yes, I screwed up. Further supporting your opinion of me as unreliable and incapable."

"That's not my opinion of you, Jasper."

"Well, you could've fooled me."

They pulled up to the two-story house next to the clinic. "Dr. Hannigan is probably sitting down to dinner. The clinic closed an hour ago."

Jasper opened his door and stepped out of the car.

James hovered for a moment as though he was deciding what he should do. "I had Maisy call your mother. She should be here soon."

Jasper looked at the man who'd never been there for him. The man who never wanted to be a father to his son. "Thanks for the ride."

Before Jasper closed the door, James said, "After the doc fixes you up, go home and get some rest. We'll talk in the morning."

As James pulled away, Jasper went up the sidewalk to the front door and rang the doorbell. A few moments later, Mrs. Hannigan opened the door.

"Jasper Goodspeed, what happened to you?" She held the door open for him, and he stepped inside.

"Is the doctor available?"

"Of course." She looked over her shoulder and called out, "Davis? Deputy Goodspeed needs your help."

She took his left arm. "You come sit down. You look like you're about to drop." She led him to a room off the foyer and turned on the lights. It was a small examination room Dr. Hannigan used after hours. Being the only doctor in town, he was always on call and welcomed patients at all hours of the day or night. He could fix most anything that didn't require surgery, deliver babies, and had pulled the occasional tooth. You could bring your house pets to him for minor issues, but he drew the line at livestock. If you had a sick horse or a goat with a stomach ache, you had to call a veterinarian from the mainland.

As she set Jasper down on the exam table, the doorbell rang again. "My goodness. Now what?" She left to answer the door, and a moment later, Jasper heard his mother's voice.

Kat came into the room and put a hand on Jasper's cheek. "Honey, what happened?"

Before he could answer her, Davis Hannigan came through the door.

"Kat. Jasper. What's going on here?"

"I think I dislocated my shoulder."

The doctor slid off the makeshift sling and handed it to Kat. He then gently prodded Jasper's shoulder. "It's sure enough dislocated. How'd this happen?"

Jasper glanced at his mother. "Got in a tussle with a…person of interest. He jumped me and hit my shoulder."

Davis picked up a pair of scissors. "I need to cut this t-shirt off of you."

It was a plain white t-shirt that had stopped being white about halfway through the day. Jasper shrugged. "Go for it."

After removing the shirt, the doctor prepared to rotate the arm back into place. "This is going to hurt like hell. But once it's done, it'll start feeling better."

"Okay. I'm ready when you are."

Kat took Jasper's hand. "I'm not ready, but go ahead."

The doctor smiled at her, then placed one hand on Jasper's shoulder and one under his bent elbow. "On three. One, two…" He jerked the arm forward, then up, and it popped into place.

Jasper gasped and held back the curse he wanted to yell out.

Davis grinned. "I'm not sure what hurt you more, the procedure or holding back from swearing in front of your mother."

Kat shook her head. "I'll say it for him. Son of a bitch!"

Jasper put his left arm around her and pulled her in close. "I love you, Mom." He looked at the doctor. "What happened to three?"

Davis chuckled. "Let's get a sling for you." He dug in a drawer and pulled out a blue cloth sling. "I want you to wear this for at least two days. Even if it feels like you don't need it. Then take it easy for two weeks. Again, I know you'll want to return to full speed, but the long-term recovery will be much shorter if you heed my advice."

"I hear you."

Kat spoke up. "What do you mean by long-term recovery?"

"It'll feel fine most of the time. But if he overdoes it, he'll feel it. It won't be completely healed for about six weeks."

She looked at Jasper. "You listen to the man. Don't overdo it."

"Yes, ma'am."

Kat drove Jasper home and went into the house with him. He went to the couch and sat down with a sigh. Penny came running in from the kitchen and jumped around his boots until Jasper picked her up and held her in front of his face. "Hey, girl. Did you miss me?" The dog wiggled in response and licked his nose.

Kat watched him. "You must be hungry. When did you eat last?"

"Um... This morning." He put Penny on his lap, and she curled up with a sigh. "Late, though. Around eleven before I headed out."

"I'll order you something and have Deidre bring it by before it gets too busy. Steak? Fish?"

"Just a burger will be fine. Fries. Clam Chowder."

"Okay." She went to the phone and called The Sailor's Loft.

Jasper laid his head back and closed his eyes but opened them when Pepper jumped up next to him. He laid down next to Jasper's thigh and began purring. Jasper stroked the cat's back and closed his eyes again.

When Kat finished her conversation with the restaurant, she sat on a chair near the couch, and Jasper straightened and gave her a smile. "Thanks."

"For what?"

"Everything. For being here. For taking care of me. For not being Dad."

"It's all I ever wanted to do since the day you were born."

"Full-time job?"

She laughed. "Sometimes." She looked around the cluttered room. "Would you like me to straighten up a little for you?"

"No. Everything is just the way I want it."

"Really?" She frowned at the pile of books next to the couch and the months' worth of Lighthouse Couriers stacked on the coffee table. "Are you sure?"

"I'm sure." He hadn't taken the time to clean up his messy house since Ivy died. It seemed pointless to him. There was no one to see it. And no reason to pick it up. He'd also been sleeping on the couch for the last eighteen months, two weeks, and three days. His clothes hung on a tension rod at the end of the hallway between the bathroom and the bedroom. The rest of his things he kept in the linen closet.

He'd lived in the one-bedroom house for four years. Two-and-a-half with Ivy and one-and-a-half without her. Everything about the house was small except the porch on the backside of it, which faced the ocean two-hundred yards away during high tide. They'd spent a lot of time on the porch, and he was only recently able to go out there and sit without the grief overwhelming him. He supposed that was progress. But it made him feel like her memory was fading.

Kat moved to the couch and sat next to him. "Tell me about this girl."

"Girl?"

"The one who was with you today."

"How do you know there was someone with me today?"

She tilted her head. "Maisy told me."

"Of course. Poppie is Lewis' sister."

"And you're fond of her?"

He laughed. "No. We're not even friends. More like sparring partners. She's stubborn and sarcastic. She won't listen to anything I say, even if it's meant to keep her safe." He took a breath. "No. I'm not *fond* of her."

"Stubborn, huh?"

Jasper frowned at Kat. "I'm not stubborn. Not like her. She's..." He shook his head.

"Okay. How'd she come to be with you today?"

"I was headed out Lighthouse Road and found her on the side of it up to her...axles in mud. I should've taken her back to town, but... I'm not sure why I didn't. I guess because I knew she wanted me to."

"But you're not stubborn?"

"No."

Chapter Nine

"Give me back my dog."

After Deidre brought Jasper's meal, Kat left to help out with the dinner rush and close up the restaurant for the night. Before leaving, she promised to check in on him in the morning to make sure he didn't go to work.

He told her he wouldn't. But he knew he would. If he didn't show up to give a full report to the chief, his father would probably show up at his door. And that was the last thing he wanted.

As he ate, he realized just how hungry he was and wished he'd asked for more. But he ended the meal satisfied he'd make it until morning.

After dinner, he took a long shower, then carefully slipped into a tank-style t-shirt and a pair of sweatpants. The pills had kicked in, the shower helped, and he was almost full. Considering the day he had, he couldn't ask for more than that.

He settled onto the couch with Penny on his chest and Pepper at his feet and read two chapters of a book until he couldn't keep his eyes open anymore.

The next thing he knew, he was awakened by someone knocking on the door. He rolled onto his side and ignored the intruder. The sun was coming through the window he wished he'd closed last night, and the cat was lying on the warm spot it made in the worn carpet.

With the second knock, Penny released a tiny growl, and Jasper mumbled, "Down, girl." He then glared at the door, willing the intruder to go away.

When the door opened a crack, he heard Poppie say, "Are you decent?"

He groaned. When she opened the door all the way, he sat up and swung his legs over the edge of the couch. "What are you doing here?" He rubbed the sleep from his eyes and tried unsuccessfully to straighten his hair. The bump on his head hurt more than it had yesterday, and his shoulder throbbed. The last thing he wanted was visitors. Especially Poppie.

She held up a Styrofoam container. "I brought you breakfast."

"Why?"

He glanced at Lewis, who was standing behind Poppie, mouthing, "Sorry."

Poppie stepped into the room. "You said if someone brought you food, they'd be welcome."

"No. That's not what I said." He fingered the bruise on his head. "I said my mother is welcome because she brings me food. She's also my mother. You're...not."

Undeterred by his comment, he looked around the room. "This is not what I was expecting. I thought you'd have a mancave. Flat-screen TV. A weight set in the corner. Instead, it looks like a sixteen-year-old boy lives here. A very messy sixteen-year-old boy."

He couldn't argue with that. She was right. He nodded toward the food container. "What did you bring?"

She handed it to him. "Ham and cheese omelet with Tabasco, country fried potatoes and sourdough toast with marmalade."

"How'd... Who'd you talk to down there?"

"A very nice waitress named Peggy. She seemed to be quite fond of you in an Aunt Peg sort of way."

"Probably because she *is* my Aunt Peg."

Poppie laughed. "How cute."

"And she's not just a waitress. She's part-owner." He set the food on top of the newspapers. "So why else are you here?"

"Since you didn't call last night and let us know how you were, we thought we better check up on you."

Lewis cleared his throat. "*She* thought. I just came to drag her back home. Come on, sis."

At the sound of Lewis' voice, Penny growled again from under the blankets.

Poppie put her hands to her face. "Aww, is that little Penny I hear?"

"No. Thanks for breakfast." Jasper waved at her. "Bye."

"Just let me see her. Then I'll go."

Jasper doubted her word but sighed and took Penny out from under the blankets.

Poppie squealed. "Oh my gosh, she's adorable. Let me hold her."

"No. She doesn't like strangers."

"I'm not a stranger. See. She's wagging her tail. She wants me to hold her."

Jasper frowned, then handed Penny to Poppie, who hugged and kissed Penny's nose and got a lick in response.

"See. I'm not a stranger." She kissed the dog again and nuzzled her neck.

Jasper held out his hand. "Alright. Give me back my dog."

Poppie gave Penny one more kiss, then handed her back to Jasper. "Fine, Mr. Grumpy Pants."

Lewis took her arm. "Come on. Let's leave him alone, now." He looked at Jasper. "Again, sorry."

"Not your fault, man. I don't think Poppie listens to anybody."

She let Lewis lead her to the door. "Okay. I'll see you around."

"Not if I see you first."

She laughed and pointed a finger at him. "You know you want to see me again."

Lewis pulled her through the door and closed it behind them.

Jasper shook his head. "Crazy, crazy woman." Penny barked at them as they walked across the porch. "Don't give me that. You were making out with her a minute ago."

❦ • ◆ • ❦

Halfway through his breakfast, the phone rang. When he answered it, his mother said, "Good boy. You stayed home."

"Morning, Mom." He fed Penny a small cube of ham.

"Peg said your friends brought you some breakfast."

Only one friend. Singular. The other is... "Yeah."

"Good, then I won't worry about you for a while."

"Mom, I need to go into the station. The chief is expecting a report."

"Your father can wait."

"I'll take it easy."

"No more tussling with persons of interest?"

"No. I promise." He picked up a piece of toast and took a bite.

"Okay. Come in for a late lunch or an early dinner. I know you want to avoid the brunch crowd. At least check in with me."

"Will do. Love you, Mom."

"I love you more."

Jasper hung up the phone and resumed eating his breakfast. His mother worried about him unnecessarily. Ninety percent of the time, he was in absolutely no danger doing his job. Gracie Island was virtually crime-free, and his days were spent taking care of traffic violations, neighbor disputes, and a few domestic situations. The most dangerous thing he did was dealing with the occasional drunk and disorderly.

Putting up with his father was the hardest part of the job. "Chief Goodspeed, father of the year." He shared some more ham with Penny, then offered some to Pepper. The cat sniffed it, then looked insulted. Penny was all too happy to eat it for him.

Poppie and Lewis were on the rocks, uncovered by the low tide. The sun was shining, which was a rare occasion on Gracie Island. They got an average of eighty days of sunshine a year. Most of them in the summer and fall. It rained sixty days a year, dropping seventy inches of rain during the winter and spring. The fog rolled in most mornings as the sun was coming up and burned off by noon. Today it was only ten, and the sky was clear.

From her perch on a flat-topped rock, Poppie watched Lewis throw fist-sized rocks into the water. "You really love it here, don't you?"

He turned and smiled at her. "I do. How about you? Is it growing on you yet?"

"Hmm. Maybe a little. I definitely won't wait six years to come see you again."

"I don't know when they're going to release the ferry. You're probably about ready to go home."

She shrugged. "It's fine. I might stay a little longer if that's okay with you."

"As long as you're staying to spend time with me and not Deputy Goodspeed."

She frowned. "Of course not. I mean, it's fun harassing him. But I've missed you. And I like seeing you so happy on this weird little backward island, rainy, muddy, foggy, interesting community, where everyone knows everyone."

"Thanks. I think." He walked to her and sat on a close-by rock. "You really need to steer clear of Jasper. Or, at the very least, leave him alone."

"Have I gone too far?"

"Little bit, yeah."

"But it's so fun."

"Probably not for him."

She picked up a rock next to her and threw it at an incoming wave. "Fine. I'll leave Deputy Goodspeed alone."

"Thank you."

Jasper didn't want to put on his uniform, so he put on some jeans and a button-up over his t-shirt. He figured the chief was lucky he was coming in at all. He had a little trouble with his boots but managed to get them tied. Then instead of trying to tame his hair, which was extra crazy today since it was wet when he went to bed, he put on a ball cap. The last thing was the sling the doctor told him to wear for two days.

He frowned at it and left it lying on the table. "Sorry, Doc."

James was waiting for him when he came through the front door. Maisy set down her knitting and jumped up to give Jasper a gentle hug.

"How're you doing today?"

"I'm all good. Thanks."

"I'm sure that's not true. You take it easy now." She looked at James, who was pouring himself a cup of coffee. "Don't you send him out to work today."

Without responding, James headed for his office. Jasper patted Maisy's hand before he poured himself a cup and followed.

The chief was sitting at his desk when Jasper came through the door. "Take a seat."

Jasper sat in the metal chair in front of the desk and took a sip of his coffee, then proceeded to relay all the previous day's events. James listened without interruption until the very end, then leaned back in his seat.

"You swam, walked, and rode a horse with a dislocated shoulder?"

"Not sure how else I would've gotten home."

James chuckled, which meant he probably had a little bourbon in his coffee. "So, I don't suppose you got the man to identify himself?"

"No." He took his holster and gun off his belt and set them on the desk. "But I'm pretty sure he touched my gun before he went overboard. Of course, I dried it out after it went in the water with me, but I didn't mess with the handle too much. Might be something there. Or on the holster."

James carefully picked up the leather holster and studied the wooden handle of the gun. "Let's find out." He took a fingerprint kit from his desk drawer. "Anybody touch this besides you?"

Jasper shook his head. "No. After I dried it out, I put it in the holster and haven't touched it since."

"Okay. So if there are any prints besides yours, we might get an ID." He put on some reading glasses and looked at Jasper over the rim. "You should've given this to me last night."

"I didn't think about it until this morning. The fact that he might have touched it, that is."

"Okay, let's take a look."

James spent the next fifteen minutes dusting the handle of the gun and the leather holster. He came up with three partial prints and ran them through their basic system. Two of them were Jasper's. The third was possibly the killers.

"I'll send this off to Augusta." He studied Jasper for a moment. "Go home. You don't look like you're quite recovered yet. Besides, your mother will kill me if I let you work today."

Jasper got to his feet. "I'll see you tomorrow." He headed for the door but stopped when James called after him.

"I'm calling an emergency town meeting tonight. You should be there if you're up to it."

"Are you going to let everyone know what's going on?"

"I think it's time."

"Okay. I'll be there."

Jasper left the sheriff's station and went two blocks to The Sailor's Loft. After ringing the bell, he went in and was greeted by Aunt Peg.

"Oh, sweetheart. What are you doing out and about?"

"I'm fine. Just a little sore."

"Are you working?"

"No. Just had to give my report to the chief. I'm headed home."

"Well, go say hi to your mother. She's in the office. Can I get you something to eat?"

He patted his stomach. "I'm still digesting that ham and cheese omelet. But you could make me a Cobb salad to take home with me."

"Coming right up."

Jasper walked through the mostly empty restaurant toward the office. It was the mid-morning lull between the early breakfast crowd and the brunch crowd, who'd start showing up around noon. He found Kat at the desk, frowning over some paperwork.

"Hey, Mom. Everything okay?"

"Darn Skeeter overcharged me again."

"Want me to have a talk with him?"

She smiled. "No. It's not sheriff business. I can handle Skeeter Mac-Donald." She pointed toward a chair. "Have a seat."

Jasper sat. "I'm headed home. I just wanted to check in with you."

"Thank you. I appreciate that. Are you hungry?"

"Aunt Peg is making me a Cobb salad."

"Good. And you had a good breakfast this morning."

"Yes."

"It sounds like your sparring partner is trying to be nice to you."

"No, Mom, she's not. She just used the food as a ploy to come harass me."

Kat shook her head. "I'm sure that's not true."

"Trust me. It's true." He got up. "I'm going to go home before church lets out."

"Are you going to the game?"

"Of course."

"But you're not playing."

"No. I'll sit in the stands like a good boy."

Kat went to him and patted his cheek. "You *are* a good boy."

Jasper stepped away from her. "You know I'm going to be thirty in a few months."

She put her hands over her ears. "Don't remind me. It makes me feel so old."

He leaned in and kissed her on the cheek. "You, Mother, will never be old."

"You're sweet. But the mirror tells a different story."

"Don't believe the mirror. Mirrors only show you what's on the surface. They don't show you the beauty within."

Kat shook her head. "You know, your father used to say stuff like that to me."

"Was he drunk or sober at the time?"

She shook a finger at him. "You behave."

"Sorry."

Chapter Ten

The Gazebo

Instead of heading home, Jasper went to the park at the edge of town and sat on a wooden bench under the large gazebo in the middle of a grassy area. Due to the unsettled weather, the park didn't get much use. But the gazebo was a landmark of the town, and every few years, the volunteer fire department sanded it down and repainted it to keep it from deteriorating in the soggy weather.

Jasper knew he'd have the park to himself today because everyone else would soon be having brunch. The sun was still low enough to hit the bench, so he leaned back and soaked in its warmth on his face. When the sun shone on Gracie Island, everything was beautiful.

When he heard, "Okay, I'm totally not stalking you," he sat up.

"You expect me to believe that?"

"Yes." Poppie came to the steps holding a small white paper bag but didn't go up them. "I figured you'd be hiding out at home."

"Had to check in with the chief."

She tilted her head. "If I may be so bold, why do you call him 'the chief' instead of Dad?"

"You may not."

She shrugged. "I believe you and I are the only two people on the island not at brunch."

"That's probably true."

"Can I come up?"

"It's public property. I can't stop you."

She took a step back. "Never mind. I'll leave you to your contemplation."

"Poppie. Get your ass up here."

She smiled, then climbed the four steps. "Can I sit next to you?"

He slid over to make room for her. She sat and put her bag down, then studied the gazebo for a few moments. "This is nice. Compared to everything else in town, it looks new."

"It was built in 1947."

"Oh. Well, it's very well maintained."

"Unlike the rest of the town?"

"That's not what I meant."

"It's a constant battle to keep the elements from eating away our town. Everything gets a new coat of paint every few years. We start at one end, and by the time we get to the other, it's time to start over again."

"Sounds tedious." She peered over his lap at his food container. "Hungry already?"

"Cobb salad for my lunch."

"I've never had Cobb salad."

He smiled. "Well, if you try this Cobb salad, you'll be disappointed in anyone else's."

"How would you know that if you've only eaten it here?"

"I've tried it elsewhere."

"Where?"

He adjusted his ball cap. "In Augusta."

"Oh, right. When you went to sheriff school." She looked at his container again. "Maybe you could give me a taste."

He nodded toward her bag. "What's in yours?"

"A brownie from the bakery. Buns of Steele?"

"Ah. Randy Steele makes the best brownies ever."

"Steele? Oh. I get it now."

Jasper stretched his legs out and crossed his ankles. "I'll trade you half my Cobb salad for half your brownie."

She folded her arms across her chest. "Hmm. I don't know. You just said it was the best brownie ever. So…" She shrugged again. "But I'm curious to try the best Cobb salad ever." She took another moment. "Sure. I'll share."

Jasper checked his watch.

She frowned. "Do you have to be somewhere?"

"No. Just confirming. It's been five minutes, and you haven't said anything that makes me want to strangle you."

"A new record." She took a fork out of the paper bag. "So, salad first?"

Jasper set the food container on his lap and opened it. Then took a fork and napkin out of his shirt pocket.

"That looks good. Did Aunt Peg make this for you?"

"Yes."

"Do you eat all your meals there?"

"No. I cook sometimes. Actually, more like make a sandwich. I grew up eating at the Loft. Why stop now?"

"Do you ever eat at the café?"

"No. That'd be giving business to the competition."

"Wow. Really?"

He laughed. "No. It's actually owned by my great-uncle."

"No way."

"He and my grandpa both wanted to start a restaurant. But they couldn't agree on whether it should be a restaurant/bar combination catering to the dinner crowd or a café for breakfast and a quick bite."

"So they each opened their own restaurant?"

"Yep."

"So what other Gracie Island pies does your family have their fingers in?"

"That's it."

Poppie took a bite of the salad. "Oh my gosh. This is good."

"It's the dressing. Peg's secret recipe."

"What's in it?"

"*Secret* recipe."

"Hmm. So is there an uncle to go with Aunt Peg?"

"Yes. Uncle Beryl."

"And what does Uncle Beryl do?"

"He's retired, sort of. He's a very talented craftsman. He makes beautiful furniture. One piece at a time. When he feels like it."

"That's very cool." She took another bite. "Oh, look, there's someone else who didn't go to brunch."

Jasper spotted the man she was referring to. "Oh. That's Burt." He handed her the salad and got to his feet. "I'll be right back."

Poppie watched Jasper jog across the grass to the older man walking slowly along a gravel path. He talked to Burt for a few minutes, then took something from his wallet and put it in the man's hand. A few moments later, the man wandered off, and Jasper headed back to the gazebo.

He sat and took the salad back.

"So, who's Burt?"

Jasper took a bite of chicken and lettuce. "Burt is a ward of Gracie Island."

"Ward. Do you mean homeless person?"

"No. He has a home. But he's a little addled, and he lives off of a small pension. Everyone takes care of Burt. Makes sure he eats and makes it home at night."

"That's very sweet."

"We take care of our own."

Poppie took another bite of salad and chewed it thoughtfully, then sighed. "I have a confession to make."

"Uh oh."

"Lewis told me the reason you get drunk on the fifth of every month."

"I figured."

"And we'll change the subject. I just want to say how sorry I am."

Jasper nodded, then stuck his fork in the last piece of bacon.

"Hey. I wanted that. You've eaten all the bacon."

"No way." He glanced at her, then put his fork a few inches in front of her mouth. She moved back from it, and he asked, "Do you think I have cooties?"

"No." She took a moment before eating the bacon off of his fork, then glanced at him. "*Do* you have cooties?"

"No." He pointed to the side of his mouth. "But I do have this canker sore—"

Poppie nudged his right shoulder, and he yelped as he jumped to his feet, knocking the remains of the salad onto the floor. He circled the gazebo, rubbing his arm.

"I'm so sorry." She stood. "I forgot."

"You forgot about our day of hell? It was just yesterday!"

"No. I just forgot you were hurt. You're not wearing your sling. You should wear your sling."

"I didn't think I needed it. But now..."

"I'm really sorry. Did I dislocate it again?"

He sat back down. "It was my fault." He picked up the food container and kicked the salad toward a space in the wood floor. He leaned back and looked at her. "It's going to take more than you're wimpy little self to dislocate my shoulder."

She glared at him. "Why do you keep referring to me as little? I'm not that little. I'm average height."

"How tall are you?"

"Five-seven."

He cocked his head.

"Okay, five-six and a quarter."

Jasper smiled. "Like I said, little."

"Just because you're what? Six something?"

"Six-three."

She looked at him. "You're not nine inches taller than me."

"Apparently, I am." He nodded toward the paper bag. "Time for some dessert?"

She opened the bag and took out the brownie.

Jasper took it from her. "Since you've re-injured my shoulder, I should get a bigger half."

"Says who?"

"Says the man holding the brownie." She tried to grab it from him, but he held it out of her reach.

"Fine. Whatever. I don't care. Take it all."

"Really?"

"No. Give me some."

He broke the brownie in half and gave her the slightly smaller side.

She took a bite and rolled her eyes. "Oh my gosh."

"I know. I told you."

They ate for a few minutes in silence, then, as Jasper finished his half, he asked, "So, did you take time off from a job to come here?"

"No. I just graduated in April."

"High school?" She almost nudged him again but stopped herself. He, however, seemed to expect it and moved over on the bench. "Maybe we should switch sides." He stood, and after frowning at him, she moved over to where he was sitting. He sat back down on her right side. "What's your degree?"

"Urban planning and development."

He turned toward her. "Really?"

"Yes."

"Huh. Interesting."

"Do you really think so? Or are you just saying that?"

"No. Really."

She still didn't know if she believed him or not. "My dad's a contractor and builds a lot of lower-income housing. My Mom's a nurse in the county health department. It just seemed like a good direction to go. I have a job waiting for me. I start next Monday."

"So your parents are still together?"

"Yes. Married thirty years and still embarrassingly in love with each other."

"'Embarrassingly?'"

"It's a little awkward when your parents are getting more action than you are." She suddenly hated that she'd said that, and she felt her cheeks flush.

Jasper laughed. "Don't worry. I'm just going to leave that alone." He got to his feet. "Oh, cool. It's raining."

She looked out at the light rain falling on the grass. "The sun's still shining."

He went down the steps and looked toward the sky. "I love it when the sun is shining, and it's raining."

Poppie watched him as he took his cap off and walked a few feet away from the gazebo, then turned his face to the rain. She sighed. *Don't even go there, girl.* "You're going to get soaked." He turned and smiled at her, and she knew it was too late. She was already gone.

He came back up the steps, shook his head, then brushed his hair back off his face. He tossed his hat on the bench and leaned against the railing.

She shook her head. "You're insane."

"What can I say? I love the rain."

"Good thing since you live in the rainiest place on earth."

"Not quite the rainiest. But close."

"Is this going to rain out your softball game?"

"No way. If we canceled the game every time it rained, we'd never play." He wiped the rain from his face with the crook of his left arm. "Are you going to come watch?"

"Of course. But you can't play. Not with one good arm."

"If it wasn't for the fact my mom and Dr. Hannigan will be there, I'd sure as hell try."

"Men and their games."

"Yeah, yeah, yeah. We never grow up. I've heard it all before."

"Only because it's true."

"Because women are so much more mature?"

"Not mature. We just don't get off on competition."

Jasper went to the bench and picked up his hat, then put it on. "If you think that's true, you need to come to the Fall festival."

"Why?"

"Because the baking contest is cutthroat, and there aren't any men in it."

"What else happens at the Fall festival?"

"Lots of booths selling local stuff like honey, produce, crafts. You name it, it's there. There's also music, dancing, beer. Lots of beer."

"Sounds fun."

Jasper sat on the bench and checked his watch again.

Poppie frowned. "Another new record?"

He laughed. "No, just seeing how much time I have before the game."

"Am I keeping you?"

"No. Actually, I want to show you something."

"Should I be scared?"

Jasper stood. "No. Come on."

Chapter Eleven

Sharks vs Barracudas

J asper and Poppie walked through the park, then down an alley to the garage at the end of the street. They found Jasper's Jeep parked in front of the building. He went to it and took a folded paper from under the windshield wiper.

He opened it and read it. "Good man."

"Is it fixed?"

"Yeah. Hop in."

"I'm not driving."

Jasper opened the driver's side door. "I wasn't going to ask you to." The key was in the ignition, and he turned the engine over, then buckled his seatbelt.

Poppie got in and looked at him. "Where are we going?"

"It's not far." He backed onto the street, then drove around the corner and down one block. When he stopped and parked, Poppie frowned.

"We could've walked."

He opened his door and went up the steps to the bright red building. Poppie got out and watched as he lifted a flower pot and uncovered a key. She read the sign above the door.

"Who's Alma Gracie, and why does she have a museum named after her?"

"Alma and Walter were the original Gracies. They built the first house here on the island." He unlocked the door and held it open for her.

She peered into the dark room. "Are we supposed to go in here when it's closed?"

"One of the perks of being law enforcement. Who's going to tell me I can't?"

"Okay, then." She followed him inside and waited while he turned on the lights. "Wow. I thought it was going to be full of old sailing stuff."

"Disappointed?"

"Not at all. This is amazing." There were multiple glass cabinets filled with everything imaginable, from seashells to silverware to jewelry. On the walls were glass floats, fishing nets, lures, the full skeletal remains of various sea creatures, and many things Poppie couldn't identify.

"Everything in here washed up on the beach."

"Like the Anderson's collection?"

"Yeah. But this stuff dates back a hundred years. Alma and Walter moved here right after they were married. The island was a wedding present from her father. She fell in love with the beach and all the treasures that washed up on it. The story goes, she went out every morning, and she kept everything she ever found."

"She found all this stuff?"

"Everything in this room, yes. But over the years, the residents continue to donate stuff. The collection gets newer as you make your way through the building. The last thirty years or so, the curator will only take something unique. If there's already one here, he won't take another."

Poppie looked at several glass cabinets. "How does this stuff get lost in the first place and end up on your beach?"

"Don't know. Careless people, I guess. Some of it's from shipwrecks." He went to a collection of coins and various metal objects. Some were so rusted or covered with barnacles that it was hard to tell what the item was originally. "This stuff here is old. It generally washes up after a big storm." She joined him and looked at it all.

"Thank you for showing me this. I could stay here all day."

Jasper checked his watch again. "You have an hour until the game."

After spending forty-five minutes at the museum, Jasper and Poppie drove back to the park. The baseball diamond was on the other side of the park from the gazebo, with a pond and a stand of trees between them.

Like The Sailor's Loft on Friday night, it seemed like most everyone in town was there. Jasper stopped for a moment in front of the bleachers.

"Go get us a couple of seats. I'm going to go check in with the team."

Poppie watched as he headed for the team in blue. The other team was wearing red. The spectators seemed to be divided into two groups representing each team, with most of them wearing something in the appropriate color. Red sat on the left, blue on the right.

Poppie smiled at Jasper's blue plaid shirt. "He came prepared." She found two seats near the top of the stands and set her jacket next to her to reserve the space for Jasper. She watched him with the other guys, who all seemed unhappy he wouldn't be playing. When he talked with Lewis, they both looked toward the stands and waved at her.

After a few minutes, Jasper returned to the bleachers. He stopped to kiss his mother, hug Aunt Peg, and shake hands with a man, Poppie presumed was Uncle Beryl. They were sitting on the first row of seats and they glanced up at Poppie and gave her a wave. After a few minutes of conversation, Jasper made his way up, stopping several times to talk to people. When he finally made it to her, he sat down with a sigh.

"I think this town likes you, Deputy."

He shrugged. "They're just kissing up."

"I don't think so."

He handed her a blue Shark's t-shirt. "Here. Put this on."

"Why?"

"Because you're wearing a red shirt."

She glanced at her white shirt with red sleeves, buttons, and collar, then took the shirt from him and slipped it on. It was too big but went on easily over her other shirt.

"Happy?"

"Yes. Thank you. You need to make it clear what side you're on." He took off his plaid shirt, which he was wearing over his own Sharks t-shirt. "Go, Sharks!"

"Go, Sharks!"

When Poppie spotted Deidre headed for them, she glanced at Jasper to see his reaction. But he seemed oblivious to the smile Deidre gave him as she squeezed in between him and an older man who didn't seem to appreciate the intrusion.

She touched Jasper's arm. "Hey. How's the shoulder?"

"It's coming along. I should be able to play next week." He glanced at Poppie. "Or maybe the week after next."

"Well, the team's going to miss you."

"I'm sure they'll do fine without me."

Poppie smiled at her and nodded at her jersey-style shirt with a blue torso and red sleeves. "Playing both sides?"

"They all come into the bar. Got to keep my customers happy." She turned her attention back to Jasper. "I hope you'll be able to play guitar Friday night."

"Oh. No problem. I'll be there."

She smiled. "Good." She still had her hand on his arm, but he seemed unaware of her flirting. Poppie wondered if he was truly unaware or just trying politely to ignore her. When Deidre couldn't get a favorable reaction from him, she sighed, then stood. "I'm going to go sit with Kat and Peg."

"Okay. Enjoy the game."

Poppie watched her go down the bleachers, then leaned toward Jasper. "You know she's totally into you, right?"

Jasper glanced at her. "Deidre? No way. I've known her since I was ten."

"You went to school with her?"

"No. She was my babysitter until I turned twelve, and I convinced my mom I didn't need one anymore."

"So she's older than you?"

"A couple years. Yeah." He turned and looked at Poppie. "Why do you care?"

"I don't. I just can't believe you don't see it. She was practically drooling over you."

"Bull." He glanced at Deidre's back as she made her way down the bleachers.

"And she's not the only one. These women in town are ready and willing to get to know the deputy."

"Everyone in town knows…"

"I realize that. But it doesn't keep them from hoping."

"You're nuts."

"Alright. But I'm pretty sure they consider you Gracie Island's most eligible bachelor. The fact you're not available makes you even more appealing."

He frowned, then turned his attention to the field. "The game's starting."

She still wasn't convinced he was as clueless as he acted. The women of Gracie Island were all enamored by their handsome deputy. And every one of them had a better chance than she did. They were here. She'd be in Boston soon and just an annoying memory for him.

She tried not to think about it. "So, blue versus red?"

"Sharks versus Barracudas. Are you going to talk through the whole game?"

"Fine. I'll be quiet." She leaned toward him again. "Who's that nice looking older gentleman playing referee?"

"Dr. Hannigan. I'll be sure and tell is wife you think he's attractive."

She was quiet for a moment, then asked, "What position do you usually play?"

Jasper sighed. "First base."

"So, you're good. If you stunk, you'd be in the outfield."

"That's not necessarily true. Are you a baseball fan?"

"I went to all of Lewis' high school games. He could've played in college. But he didn't go to college. He hit the road, traveled, and ended up here."

"Best education you can get."

"My parents didn't think so."

"Their son's happy. What more could they want for him?" The Sharks came up to bat, and Jasper stood and whistled. When he sat back down, she smiled at him.

"You're one of those."

"One of what?"

"A boisterous fan."

"Shh. You're brother's about to bat."

Lewis came up to the plate and went through his usual good luck routine. He tapped the bat to the base twice, adjusted his hat, then shuffled his feet. Poppie had seen him do it since he was a sophomore in high school. He was the only tenth-grader on the varsity team. After two low pitches, he got a hit and made it to third base. Jasper stood, cheered him on, and whistled again.

When he sat again, he looked at Poppie. "What?"

"Nothing. I like your enthusiasm."

Jasper whistled for the next batter, who got a hit and brought Lewis home.

Standing when Jasper did, Poppie talked loud over the cheering blue crowd. "So, how many teams does Gracie Island have?"

"Just two."

"You play the same guys every week?" They both sat.

"Yeah."

She looked at the fans in red. "So, it's more of a rivalry than a sporting event."

"I guess you could say that. The Sharks and the Barracudas have been playing each other for about fifty years."

"Oh my gosh. That's wild. So when you're a kid growing up, how do you decide what team to back?"

"It's pretty much inherited. But sometimes, you get a couple from two different sides. My parents, for instance."

She took a moment to think about it. "Your dad was a Barracuda, and your mom was a Shark."

"Yeah. In that situation, the kid can decide red or blue."

"Is the chief over there on the red side?"

"No. He hasn't come to a game in years. Not since he played."

"Did he play against you?"

"He stopped when I was a kid. Long before I started playing. That would've been cool, though. Although, I heard he was pretty good."

"And what about newcomers like Lewis?"

"As soon as I found out Lewis played in high school, I convinced him to come play with the Sharks."

"I'm glad you and Lewis are friends. I was afraid he was all alone here."

"No one is alone on Gracie Island."

By the fifth inning, the Sharks were ahead by two runs, thanks to Lewis. As the team came off the field, Jasper checked the sky above them, then took Poppie's hand and stood.

"Come on."

She got to her feet. "Why?"

"It's about to start pouring."

She looked at the sky above them. It was cloudy now but didn't seem that ominous. "How do you know that?"

"Trust me." He led her down the bleachers, excusing their way through the crowd, then got to the ground and headed for the dugout.

"Where are we going?"

"The only dry place on the field." They went down the steps to the dugout, and Lewis gave Jasper a smile.

"How long do we have?"

"Ten minutes." They sat at one end of the bench while the game proceeded. Nine and a half minutes later, it started raining.

Lewis checked his watch. "Thirty seconds early."

Jasper laughed, then looked at Poppie. "If I say it's going to rain. It's going to rain."

"Okay, Rain God. I believe you."

The game continued in the rain as the spectators pulled out rain gear and umbrellas. No one left, though some of them retreated to stand under trees. The field got muddy after a few minutes, and the ball appeared to be hard to see because there were a lot of strikeouts and missed catches.

Poppie leaned into Jasper's ear to be heard over the rain on the metal roof above them. "I can't believe this!."

Jasper grinned. "This is baseball on Gracie Island."

Chapter Twelve

The Town Meeting

Poppie was on the porch, trying not to think about Deputy Goodspeed. The rain had ended, and the sun had returned, though the clouds that still remained partially obscured it. She expected seeing the sun was rare on Gracie Island, so she thought she should enjoy it while it lasted. When Lewis came through the front door, she turned in her seat.

He was slipping on a jacket. "Come on. We're going to be late."

"For what?"

"The town meeting."

"Like a town meeting, town meeting?"

He frowned. "What other kind is there?"

She got to her feet. "Give me a minute to get ready."

"No time. We need to get there early so we get a good seat?"

"What for?"

"Just come on."

She headed for the house. "Two minutes. I need my purse and a jacket." She went through the door. "And a shot of something. This town makes me want to drink."

When she came outside with her purse, and a jacket hung over her arm, Lewis was in the truck with the motor running. She got in, and he started driving before she got the door closed.

"Geez. Why are you so excited?"

"I love town meetings."

"You need to get off this island and back to civilization more often. Is every Sunday this crazy?"

"We don't always have town meetings on Sundays. And once winter hits, we won't play ball until spring. So, no." He glanced at her. "You should comb your hair."

"Why?"

"Everyone in town is going to be there."

"Well, if someone had given me more than a minute's notice, I'd be more put together." She took a brush from her purse and ran it through her hair. She then pulled it on top of her head, swirled it around, and secured it with a band. "Does this pass inspection?"

"Yeah. You look okay."

She sighed, then glanced at him. He seemed genuinely excited. "You're weird. You know that?"

He grinned. "It runs in the family."

He turned in the correct direction at the fork, and they drove into town, down Main Street, and arrived at a large red building near the docks.

Poppie studied it through the windshield. "What is this place?"

"It used to be the ice house. Like a giant freezer. They stored the day's catch inside until they took it to the Mainland."

"Where did they get the ice?"

"They brought it over from the Mainland."

"Seems a bit counterproductive."

"Until they had refrigeration, it worked."

Lewis found a place to park not too far away, and they got out of the vehicle. Poppie watched the townspeople head inside. "So, is everyone in town as excited as you are for this town meeting?"

"It's a special one. So yeah, probably."

"Special, how?"

"Called by Chief Goodspeed."

"Hmm."

Lewis glanced at her. "Yes. The Deputy will be here, too."

"I didn't ask."

They went inside and found two seats together in the middle of the third row. After shuffling by several people, they sat down.

Poppie glanced around the room and spotted Jasper and the chief standing in the front corner. The chief was talking to an older man, and Jasper was looking like he'd rather be somewhere else. He must've sensed her watching him because he smiled at her and gave her a wink. She gave him a nod and returned his smile, then looked away as she tried to ignore how the wink had made her stomach feel.

Lewis nudged her. "What's going on with you two?"

"Nothing."

He studied her for a moment. "Something's changed."

"No. We had a nice lunch today while everyone was at brunch. I wasn't mean to him. He wasn't grumpy. So if that's what you mean, then maybe. I guess."

"Oh, brother."

"Who's that man?"

"Scott Haskell, the mayor."

"You have a mayor?"

"Shhh."

The mayor went to the podium in the front of the room and tapped on the microphone. It made a loud thumping noise, and he adjusted it, then spoke into it.

"There we go. Thanks for your patience, folks. We're going to get started now." He cleared his throat. "Chief Goodspeed has some announcements to make, but first, a couple of items need to be discussed." He motioned at Peg, who was sitting in the front row. She got up and went behind the podium.

"Thank you, everyone. I just want to mention a situation at The Loft. As most of you know, the men's room has been out of order for a week or so."

Poppie put a hand over her mouth and whispered to Lewis. "Seriously?"

"Shhh."

"In the meantime, the women's room is available. You just need to knock first and make sure no one's in there. And the ladies asked me to mention that they'd appreciate it if you put the seat down when you've finished."

The crowd murmured, and someone called out, "If we want to get nagged at for not putting down the seat, we'll go home to use the can."

Peg ignored him and went on. "So there's absolutely no reason for any of you gentlemen to relieve yourselves behind our building."

There were a few snickers in the crowd, and Poppie held back a laugh. She glanced at Jasper, who pointed a finger at her and shook his head.

"It's become a problem, and the chief has assured me he will charge you with indecent exposure if you're caught in the act."

Poppie looked at Jasper again, but he seemed to be concentrating hard on the back of the chief's head.

Peg smiled at the mayor. "Thank you, Scotty."

"Of course." He took a breath. "The other item on the agenda is Burt's roof. It started leaking, and it needs to be fixed before the rains come. So, there will be a sign-up sheet at the sheriff's office for volunteers and donations. We'd like to get it done before the end of the month. Maisy is heading that up, so see her if you have any questions." He looked at James. "And I guess that's it. Chief Goodspeed, it's all yours."

The chief approached the podium and gave the crowd a small smile. "Good evening, folks. I'm afraid what I have to say will be alarming, but I feel transparency is the right thing to do at this point. You probably have all heard about the fatal car accident on Thursday night. I'm telling you now, it wasn't the crash that killed the driver. The man was shot and died from his wounds."

A collective gasp filled the room, followed by an outburst of questions.

James held up his hands. "Let me finish, folks." He waited for them to quiet down. "Both the victim and the suspected shooter are mainlanders, and we're working to identify them. In the meantime..." He glanced at Jasper. "We believe the suspect is still on the island."

The gasps were louder this time, and the questions didn't stop when James held up his hands again. He looked at Jasper, who joined him, then whistled loudly. It got the crowd's attention, and they quieted down.

The chief stepped aside, and Jasper moved to the microphone. "I know it's upsetting, but I've seen the man, and I want to give you a description. We could use everyone's eyes and ears. This is Gracie Island. The man picked the wrong place to try to hide."

Jasper's words turned the mood around in the room from fear to indignation and a united front. He proceeded to describe the man as six foot, medium build, light short cropped hair, wearing jeans and a blue t-shirt.

The chief stepped back up, and Jasper moved aside. "We want everyone keeping an eye out for him. But we don't want any heroes. You see him, you call the sheriff's department. He's got to be getting mighty hungry and tired. I'll take your questions now."

The room exploded with questions as everyone got to their feet, and the chief began answering them as best he could. Jasper retreated to the corner, but the crowd still surrounded him. Poppie made her way to him and waited until he noticed her.

He excused himself from the group of people around him and went to her.

"Geez. That didn't go quite as expected." He took her arm, and they went through a door to a small room that appeared to have been a kitchen at one time.

She laughed. "What were you expecting?"

"I don't know. Not that."

"You just told them there was a killer running around the island. I think, considering that, it went pretty well."

"Hmm. I guess." He went to the door and cracked it open a couple of inches. "I should go back out there."

She smiled. "But you don't want to."

"Not even a little."

There was a door on the far side of the room. "Where does that go?"

"To the dock."

She raised an eyebrow at him.

He took a breath. "The chief will kill me."

"He probably won't even notice."

"Oh, he'll notice." He looked at the door to the meeting room, then at the door to the dock. "Let's go."

They went through the door and found themselves on a four-foot-wide wooden dock extending twenty feet onto the water. There were two sailboats tied on either side of it, and the lines slapping against the masts made a musical sound. They walked to the end of the dock and sat down, dangling their legs over the water a foot below. There was a light breeze, and the smell of the ocean air was strong.

Poppie peered over the edge into the dark water. "Do you have sharks here?"

"Probably. I've never seen one. I'm pretty sure they won't jump out of the water and pull you in, though."

"Pretty sure?"

The sun was setting, leaving the partly cloudy sky a beautiful shade of orange that reflected off the water at the edge of the horizon.

"Oh my gosh. This is beautiful. So, the mainland's that way?"

"Yes. Ten miles."

"You guys are really in the middle of nowhere."

"Yep." He glanced at her. "I don't suppose you have another little bottle of rum in your purse?"

"No. I have gum."

He held out his hand. "That works."

She dug in her purse and took out a pack of spearmint gum, handed him a piece, then took one for herself.

"How is gum a replacement for rum?"

"I don't know. Taste better, though."

They sat and chewed their gum as they watched the sun go down.

After several minutes of silence, Jasper said, "So, I guess you'll be leaving soon to start your job in urban planning or whatever?"

"Yeah. Soon. But I thought I'd stay through Friday. I'd like to hear some more of that music."

"It does kind of draw you in."

After more silence, during which Poppie was hoping he was glad she was staying until Friday, she asked, "So, why did you become a deputy sheriff?"

He shrugged. "I get to wear a cool uniform and carry a gun."

"Seriously. I don't think it's because you admire your father."

"I actually do admire the man as the chief. He was just never meant to be a father."

"Do you care to elaborate on that?"

"Nope. I end up sounding like an ungrateful whiner. He never beat me or humiliated me. He was never mean. He was just never there, emotionally or physically. I barely saw him growing up. But he provided for us. Kept a roof over our heads. Food on the table. I had a great childhood. I can't complain."

"Running around with your friends?"

"Yes. Pretty much the best playground a kid could ask for."

"I guess it is. If you don't mind the rain. And the fog. And the occasional hurricane."

"We haven't had a hurricane in thirty years."

"Sounds like you're about due."

"Don't say that. You'll jinx us." He stood and held a hand out to her. "We should get back. Lewis is probably wondering what happened to you."

She took his hand, and he pulled her to her feet, then let go. He stuck his hands in his pockets and started walking toward the building.

Poppie walked beside him. "So, the whole peeing in back of the restaurant...?"

Jasper laughed. "Unfortunately, it's become a problem."

"Wow. Maybe they should get the bathroom fixed."

"They're working on it. Seems to be an issue with the plumbing. The original steel pipes rust out eventually and need to be replaced by something more modern. It happens on a regular basis around here. But sooner or later, all the pipes will be replaced."

"Well, that's a relief." They approached the door. "So, how much trouble are you going to be in for ditching the chief?"

"Aww, I'll just tell him I was reassuring some townsfolk."

"Do you think he'll buy it?"

Jasper grinned. "Probably not." He opened the door for her, and she went inside. As Jasper closed the door, Lewis came through the other one.

"Jesus, I've been looking all over for you."

Poppie smiled at him. "Sorry. We were ditching the angry mob."

Lewis glanced at Jasper. "The chief's looking for you."

"Is he mad?"

"He isn't happy."

Jasper went to a window and opened it. "You haven't seen me." He threw a leg over the windowsill. "I'll see you guys later."

After Jasper disappeared out the window, Lewis closed it, then looked at Poppie. "Where were you two?"

"On the dock." At the skeptical look he gave her, she added, "I promise you there is nothing going on."

"Hmm."

"I'm leaving in a few days. I'm not going to start anything." *Even though he's tall and handsome and...unavailable.*

"Fine. I don't believe you. But, fine."

Chapter Thirteen

"It was just a dream."

For fear of running into the chief, Jasper left his Jeep in town and walked home. As he got about halfway there, he realized it probably wasn't the smartest thing to do, seeing as the bad guy was still at large and already had a grudge against him.

The rest of the way, he imagined the man lurking in every shadow. But he made it home safe and went inside. Then, for the first time in a long time, he locked his door. He sat on the couch, and Penny came darting out from under the chair and whined at his feet.

He picked her up and let her lick his cheek. "I missed you, too." He took off his jacket, which caused some pain in his shoulder, then removed his boots. His pain pills and a half bottle of water were on the coffee table. His pain was tolerable and had been all day, but he wanted to get a good night's sleep, so he took two pills before taking off his pants and shirt, then lying down. He pulled the blanket from the back of the couch and settled into the pillow. Penny snuggled under the blanket, and Pepper took his spot at Jasper's feet.

Jasper sighed. Compared to yesterday, this had been a pretty good day. He thought about reading a book, but after a yawn, he knew he wouldn't that last long. He closed his eyes and let sleep overtake him.

Jasper sat up straight in the dark, causing Penny to yelp as she fell off his chest and Pepper to jump off the couch.

"Shit." He rubbed his eyes and fumbled for the water bottle. He drained it, then tossed it onto the table as he picked up Penny. "Sorry, girl."

He laid back down. For months after Ivy died, Jasper had nightmares, though he hadn't had one for a while now. But what woke him from a sound sleep wasn't a nightmare. It was a dream. A dream about Poppie, and they weren't sparring anymore. In fact, they weren't even talking. They were too busy with...other activities.

He shook his head to clear the dream from his mind, but it didn't really help.

"Dammit." He suddenly felt guilty. Even though he had no control over his dreams or even considered doing what he was doing in this one, he felt like he'd betrayed Ivy.

He sat up again, this time making sure to bring Penny with him. He needed to logic his way out of it. "You can't cheat on your...wife...in a dream. It was just a dream. A stupid dream." *Poppie? Really? She was the last person he'd...* He laid back down. "Shit."

Jasper had trouble falling asleep again. He finally gave up around seven and got out of bed. He assumed he was going to have a busy day chasing leads since everyone in town would be looking for the bad guy. He needed a good breakfast, and he decided to go to the café today instead of The Sailor's Loft. As much as he loved his mother's and his aunt's cooking, the café had biscuits and gravy that couldn't be beat.

He made some coffee and sat on the front porch to drink it. The fog was thick this morning, and he could barely see his Jeep parked fifteen feet away. Jasper liked the fog. He liked how it felt in the air, and watching it burn off slowly fascinated him. Next to the rain in the sunshine, the fog was his favorite Gracie Island weather phenomenon.

He finished his coffee and went to take a shower, hoping the fog would wait to lift until he drove into town. Fog at night was dangerous to drive in. But in the daytime, he liked how it made him feel alone in the world.

The fog had cooperated, and he drove slowly to the café, arriving by eight, then settled into a booth in the back of the restaurant. He wanted to be as incognito as possible since he'd be dealing with the townsfolk soon enough.

He'd at first disagreed with the chief not letting everyone know about the man running around their island, but now that the news was out, he wondered if maybe they should've kept it to themselves. Three people had stopped him on the street between the Jeep and the café. They were understandably nervous and wanted answers Jasper didn't have. He tried to assure them as best he could without promising a miracle.

He ordered his breakfast and was taking his last bite when he saw Lewis and Poppie come through the door. He slid toward the wall and hoped the divider between the booths blocked him from their view. But no such luck. As Lewis headed toward the restroom, Poppie spotted Jasper and gave him a wave.

He gave her a nod, then sighed when she headed for his table.

He mumbled, "Shit," then gave her a small smile when she slid into the seat across the table.

"Good morning, Deputy. Why are you doing hiding back here?"

"I didn't want to deal with any concerned citizens until I had my breakfast."

"Having met the man face to face, they have a right to be concerned." She watched him as he finished his coffee. "So, how mad was the chief that you ditched him last night?"

"I haven't seen him." Jasper was irrationally bothered by her intrusion. The dream was still too fresh in his mind.

"Well, good luck with that." She smiled. "Are you okay?"

"Yeah. Sure. Why wouldn't I be?" She looked good today in a blue, double-breasted, corduroy coat.

She frowned. "No reason. Just asking."

"Hmm."

"I thought the cafe was your mother's competition."

"I was joking."

"Okay. What's good here? What did Deputy Goodspeed order from his great-uncle's café?"

Why was she always so perky? "Biscuits and gravy."

"Mmm. Sounds good."

He took his wallet out and put a five and a ten on the table. "I need to get to the station." He slid out of the booth and got to his feet. "I'll see you around."

"Oh, um…Okay. See you later."

Lewis sat at the table as Jasper walked by the window, then jogged across the street.

"Your best buddy was here?"

She sighed. "For a minute. He basically blew me off."

He pushed Jasper's plate to the edge of the table. "I told you to leave him alone."

"I just came to say hi, and... Whatever. He's back to being Deputy Grumpy."

"Maybe the chief reamed him."

She shook her head. "He hasn't seen the chief yet."

Lewis took a menu from the slot at the end of the table. "Don't take it personally."

She folded her hands and stared out the window. It was hard not to. She thought last night they'd finally gotten past the dueling and settled into something resembling a friendship.

Lewis looked at her over his menu. "What are you going to have?"

"Biscuits and gravy."

"Really? I thought you hated biscuits and gravy."

"I do."

As he feared, Jasper spent the day chasing leads reported by a citizenry with overactive imaginations. The man was spotted in the woods behind the Ice House and at the park. Someone else swore they saw him on a small boat headed for open water. Another said he was in the alley behind the grocery store. And so the day went with Jasper obligated to check out every lead. The chief helped, but he only took the calls in town, leaving Jasper to cover most of the populated and unpopulated areas of the island. By the end of the day, he was tired and frustrated and was wishing they'd never called the town meeting.

He ate a late dinner at The Sailor's Loft, then went to the Rusty Pelican for a beer. Even though his mother's restaurant had a bar, he didn't feel comfortable drinking there. She'd never judge him, but he felt like he'd be disappointing her. She was married to an alcoholic for sixteen years. She didn't need to see her son throwing back a few.

Aside from his monthly binge, he didn't drink much. He, too, knew what it was like being around an alcoholic. Tonight, however, he was on his second beer when Lewis came in and sat next to him.

He glanced at Jasper. "Rough day?"

"Gruesome. Apparently, the offender has the ability to be several places at once, miles away from each other."

"Well, if it's any consolation, I didn't see him today."

"You're the only one in town. Aside from me, of course."

Mellie came over, and Lewis ordered a beer. When she looked at Jasper, he shook his head.

"I'm good, thanks."

When Mellie left, Lewis said, "So I just missed you this morning at the café."

"Yeah. I had to run."

"Hmm. None of my business, really, but Poppie seems to think you blew her off."

Jasper looked at him. "Well, she's imagining things. I needed to go to work. It had nothing to do with her."

"Okay. I know she can be a pain in the ass. I wouldn't blame you if you did."

Jasper finished his beer. "Well, I didn't."

"Right. Gotcha." Mellie delivered Lewis' beer, and he took a drink. "So, I'm going out with Sarah on Saturday."

Jasper turned in his seat. "I knew you two would hit it off."

"Yeah. Of course, I'll be there Friday, with my harmonica."

"Good. You round out our sound." Jasper rubbed his shoulder. The doctor was right about the sling. He should've worn it. "I think I should be able to play by then." He got to his feet. "I'm going to head out. It's been a long day."

"Sure. Have a good night."

Jasper left some money on the bar and headed for the door. Lewis had nothing to do with him and Poppie and the dream, but he didn't want to talk to him either. As he got to the door, he considered going back and having another beer with Lewis.

Screw it. I'll be nice to him next time I see him. He went out to the parking lot and got into his Jeep, then drove the mile to his house. When he pulled in front of the house, Poppie was sitting on his porch.

He got out slowly, then went up the steps.

"What are you doing here?" He checked the time on his watch. "Kind of late."

"I was getting some groceries while Lewis went to have a beer. I think he was hoping to run into Sarah."

He leaned against a support beam. "He ran into me instead."

"I thought you didn't drink much other than...you know."

"I don't. But an occasional beer or two is normal. Especially after a day like today."

"A lot of supposed sightings of the guy you're looking for?"

Jasper sat in the only other chair. "Crazy day."

"Do you think they'll calm down after a day or two?"

"I doubt it. Not until we find him." He rubbed his face and covered a yawn. "My own fault, I guess. He should be in a jail cell right now."

"I appreciate you taking the blame, but it's my fault. I'm the one who, unsuccessfully, macraméd him."

Jasper rested his feet on a small table. "It's not your fault."

She leaned back in her chair. "Where do you think he is?"

"If I knew that, I wouldn't have been running all over the island today. He's a sneaky bastard. I'll give him that."

"Can I ask you something?"

"Sure."

She leaned forward and rested her forearms on her knees. "Are you mad at me?"

"No. Why would I be?"

"I don't know. We had a pretty good day yesterday. And today, it's like you're annoyed with me again. Not that that's not fun. But you *not* being annoyed at me is more fun."

Jasper smiled. "I'm not annoyed with you. And yesterday *was* a good day. Especially compared to Saturday. My attitude today has nothing to do with you."

"You sure?"

"Yes." He had to lie to her. He couldn't tell her he felt guilty just talking to her. Especially here on the porch, where he'd spent countless hours with Ivy.

She stood. "Okay. Sorry to waylay you on your porch. I was worried I'd said something stupid or, you know…inconsiderate."

He shook his head and stood, too. "Have a good night."

"Thanks. You too."

Jasper watched her walk to the truck and get in. She gave him a little wave before driving off, and he sat back down.

He'd be glad when she went home.

Chapter Fourteen

"Of course it's not a good thing."

The smell of smoke woke Jasper from a sound sleep. Sitting up, he turned on the light next to the couch. He couldn't tell where it was coming from, but it was close, and he got up to follow the scent. It got stronger as he went down the hall to the bedroom, and he pushed his hanging clothes out of the way. Smoke curled up from under the door.

Even though he hadn't worked many fires, Jasper knew the signs to look for. Before opening the door, he put a hand on it to see if it was hot. It wasn't, nor was the doorknob. He opened it slowly and put an arm up to shield his face as a blast of hot air hit him.

The back wall of the room was on fire, along with the bed and his grandmother's dresser. The candles in front of a picture of him and Ivy on their wedding day were melted, and the glass on the frame was cracked. He considered briefly running in to grab it but instead closed the door and ran down the hall.

Penny was still on the couch, but Pepper was nowhere to be seen. Jasper put on his pants, then picked up Penny and headed for the front door, hesitating again. Wondering what he should take with him. He looked at Penny, then took his jacket and keys off the rack by the door, stepped into his boots, and went outside, leaving the door open for the cat to run through if he was still inside. He put Penny in his Jeep, stuck his key in the ignition, and picked up his radio.

"Stan, this is Jasper. My house is on fire. Send everyone."

He closed Penny in the Jeep, then ran around to the back of the house. He turned on his hose and started spraying the fire, but as he did it, he knew it was hopeless. The porch was gone, and the fire had already spread to the roof of the old house. He kept spraying, and within minutes, the neighbors started arriving. He handed the hose to one of them, then ran to the front. As he tried to go inside, someone took his arm and stopped him.

He turned to see his father. "Don't, Son. It's too late."

"I didn't get anything out."

"It's too late. You got yourself out. That's all that matters."

"But—"

"Jasper. No."

Jasper sighed and nodded. James was right. It was too late. He could see the fire through the front window now. The couch he was just sleeping on was burning, along with the table and the stack of books he hadn't finished reading.

James held out his hand. "Do you have the keys to your Jeep?"

"In the ignition."

James left him and moved the Jeep back a safe distance. Jasper watched his father take a moment to pet Penny and put a blanket from the backseat around her. When he got out of the vehicle, he became the chief again and took over the operation. Jasper watched, unable to move from the spot he was in or help out. He was frozen and unbearably sad. The house wasn't much, but it was all he had left of Ivy.

Time seemed to have no meaning, but after a while, the activity died down. Everyone seemed to know there was nothing to do now but keep the fire from spreading. They kept an eye on flying embers and stopped spot fires before they took hold. In the damp soil, it wasn't hard to do. There was a propane tank twenty yards from the house, and two men stationed themselves by it. If the fire got too close to it, it'd blow.

Jasper was standing too close to his burning house, but he couldn't make himself move. He was mesmerized by the flames, now on the front porch. He could feel the heat on his face and his bare arms.

He felt a hand on his back, then heard Poppie whispering. "Oh my gosh, Jasper, I'm so sorry." She moved in front of him, then put her arms around him and pulled him in for a hug. She spoke into his ear. "Penny?"

Jasper stepped away from her. "She's in the Jeep."

Poppie wiped her eyes. "Thank God. Pepper?"

Jasper shrugged. "I don't know." He glanced at the Jeep. "Would you mind...?"

"Of course not." But please, move back a little. He took a few steps back as she headed for the Jeep and opened the door. He watched her pick up Penny and carry her away from the fire, the confusion, and the noise.

Lewis appeared beside Jasper. "What happened?"

"I don't know. The smoke woke me."

When the roof caved in, everyone retreated as embers filled the sky. Lewis took Jasper's arm and pulled him another ten feet away. There were at least twenty people there now trying to help.

Jasper watched the chief, still in charge, start thanking them all for showing up but telling them to go home. The men from the volunteer fire department were spraying the edges of the fire to keep it contained, using the neighbor's hoses from either side of Jasper's house and the fire department water truck.

Jasper shook his head. "It's like pissing on a forest fire."

Lewis patted his back but didn't say anything.

When one of the men from the fire department came up to them with a melted gas can in his hand, he asked, "Is this yours?"

Jasper shook his head. "No. Mine's on my Jeep." Jasper started walking toward the vehicle. In the back, where his gas can was supposed to be tied to his bumper, were two pieces of cut rope. "Son of a bitch. Someone burned my house down."

It took an hour for the house to burn to the ground, and within two hours, most everyone had given their condolences to Jasper and left. The only people remaining were three men from the fire department, James, Kat, Lewis, and Poppie. She'd been sitting in the passenger seat of Lewis' truck with Penny.

When he was finally able to move away from the fire, Jasper went to the truck and got in behind the wheel. Penny whined, then jumped from Poppie's lap to his.

Poppie turned toward them. "Lewis said fires are rare around here."

"They are."

"Was it him? From the lighthouse?"

"I don't know who else it'd be."

"I don't get it. Why would he do this?"

Jasper shrugged. "I don't know. I saved his ass twice. I guess I should've let the ocean take him."

"If you had, you never would've forgiven yourself. I at least know that much about you."

He glanced at her. "I have a confession to make to you."

"You don't owe me anything."

He took a deep breath. "You were right about Sunday and about this morning."

"Jasper, really, it's okay."

"No. I was an ass...*I mean...A* hole." He gave her a little smile. "And I'm sorry." He watched the smoldering ruins of his house for a moment while he scratched Penny behind the ears. "I found myself...enjoying your company and—"

"Jasper, please. You don't need to—"

"Just let me say the hell what I want to say."

"Okay."

"I loved my wife so much. I still do. Losing her—" He took a moment. "Having fun or enjoying the company of someone else. Anyone else. Seems like a betrayal." He glanced at her, then looked at Penny. "You're...annoying as hell. But I like you, and you don't deserve to be treated badly just because I don't have my shit together. So, I'm sorry for this morning."

She reached over and petted Penny's back. "You can make it up to me."

"How so?"

"When you're up to it, but before Saturday because I'll be headed home, you can take me to breakfast."

"Biscuits and gravy?"

She smiled. "I've always hated biscuits and gravy. But this morning, after you left, I ordered some."

"What did you think?"

"I still hate biscuits and gravy."

He chuckled. "How do you feel about French toast and bacon?"

"I love French toast and bacon."

"Coffee?"

She shook her head. "I don't drink coffee."

He turned toward her. "What? How do you function?" She shrugged, and he said, "*That's* what the little bottle of rum was for."

She rubbed Penny's head, then removed her hand when she brushed Jasper's. "Do you really want to see what I'm like on caffeine?"

"God, no. Stick to rum."

When Lewis tapped on the window, they both turned toward him as he opened the driver's side door.

"Sorry to interrupt. I think your mom's ready to take you home."

Jasper nodded and stepped out of the car with Penny in his arms.

Lewis put a hand on his arm. "If you need anything…"

"I love my mom, but after a couple of days at her house, I'll be ready to shoot myself."

"You're welcome to my couch anytime."

"I might take you up on that." He peered back in at Poppie. "Give me a couple of days."

She nodded. "See ya, Deputy."

As Jasper walked away, Lewis got into the truck. When he looked at Poppie, she started to cry, and he put his arms around her and stroked her hair.

"I know. I know."

A few minutes later, she sat up and wiped her eyes. Then he handed her a napkin from the glove box, and she blew her nose.

She glanced at him and said, "Sorry," as she deposited the used napkin in the pocket on the door. "He's lost everything now. His wife. And now this. It was all he had left of her."

"It's tragic. I know."

"So what happens now? What's he going to do?"

"Jasper has a family of three hundred here on the island. We'll take care of him."

"I think I'm going to miss Gracie Island." She smiled at him. "And you, of course."

"And Deputy Goodspeed?"

"A little." She could see Jasper through the windshield, talking with his parents. "Okay. A lot." She glanced at Lewis. "Just look at him! He's...really...hot."

"Thanks for cleaning that up for me."

"It's so much more than that, though."

"I know. I knew the second you laid eyes on him."

She swung and hit Lewis on the shoulder. "You did not."

He nodded.

"So, was it when he was throwing up in the grass? Or when he inferred my name was stupid? Or maybe it was the next morning—"

"All of the above."

She frowned. "I think I could've fallen in love with Deputy Jasper Goodspeed."

Lewis sighed. "He's not going anywhere."

"Do you think he'll be ready someday?"

"Of course. You just need to keep coming to visit me until he is."

"I can do that."

He nodded again, and chuckled. "I wish you were coming to see me. But I'll take you however I can get you."

She hugged him. "I love you, Lewis. And I'll be coming back to see you. The deputy is a side project."

"Sure he is." Lewis started the truck. "Let's go home."

It wasn't until he was taking off his smoky, fire-singed clothing that Jasper started let the reality of what happened sink in. He stepped into the shower in his mother's guest bathroom and, for a moment, let the emotions overtake him.

When his mother knocked on the door, he took a deep breath, rubbed his face, and brushed his hair out of his eyes.

"Are you okay, honey? Do you need anything?"

He cleared his throat. "I'm fine, Mom."

"Okay. A couple of the boys brought some clothes over for you. I'll put them on your bed."

"Thank you."

"And I'm sorry the shampoo smells like flowers. I'll get something more appropriate for you tomorrow."

Jasper picked up the bottle and read the label. *Lilac and Jasmine. Could be worse.* "It's fine, Mom."

"Okay. I'll leave you be."

He took another breath. "Get it together. It's just a house." He closed his eyes and stuck his face under the water. "You can build another house. A house where you won't see Ivy in every room. Maybe this was a good thing." *You're talking to yourself. Of course, it wasn't a good thing. It was a horrible thing.* He turned his back to the shower spray and got his hair wet. *You're going to be wearing someone else's clothes tomorrow smelling like lilac and jasmine.*

James was sitting at the kitchen counter on one of three barstools in Kat's kitchen. She set a cup of coffee in front of him.

He took a sip. "How'd he do last night?"

"I think he was awake most of the night, but he's sleeping now. I just checked on him." She went to a box of pastries on the counter and opened it. "Bear claw?"

"Yes. Thanks."

She put one on a plate, and set it in the microwave, then turned back to James. "You need to give him time to get over this."

"Of course. I know." When she frowned at James, he said, "I've let him have his fifth of the month thing. I know he has his own way of processing."

"Yet you interrupted him last week."

"There was a man with a bullet in his head. I needed him."

The microwave dinged, and Kat set the pastry in front of James. "Why would this man, loose on our island, choose to burn Jasper's house?"

"I'm thinking Jasper wasn't completely forthcoming on the events of Saturday."

When Jasper walked into the room, they both looked at him as he sat at the counter, leaving an empty stool between him and James.

"There's nothing I haven't told you." Kat set a cup of coffee in front of him. "All I did to him was save his life. Twice."

Kat put another bear claw into the microwave. "Maybe he didn't want to be saved."

"They may think that. But when they're facing heaven, or in his case, hell, they'll grab the hand offering to pull them from the abyss." His parents both looked at him, and he shrugged. "I can be prophetic when I want to be."

Kat handed him the pastry. "Maybe it was random. Maybe he was trying to create a diversion."

"He took the gas can from my Jeep. The Jeep he cut the gas line on. He knew whose house that was."

James ate his last bite and drained his coffee cup. "We'll have to ask the man his motives when we catch him." He got to his feet and put a hand on Jasper's shoulder. "Take some time. Come in when you're ready."

Jasper watched James leave through the kitchen door, then turned to his mother. "Who the hell was that?"

"He's trying, Jasper."

"Hmm. He's about thirty years too late."

Chapter Fifteen

"Here, kitty, kitty."

Jasper looked through the local phone directory for Lewis' number. They were good friends, but he rarely called him. He also had the annoying problem of remembering numbers. Names he was good at. Phone numbers, not so much.

The Lighthouse Courier put a phone book out once a year. But only made changes to it if someone moved in or out or died. His mother was busy in the kitchen, so he found the number, then dialed the phone.

Poppie answered the call. "Hello?"

"Poppie?"

"Yes, Deputy Goodspeed. Is this official business?"

"No." The phone was on a desk, and he sat on the chair. "I'm going into the office today. I need to find this bastard."

"I don't blame you."

Penny came to Jasper's feet, and he picked her up and set her in his lap. "But I was wondering if you wanted to let me buy you that apology breakfast tomorrow?"

"Sure. I'd like that."

"Okay."

"Have you been back to your house?"

He took a moment. "No. I'm going there now. I need to see if Pepper showed up. He's probably pretty hungry by now."

"Do you want some help?"

"Well, hopefully, he's sitting there wondering what happened to his house."

"But if he isn't?"

"Sure. If you want to swing by." The thought of having company was actually quite appealing. He wasn't looking forward to returning to the pile of ash that, just yesterday, was his home.

"Okay. I'll see you in a little bit, then."

As he hung up the phone, Kat came into the room. "Did I hear you say you were going into the office today?"

"Yes. I can't sit here and do nothing. I'm physically able to work. I need to work."

She studied him for a moment, then nodded. "Come see me later to check in, please. I'll feed you lunch."

"I will."

She went to him and hugged him. "I have some of old Jack's food. I couldn't bear to part with it." She went to the kitchen pantry and retrieved a bag of cat food. "Take it with you. Pepper will be hungry when you find him."

Jasper took the bag. "Thank you." He set Penny on the floor. "Would you mind bringing her to the restaurant today? I don't want to leave her here all alone. She's a little confused."

"Of course. Peg and I will spoil her rotten."

Jasper frowned. "Not too rotten."

Kat patted him on the cheek. "Go find Pepper."

Jasper drove to his house and parked in front of the pile of ash with a few black boards sticking out of it. It was still smoldering, but it was supposed to rain soon, so that'd extinguish any hot spots that were left. He shook off the feeling of overwhelming loss that hit him as he tried to picture the house as it'd been yesterday. For some reason, he couldn't quite pull up the image. He sighed and got out of the Jeep.

Pepper wasn't sitting there as he had hoped, and he feared the worse. If the cat was able to come home, he would've. Even if home was a pile of ash. Jasper called Pepper's name, then shook the bag of food.

When he heard a vehicle, he turned to see Lewis' truck approaching. Poppie parked next to the Jeep, then got out of the truck.

She seemed to be as devastated as he felt, but she produced a smile. "Any luck?"

Jasper shook his head. "No. But I just got here. I was hoping..."

Poppie looked at the remains of the house, then glanced at Jasper. "Where should we start?"

"He probably wouldn't have gone down by the water, so in the trees, maybe." He headed for the stand of trees that stood between his house and the neighbor's. There was a lot of brush and tall grass between the trees. Perfect for a freaked-out cat to hide in.

"Would he go to the neighbor's house?"

"No. Jake has two big dogs. Pepper steers clear of them."

They took it slow, calling Pepper's name, interspersed with "Here, kitty, kitty."

When they made it halfway through the quarter-acre stand of trees, Jasper stopped.

"Shh."

Poppie stopped, too. "Did you hear something?"

He held up his hand. "Pepper?"

A small meow came from under a nearby fern. Jasper went to it and knelt. He lifted the leaves a few inches and spotted the cat's blue eyes.

"Hey, buddy." He reached in and petted Pepper's ears. "It's okay. I'm going to lift you out of there."

Jasper gently lifted the cat and pulled him out of the bush.

Poppie gasped when she saw Pepper. His front paws were burned, as were the tip of his tail and one of his ears. The ends of his whiskers were singed, and there was a pink spot on the end of his black nose.

Jasper stood and tucked the cat inside his coat. "I need to take him to Dr. Hannigan."

"He's a vet?"

"No. But he's the only doctor we've got." He started walking toward the Jeep.

"I'll come with you. Let me hold him while you drive." She got into the Jeep, and Jasper put Pepper in her lap, then took his jacket off and put it over him.

He got in behind the wheel, swearing beneath his breath. "Now I'm really pissed."

They drove to the clinic, and Jasper carried Pepper inside to the empty waiting room. Amy, the receptionist, looked up and smiled, then lost it when she saw who it was.

"Oh, Jasper, I'm so sorry about your house."

He nodded and uncovered Pepper's head. "I need to see the doc."

"Oh my goodness." She came from behind the desk. "Come into room one. Dr. Hannigan is with a patient. But he shouldn't be too long. I'll let him know you're here."

They followed her down the hall and into a small examination room.

"Can I get you anything? Coffee? Water?"

He shook his head, then glanced at Poppie.

"I'm fine." Amy left, and Poppie looked around the room. "It's like you guys live in a time-warp. This is so 1960s."

"Yeah, well, I bet you couldn't take an injured animal into your fancy modern medical facility."

"That's true." She rubbed Pepper's good ear. "He's going to be alright." She glanced at Jasper. "Isn't he?"

"Doc will fix him right up." He wanted that to be true, but he wasn't sure. Pepper looked bad and was uncharacteristically quiet and docile.

She looked closely at Jasper. "Is that Lewis' shirt?"

"I don't know. Is it? There were a bunch of clothes lying on the bed this morning. I picked one and put it on."

"Oh my gosh. You lost all your clothes. So everything you have on—"

"Isn't mine. Yes."

"Even your—"

"Do you really want to know the answer to that question?"

"Um. No. I guess not."

"I don't know why you're so obsessed with my underwear. Whether I'm wearing them or not. Or who they belong to."

She started to argue with him but stopped when Dr. Hannigan came through the door.

"Am I interrupting?"

They both said, "No," at the same time.

He put a hand on Jasper's shoulder. "I'm so sorry about the fire."

Jasper nodded.

"If you need anything, just ask."

"Thank you."

Dr. Hannigan took Pepper out of Jasper's arms and set him on the examination table. After a few minutes, he said, "Well, the good news is it looks worse than it is. He'll be fine. Though his hair may not grow back in these burned areas. Hold on to him. Don't let him jump off the table. I'll be right back."

Jasper sat on the table next to Pepper and put a hand on his back.

When the door closed behind the doctor, Poppie whispered, "I'm not at all obsessed with your underwear, or lack thereof."

Jasper smiled. "Okay." He stroked Pepper's back. "You're going to be fine, pal."

Poppie went to a wooden chair and sat, then picked up a magazine and flipped through it. She frowned and looked at the cover and then at the date. She held it up and tapped it with her finger. "Issue date is March 2017."

"So?"

She shook her head and set the magazine down as Dr. Hannigan returned with a large wooden container resembling a tackle box. He set it on the counter and opened it.

"I'm going to give Pepper a sedative before I clean these burns. Once he's relaxed, I'll insert an IV and give him some fluids and an antibiotic." With a syringe in his hand, he went to the cat. "Hold him still."

Jasper held onto Pepper but couldn't watch the doctor give the shot. He looked at Poppie, and she smiled at him.

He mouthed, "What?"

She mouthed back. "You're so cute."

He frowned, and then Dr. Hannigan stepped away and deposited the syringe in a plastic container. "That'll take a few minutes to work." He looked at Jasper. "How's the shoulder?"

"It's fine."

"Did you wear the sling at all?"

Jasper glanced at Poppie. "No. I... Sorry." He shrugged.

The doctor said, "Turn a little and sit straight." Jasper complied, and Dr. Hannigan began probing the shoulder. When Jasper winced and released a small groan, Dr. Hannigan stepped back. "Let me see your range of movement?"

Jasper moved the shoulder in a limited circular motion, this time holding in the groan.

Hannigan went to the counter and retrieved a sling. "I can't make you wear it. But you're going to heal much faster if you do. Just a couple days of limited use, and it'll start feeling much better."

Jasper took the sling from him. "Thank you."

"How are your pain meds? Did you lose them in the fire?"

"Yeah. But I'm fine."

"Okay. If you change your mind, let me know."

Dr. Hannigan spent the next thirty minutes cleaning and dressing Pepper's burns. Again, Jasper couldn't watch. He sat in the chair next to Poppie and looked through the magazine she'd discarded. He wasn't interested in the content anyway, so it didn't matter that it was several years old.

When the doctor was finished, Pepper had his two front paws wrapped and a bandage around his head and under his chin, covering his one ear. The tail was left uncovered since there was no way to bandage it.

"He's going to be out of it for another hour or so. And probably won't feel like doing much for a day or two. But he'll be back to himself soon enough. Keep him dry, clean, and hydrated. He might not eat much at first. Don't worry about it. He'll eat when he's ready." He lifted Pepper and handed him to Jasper. "Are you staying with your mother?"

"Yeah. For now."

"And your little pooch...?"

"Penny. She's fine. I got her out. I just couldn't find Pepper."

"Well, he did alright, considering." He gave Pepper a pat on the head. "Bring him back next week, and I'll check his progress."

"Okay. Thanks, Doc."

"You take care, now." He glanced at Poppie. "You're Lewis' sister?"

"Yes."

"Right, I heard you were in town. What do you think of our little island?"

She glanced at Jasper. "It's quite unique."

Dr. Hannigan laughed. "That's one word for it."

Chapter Sixteen

"Save the fireplace."

As Jasper drove Poppie back to his house and Lewis' truck, he reached over and rubbed Pepper's undamaged ear. The cat was still drowsy from the sedative and purred quietly.

"I don't suppose you'd be willing to watch him today for me? If not, I'll just stay home with him."

"Of course I can watch him. You go to work." She looked at his shoulder. "Are you going to wear your sling?"

"Um, probably not."

"I guess it's hard to look official with your arm in a sling. Of course, without your uniform..."

"I have a uniform at work. And some spare clothes. So, I'm good to go."

"Well, I'll take good care of Pepper and call you if anything weird happens. But I'm sure he'll probably sleep all day."

They arrived at the house, and Jasper sat for a moment after turning off the engine. He sighed as he looked at what used to be his house.

Poppie glanced at him. "Did you own the house?"

"Yeah. Which means I still have the two acres."

"So you can rebuild?"

"Eventually. The chief has an old travel trailer I can haul over here. At least, I think he'll let me use it. It's just sitting on his property."

Poppie turned in the seat. "I know today is not the day for it, but someday, maybe you can tell me what the deal is between you and your father."

"It's a long story. Probably need a whole bag of tiny rum bottles to get through it."

She opened her door and got out with Pepper in her arms. Jasper handed her the bag of cat food. "Take this in case he wants to eat."

"Okay. Don't worry about him. He'll be fine."

"I'm not worried."

"Go do your deputy thing. I'll see you later."

"Thanks, Poppie. And thanks for helping me find him and taking him to Doc's."

She shrugged. "I was happy to do it. That's what you guys do around here, right? Help each other out? Take care of each other? Be there when you're down?"

"Yeah. That's what we do around here. But you're not from around here."

"Thank goodness."

"Are you looking forward to going home to the big city?"

She took a moment. "Honestly, I don't know. I'm oddly intrigued by all of you."

"Hmm. Well, if you miss us, you know where to find us."

Poppie smiled. "See ya, Deputy."

"You take care, Poppie."

Jasper waited until she pulled away before getting out of the Jeep and walking to the pile of ashes. The fire had burned so fast and hot, there was nothing left. The stone fireplace was intact, and the charred refrigerator was lying on its side next to the stove. Nothing else was identifiable. He circled the ruins to where the bedroom had been and squatted a foot from the ashes. When he saw a small shape he thought he recognized, he stood and took a few careful steps into the debris. He kicked at the small cylindrical item that had caught his eye.

"Shit." He bent and picked it up. "Son of a bitch." He stepped out of the ashes and blew the dust from the metal film cartridge he'd had since he was a kid, then opened it. He dumped the contents into his hand. Six months after Ivy died, he'd taken his wedding ring off and put it into the container, then stashed it in the top drawer of his grandmother's dresser.

He studied the gold band in the palm of his hand, then looked at the sky.

"Thank you. You always did know what I needed before I did."

He returned the ring to the canister and dropped it into his pocket. When he got to the Jeep, he picked up the radio. "Maisy, can you connect me to Hal Walker?"

"Sure thing, hon."

The radio was silent for a few moments, then crackled. "Walker Excavation."

"Hal, this is Jasper. How soon can you come clear my house?"

"As soon as the insurance company gives me the okay. But don't you want to take some time to sift through it? Might be something salvageable."

Jasper put his hand on the canister in his pocket. "I've got all I need. Just want it gone."

"Okay. I'll call Rick Haven and have him wrap up the paperwork, then clear my schedule. Do you want me to save the fireplace?"

Jasper looked at the stone chimney he'd built with help from his grandfather a year before he died. "Yeah. Save the fireplace."

When Jasper came through the office door, Maisy came around the counter and hugged him. "Honey, I'm so sorry."

She let go of him, and Jasper took a few steps back. "Thank you. Is he in?"

"No. He ran out of here pretty quick about forty-five minutes ago."

"If he checks in, will you let him know I'm here?"

"Sure."

Jasper headed for his office and closed the door. His spare uniform was hanging from a hook on the back of the door. He took the film canister out of his pocket and set it on the desk, then locked the door and changed into his uniform. Somehow, it made him feel a little better.

He unlocked the door, then sat at his desk before picking up the canister and opening it again. He took his ring out and looked at it for a moment, then slipped it on. He held out his hand, then shook his head. That *didn't* make him feel better. He took it off, put it back into the canister, and then stashed it in the top drawer of his desk.

The sound of the phone ringing startled him, and he took a breath. "Jesus. Chill out." He lifted the receiver. "Deputy Goodspeed."

"The chief needs you at the old Meyer's place."

"Thank you, Maisy." Working would help. But catching the bastard would make him feel almost whole again.

Jasper left his office and went into the reception area. Maisy came out from behind her desk. "The chief shouldn't be asking you to work today."

"It's fine." He put his hand on his belt where his holster should've been.

She held up a finger, opened a cupboard, and handed him his gun and holster. "The chief cleaned this for you."

He took it and clipped it onto his belt. When the fax machine kicked on, they both went to it and watched as the paper slowly fed through the machine. When it finished, Maisy handed it to Jasper.

He glanced at it, then took a closer look. "Son of a—" He glanced at Maisy. "This is what we've been waiting for. We have an ID." He read the report again, then asked Maisy for the key to the gun safe.

"Are you sure?"

"Yeah. This guy's a bit of a loose cannon. I want to be prepared next time I see him."

She handed him the key, and he opened the gun safe and took out a pump action, twelve gauge shotgun.

She frowned. "Well, that should slow him down."

He gave her a wink, then left the office and drove the four miles to the old Meyer's house. It was a mile from the nearest house and had been abandoned for several years. Jasper had checked it out on Friday and found it empty. The chief was standing on the porch when Jasper arrived and parked next to the Bronco.

"What did you find?"

James waved him toward the door, then went inside. Jasper followed him. The open windows let in enough light to see by, and it was clear someone had been staying in the house. There were empty cans of food and several water bottles. Six empty beer cans were piled in a corner next to an unopened six-pack.

Jasper looked around. "Where the hell is he getting this stuff?"

"No one locks their doors. Pretty easy to sneak in and take a couple cans of food. Not enough for anyone to notice."

"I'd notice if a six-pack of beer was missing from my fridge."

James glanced at him but didn't say anything.

Jasper pulled the fax out of his pocket. "This came in as I was leaving."

James looked it over. "The men were related?"

"Apparently."

"How can you be angry enough to shoot someone you're related to?"

This time, Jasper glanced at the chief without commenting. He walked to a half-empty can of chili with a spoon sticking out of it and an almost full can of beer. He glanced at James.

"Does this look like someone left halfway through their meal?"

James came up beside Jasper. "Might be." He looked through the window. "Could be he's out there watching us."

Jasper checked the window on the opposite wall. There was a stand of trees, perfect for hiding in while keeping an eye on intruders. "The trees?"

James headed for the door. "Come outside. Let's have a conversation by the trucks."

Standing next to the vehicles would give them a clear view of the trees. James put his back to them. "Your eyes are better than mine."

Jasper stood in front of him, and as they talked randomly about nothing, he scanned the trees for any movement or something that didn't belong in the gray-green foliage of the red oaks. After a few moments, he said, "Got him."

"How far in?"

"About ten feet. Maybe more. If you can make sure he stays there, I can come in behind him using the ravine at the end of Newman's property."

"Do it. I'll stay busy here."

Jasper headed for his Jeep and got in, then with a wave for effect, he backed up and drove away.

He went to the main road, drove a half-mile, then turned onto a runoff ditch that followed the backside of the stand of trees. It was currently dry with spots of mud, an occasional boulder, and plenty of potholes. He bounced along, gritting his teeth against the pain it caused in his shoulder until he figured he was about even with where he'd seen the man. The man they now knew was named Roger Ingram from Bayridge, Massachusetts. Age thirty-two. Brother of Mark, the deceased.

Jasper made a U-turn and then stopped the Jeep and got out, bringing the shotgun with him. The bank was about four feet tall, and he zigzagged his way up since climbing with his bad shoulder was out of the question. He slipped once but caught himself before reaching the top and moving into the trees. There was a lot of open space between the oaks, and the brush was low, so he made his way, slowly moving from tree to tree as best he could.

When he spotted Roger twenty feet ahead, he slowed down, then stopped behind a large holly tree. He watched for a moment. Roger seemed to be intently keeping an eye on the chief. Jasper moved closer, careful not to step on anything that'd give his presence away. He got within ten feet, stopped to collect himself, then cocked the shotgun.

Roger heard him and turned around and smiled. "Well, if it isn't the deputy."

"Put your hands on your head. Interlock your fingers."

"You going to shoot me if I don't?"

Jasper could see James heading across the field toward them. "You burned my house and my cat. Yes, I'll shoot you if you don't."

Roger put his hands on top of his head, then glanced back when he heard James approaching.

James took out his cuffs and put a hand on Roger's wrist. "Let's do this nice and slow. One at a time." He lowered Roger's right arm and put a cuff around his wrist.

Jasper pointed the shotgun at the ground and took a step toward them. As James took Roger's other hand, Roger threw his head back, hitting James in the nose. James dropped to one knee as Roger made a dive toward Jasper, who didn't have time to get out of the way. Roger hit him full force on the right shoulder, knocking him to the ground, grabbed the shotgun, and took off running.

James got to his feet and went to Jasper. "You okay, Son?"

"Go. I'm fine."

James took off after Roger, who had a good head start on him.

Jasper took a moment before struggling to his feet and following James. As he wove through the trees, he caught glimpses of the chief fifty or so yards ahead. When he heard the shotgun go off, Jasper started running.

He found James on the ground, and Roger was gone. Jasper knelt next to James.

"Chief." There was no blood on James' back, so Jasper rolled him over.

James grumbled. "I'm fine, dammit. The bastard missed."

Jasper suddenly felt his knees give out, and he sat down next to James. "Shit. I thought—"

"If it wasn't for me tripping on that root at the perfect moment, I might be."

Jasper took a moment, then got to his feet. "I'll go after him."

"Don't bother. He's long gone." James looked at Jasper. "Did you leave your keys in the Jeep?"

Jasper sunk back down to the ground and leaned against a tree. There were no words to convey his level of frustration. Jasper shook his head. "He took my damn Jeep?"

James sat up, pulled a handkerchief from his pocket, and dabbed at his nose.

"Don't worry. He'll leave it somewhere. We'll find it."

Jasper nodded toward James' nose. "Is it broken?"

"No. I don't think so. How's the shoulder?"

"Pretty sure it's dislocated again."

"Damn."

Jasper picked up a rock and threw it over the edge of the ravine. "We're either the worst members of the sheriff's department or—"

"He's crazy. And he doesn't give a shit. Most dangerous criminal there is."

"I should've kept the twelve-gauge on him."

"And take the chance of shooting me? You followed protocol." He glanced at Jasper. "For once." He shrugged. "I shouldn't have let him head bang me. Second guessing won't help." He got slowly to his feet, then held a hand out to Jasper. "Let's get you back to town and to the clinic."

Jasper let James pull him to his feet, and they headed for the Bronco. About halfway there, James said, "Next time you leave your Jeep to pursue a suspect, bring your keys."

Jasper nodded. "Roger that."

James glanced at him. "Do you want me to call your mother and let her know you're at the clinic?"

Jasper sighed. "Can we just keep this one between us?"

"Sure."

"Probably shouldn't mention your clumsiness saved you from a load of buckshot, either."

"Probably not."

"Thanks, Dad."

Both men hesitated for a brief second before continuing on. Jasper hadn't called the chief "Dad" in ten years. And he wasn't sure why he did now. He just kept walking. He was too tired and too pissed off to try to figure it out now.

Chapter Seventeen

"I'm not falling for that, again."

As he had done on Saturday night, James dropped Jasper off in front of the clinic. It was mid-afternoon, and the waiting room had two other people in it. Jasper went to the counter and waited for Amy, who was on the phone.

When she hung up and turned to him, she said, "Oh no. Is it Pepper?"

"No. It's me this time."

She came around the counter and took his left arm. "Come sit. You look like you're in some pain." He took a chair, and she sat next to him. "What's going on?"

Jasper glanced at Max Shepard, who was sitting nearby. He owned Max's Marine and sold everything from bait to outboard motors. Max knew everyone in town. And if something was going on, Max knew about it and felt it was his duty to spread it around.

"Just having some trouble with my shoulder."

Amy patted his knee. "You stay right here, and Dr. Hannigan will be with you shortly. Would you like an icepack?"

"Um. Sure."

She rushed off, and Jasper nodded at Max. "How's it going?"

Max held up a finger wrapped in a bloody paper towel. "Damn near severed my finger."

"Ouch."

The other person waiting was Meg Turner. She taught at the school and had been new when Jasper was in high school. Now she'd been there fifteen years. She seemed to have a cold or the flu, and Jasper was glad she was sitting across the room. He smiled at her when she looked his way, and she gave him a little wave in response with the tissue in her hand, then used it to wipe her nose.

Jasper leaned back and closed his eyes, then remembered he was supposed to check in with his mother. He stood and went to the counter. "Can I use the phone?"

"Sure." She pushed it toward him and handed him the ice pack. "This should help."

Jasper dialed the restaurant. He called it often enough, so it was one number he remembered. After waiting for a few rings, Aunt Peg answered.

"The Sailor's Loft."

"Aunt Peg, this is Jasper."

She laughed into the phone. "Since you're the only one in town who calls me Aunt Peg, I kinda figured that out. How're you doing, sweetheart?"

Jasper glanced at Amy. "I'm fine. Just checking in. Is Mom available?"

"Sure thing. She said you were coming by for lunch."

"I got tied up. I'll be there for dinner."

"Good. We got some fresh salmon today."

"Sounds good."

She left the phone, and a few moments later, Kat came on the line. "I was worried about you. I called the office, and Maisy said you went off to meet James."

"Yeah. I'll tell you about it later. I'll come in for dinner."

"Okay. We got some fresh salmon today."

"Yum."

He wasn't really a fan of salmon, fresh or otherwise, but his mother and Peg were always trying to feed it to him. He hung up the phone, returned to his seat, and put the icepack on his shoulder. Meg had been called back while he was on the phone. He wondered how long it would take for Dr. Hannigan to tell her there wasn't much he could do for her, then send her home with instructions to drink plenty of fluids and get some rest.

He glanced at Max, who was peering at the end of his bandage. Max's injury might take a bit longer.

Forty minutes later, when Max came out of the exam room with a freshly bandaged finger, which presumably had stitches under it, Amy escorted Jasper to the same room he'd been in a few hours ago with Pepper. He sat on the table and waited for Dr. Hannigan to come in and reprimand him.

The doctor came in with a frown. "What's going on?"

"Pretty sure it popped out again."

Dr. Hannigan felt Jasper's shoulder. "They don't just pop out. What happened?"

"Well, believe it or not, the same...person of interest...plowed into me again."

It didn't appear the doctor believed the story. "What are the odds of that happening?"

"I know it's hard to believe, but it's actually true. He's also the same guy who burned down my house and put the hole in the head of the unidentified man in your morgue."

Hannigan took a step back and studied him for a moment. "I'm assuming you have this man in custody now?"

Jasper sighed. "You know, that would be a pretty good assumption. And I wish it were true. But unfortunately, it's not."

"He's still at large?"

"Yes. And in my Jeep." He grimaced as Dr. Hannigan probed some more. "The good news is, the man in the morgue is now identified. Along with the man in my Jeep."

"Sounds complicated. It also sounds like you've been doing too much, considering you've now dislocated your shoulder twice in four days. Let's get that shirt off."

Jasper started unbuttoning his shirt, then let the doctor help him out of it. "In my defense, since he knew I was already hurt, he purposely hit me there again."

"Sounds like a great guy. Why isn't he in custody?"

"Well, this time, he got away from the chief."

Dr. Hannigan put a hand on Jasper's shoulder and the other on his forearm. "This is going to hurt. On three."

"Right. I'm not falling for that again."

Jasper left the doctor's office with his arm in a sling and a bottle of pain pills in his pocket. Since he was without his Jeep for the second time in four days, he walked to The Sailor's Loft, a quarter mile away.

Everyone inside wanted to shake his hand and tell him how sorry they were about his house. And the ones who hadn't heard about his shoulder injury on Saturday wanted to know why he was wearing a sling.

Jasper put on a smile and graciously accepted their condolences, but he found it all annoying, and he was glad when his mother appeared, rescued him, and sat him at a quiet table.

She brought him a glass of water and a beer. "So, do you want to try the salmon?"

"Not feeling like fish tonight. How about a steak?"

"Okay." She sat at the table. "Now tell me what happened to your arm. I don't think you all of a sudden decided to start wearing the sling after four days."

"I tweaked it a little."

"Tweaked it?"

"Yeah. I'll be fine."

She got to her feet. "You know I'll find out what really happened. There are no secrets on Gracie Island."

He took a sip of his beer. "I'm fine, Mom."

She left the table, and Jasper was able to put away his brave face. His shoulder hurt. More than the first time. The doctor had said why, but Jasper had stopped listening after torn ligaments and damaged muscle tissue.

While he waited for his food, he took a pain pill and finished his beer. By the time his steak arrived, he was feeling slightly better but still worse than the original injury.

He ate slowly, fended off a few more well-wishers, and asked for another beer. When he finished his meal, he was feeling a little light-headed, but the pain was still there. While he ate the piece of apple pie Aunt Peg insisted he eat, he took another pain pill. He went out the back door to avoid any more townsfolk and family members, then headed down the alley and came out on Main Street. As he took a deep breath of fresh ocean air, he felt woozy, and he sat on a bench in front of the grocery store.

Poppie and Lewis had finished eating dinner at the café and were headed home. When she saw Jasper sitting on the bench, she told Lewis to pull over.

He stopped in front of Jasper, and Poppie rolled down her window. "Hey, Deputy. Are you okay?"

He gave her a smile. "Oh. Hey."

Poppie glanced at Lewis. "I think Deputy Goodspeed has had a few too many." She opened her door and got out. "Go park somewhere."

She walked over to the bench and sat next to Jasper. "So, big guy. What's going on?"

"Just sitting on this bench."

"Are you okay?"

"Yep." He frowned. "I'm not sure why I'm sitting on this bench. I was having dinner."

"Have you been drinking?"

"No. Well, just a beer with my steak." He thought for a moment. "And one before my steak." He held up a finger. "I know what's wrong." He took the pain pills out of his pocket and handed them to her. "Probably shouldn't have had two beers with these."

Poppie read the label. "How many did you take?"

"One before dinner and one after apple pie."

"And two beers."

He nodded. "Yes. And two beers."

"Well, according to the directions, you had one pill and two beers too many."

"Directions?"

She put the pill bottle back into his pocket. "One pill every four to six hours. No alcohol."

"That won't work."

"I thought you were on the mend. Why the sling? Why the pills?"

He rubbed his eyes and ran his hand through his hair. "Had a relapse of sorts."

"A relapse?"

Lewis joined them. "What's going on?"

"It appears Jasper has had a relapse. Whatever that means."

"Oh, right. I heard he hurt his shoulder again." Jasper and Poppie both looked at him. "Max told me."

Jasper shook his head. "Damn, Max. The town crier."

Poppie studied him for a moment. "Did you dislocate it again?"

"A little bit, yeah."

"A little bit?"

He frowned at her. "Why do you keep repeating everything I say?"

Lewis moved out of the way of two women walking down the sidewalk, then asked, "Why does he look like he's had a six-pack of beer?"

"Because he didn't know there were directions on his pill bottle." Poppie got to her feet. "Where's your Jeep? Lewis can bring it to your mom's while I drive you there."

Jasper shook his head. "Don't know. The bastard took it."

"What?"

"Right after he did this." He patted his shoulder.

Lewis moved closer to the bench. "You had him in custody again?"

"Yep. And the slippery bastard got away. Again."

Poppie sat on the bench. "Oh my gosh."

"Wasn't me this time. Well, it was partly me. But it was mostly the chief. He was cuffing the guy when he got away. Took the chief's cuffs and my Jeep. Oh, and as an extra added bonus? He has my twelve-gauge, too."

Lewis shook his head. "He's armed."

"Well, he's always had a gun. He shot his brother in the head, remember? But, yes. Now he has a shotgun, too."

"They were brothers?"

Jasper sighed. "Today has been very informative. But I think you're all caught up now."

Poppie took his left arm and stood, bringing him with her. "Let's get you home. Sounds like you've had a day."

"I've had a lot of days lately." He glanced at her. "Ever since you came to town."

They got him to the truck, and Poppie sat between the two men as they drove to Kat's house.

When they pulled in front of the house, Jasper asked, "Where's my cat?"

"I've still got him. I'll bring him over in the morning."

"You sure?"

"Yes. He's doing fine. Ate some food this afternoon. Don't worry about him."

Jasper patted her knee. "I owe you."

"You certainly do."

He frowned, then smiled. "You're joking."

"Yes. I am."

He reached with his left hand to open the door but couldn't seem to manage it. "Dammit."

Poppie touched his shoulder. "Here. Let me." She leaned over him and tried to open the door. "What is wrong with this thing?" She looked at Jasper's face inches away from hers and briefly forgot what she was doing.

He held her gaze and started to say something.

Lewis threw open his door. "Good God, you two. It's locked. I'll get it." He got out of the truck, and Poppie sat back up and glanced at Jasper.

"It's locked."

"Hmm."

"You smell like—"

"Lilac and Jasmine?"

"Yeah."

When Lewis unlocked the door and opened it, they both looked at him.

"Are you two getting out of there, or do you need some time alone?"

Jasper stepped out of the truck, then held onto the top of the door for a moment to get his balance. "Thank you for the ride."

"You're welcome. Do you need help getting inside?"

He shook his head. "I've got it."

"You sure?" He glanced at Poppie. "My sister probably wouldn't mind giving you a hand."

Jasper looked at her and frowned. "I'm fine." He headed for the front porch. Took the steps slowly, then stopped before going inside. He turned and waved.

Poppie waved back as Lewis got into the truck, then she turned to her brother and punched him in the shoulder.

Lewis rubbed his arm. "What was that for?"

"My sister wouldn't mind helping you?"

He smiled. "Well, jeez, you guys looked like you were about to...do something I didn't want to witness."

She swung at him again, but he dodged out of the way and laughed.

She glanced at the house. "Just take us home."

Chapter Eighteen

"Of course he was a Boy Scout."

Poppie had Pepper in her arms as she went up the steps to the porch and knocked on Kat's door. A few moments later, Kat opened it with a smile.

"Good morning." Kat noticed Pepper. "Oh, my poor little man."

Poppie let Kat take him from her arms. "He seems much better today."

Kat nuzzled him, then smiled at Poppie. "You're Poppie, right? Jasper's friend?"

"Yeah. He asked me to watch Pepper yesterday while he went to work."

"So very nice of you. Come on inside."

"Oh no. I don't want to be a bother."

"It's no bother, dear." She held the door open, and Poppie stepped through it. "Come sit. I'll pour us a cup of coffee."

"Oh. It's fine. I don't drink coffee."

Kat put Pepper in a pet bed next to the refrigerator, then pulled a chair back from the table. "Sit. Tea, then?"

"No. Nothing. Thank you." Poppie sat in the chair. The kitchen was big, with a blue and white tiled floor that matched the blue cupboards below the white countertops. The cupboards above the counters were a white wood frame around leaded glass panels. A bouquet of fresh flowers in a porcelain vase sat on the counter, and the window above the sink overlooked an extensive garden.

"Your kitchen is beautiful."

"Thank you. I love it. I spend most of my time here when I'm not at the restaurant. You'd think I wouldn't want to cook once I came home, but it's what I do."

"Did Jasper grow up here?"

"Yes. So did I. It was my parent's house."

"Wow. Amazing."

Kat glanced toward the living room and a hall leading to the bedrooms. "I'm afraid he's still asleep."

"Yeah. I figured. He was a little out of it last night. Lewis and I brought him home."

"Yes, he told me. At least he got a good night's sleep finally." Kat sat and patted Poppie's hand. "I'm glad you and he are friends."

Poppie shook her head. "I'm not sure we're friends exactly. He finds me pretty annoying."

Kat got up and poured herself a cup of coffee, then filled a glass with water and set it in front of Poppie. "I need to serve you something."

Poppie took a sip. "Thank you."

Kat sat back down. "Being annoyed by a pretty girl is better than being sad all the time. And I'm sure he's not as annoyed as he makes out to be."

"I don't know. I can be pretty annoying."

Kat laughed. "Well, keep it up. It's good for him. Did you come to see him? He should be awake soon."

"Yes. No. I just wanted to bring Pepper to him. And… We were supposed to have breakfast this morning. But after his day yesterday, he might've forgotten."

"The day he has yet to tell me about?"

Poppie smiled. "It's probably better that you don't know."

"Well, now I have to know." She stood again. "Don't let him off so easily. I need to run to the restaurant for a couple of hours. You wait here until he wakes up."

"Oh, no. He probably won't like that too much. His no visitor policy and all."

"This is my house, and I want you to stay. I like visitors."

"Okay. But if he gets mad, I'm going to point the finger at you."

"You go right ahead." She removed her apron and checked her hair in the reflection of one of the glass cupboards, then picked up her purse and keys. "I'll see you two in a bit."

"Okay."

Poppie watched Kat leave the house, then sighed and glanced around the kitchen again. She got up and looked at the garden through the window. It seemed to be divided in half, with one side full of wildflowers and the other with assorted vegetables. Presumably, ones that didn't need a lot of sun.

After a minute, she wandered into the living room. Like the kitchen, it was tidy and welcoming, with a large gray sofa in front of a rock fireplace. She went to the mantle and looked at the pictures it held. Most of them were of Jasper at various ages.

"Look how cute you were." They ranged from newborn infant to young adult, with the last one being a picture of him and his wife on their wedding day. She touched the frame. "You look so happy with your beautiful bride."

She turned away from the pictures and went to the bookshelf. It was full of a variety of novels, with the top shelf dedicated to a collection of books about the sea, the coastline of Maine, local flora and fauna, and sea creatures.

She sat on the couch. "You must've had a very happy childhood, despite the whole chief/ father thing." She noticed a shadow box on one wall with Jasper in a Boy Scout uniform. It also held his folded hat and the many badges he'd earned. "Of course, you were a Boy Scout." She stood again and returned to the wedding picture. "I don't think I'll ever be able to compete with you, Ivy. But I promise you. If I get the chance, I'll take good care of him."

Jasper rolled onto his back from his left side and groaned. The painless euphoria from last night was gone. He glanced at the alarm clock, but it only showed three flashing zeros. The power on the island had a habit of surging on and off. Usually, just long enough to stop the clocks. But sometimes, it'd be out for hours. Everyone on the island had backup generators to keep their refrigerators and freezers going during the long ones. Last night's surge must've been a quick one.

He remembered he was supposed to meet Poppie for breakfast, but he had no idea what time it was. His watch was on the dresser, which was too far away. He tried to gauge the time by the filtered sun coming through his window, but the clouds made it impossible to tell how high it was.

"Mom?"

A few moments passed before the door opened. "Yes, dear?" Poppie peeked around the door.

Jasper pulled the blanket higher over his bare chest. "What the hell?"

"Your mother went to the restaurant."

"Why are you here?"

"She told me to wait until you woke up and remind you you're buying me breakfast this morning."

He tried to get comfortable. "I didn't forget."

She stepped into his room and got a frown from him. "You grew up in this room, didn't you?"

"Yes."

She looked around at the furnishings, collections, and memorabilia of a younger man. "And she kept it just how you left it when you went off to sheriff school."

He watched her begin to snoop. "That's not what they call it."

She went to his bookcase stuffed with books ranging from classics to thrillers. "Stephen King?"

"He's from Maine. I'm being supportive."

She glanced at him. "I'm pretty sure he does okay without local support." She turned and smiled at him. "I saw your Boy Scout stuff. Lots of badges."

"Like I said the other day, not a lot to do around here."

She moved to his desk. "How about sports? You seem...athletic. Did you play ball in school?"

"There were ten boys in my class. Not enough for a team. Besides, who would we play?"

She pulled a snapshot from the frame of a mirror above the desk. It was Jasper with two boys, all around ten or twelve, with their arms around each other. "Aw. You *did* have friends."

"Are you done? I need to get up."

"No. I'm still snooping." She picked up two more pictures and looked at them. "Okay. Two questions." She held up a picture of Jasper standing in front of a small airplane. "Do you know how to fly this?"

"Yes."

"Seriously? That's impressive. Where do you fly?"

"Mostly medical emergencies. Special supply runs. Stuff like that."

"Even more impressive. So you *do* get off the island once in a while."

"Of course. But not by choice."

She held up the other picture. "Graduation from…the Police Academy?"

He sighed. "Yes."

She turned the picture to look at it again. He was very handsome with his shorter hair and clean-shaven face, but she preferred his look now. She pointed at the picture as she spoke. "So, you, your mom, Aunt Peg, and Uncle Beryl." She glanced at him again. "I don't see your father."

"That's because he wasn't there."

She set the pictures down. "I'm beginning to not like Chief Goodspeed very much."

Jasper grumbled, then sat up. "Can we continue this conversation at breakfast?" When she continued exploring, he sighed. "Fine." He tossed the covers back and stood up.

Poppie covered her eyes. "Jasper!"

He took his cleaned and pressed uniform from the chair it was lying over and headed for the door. Poppie peeked through her fingers and watched him go.

Hmm. Better than I imagined. And that answers the underwear question.

Jasper came out to the living room, freshly showered and dressed in his uniform and his sling, to find Poppie sitting on the couch.

"You're still here."

She glanced at him. "I'm still hungry."

"Right. Breakfast." He went to the door and picked up his boots, then sat on a gray plaid chair next to the fireplace. He loosened the laces and put them on, then frowned at them as he contemplated how to lace them with one hand.

Poppie got off the couch and knelt in front of him. "Let me do it."

"I can do it."

She tightened the laces on one of the boots. "Quit being so stubborn." She tied both boots, then stood. "Those are really cool boots, by the way."

He stood and adjusted his pant legs over the top of the boots. "You should get yourself a pair."

"I would if I was a tall, sexy deputy sheriff." She stopped breathing for a moment and looked at him. "Or a man. Any man, really."

He grinned at her.

"Shut up."

"I didn't say anything." He headed for the door. "You coming?"

She followed him to the door and went through it when he held it open for her. As they crossed the porch, he held out his hand. "Let me drive."

She turned to him. "Why? Because you're the man?"

"No. Because I'm a tall, sexy deputy sheriff."

She swung at him, but he stopped her with a hand around her wrist. "Penelope, I could arrest you for assaulting an officer."

She pulled her hand away and went down the steps. He went around her and opened the truck door for her. "You could get a year in jail plus a fine."

She got into the car, and he closed the door, then went around and got behind the wheel.

She glanced at him. "It'd be worth it." She handed him the keys, then aggressively put on her seatbelt.

Jasper put the key in the ignition and started to laugh. "Poppie, Poppie, Poppie."

"What?"

"You make me laugh. And I haven't felt like laughing in a very long time."

She crossed her arms. "Well, then, I guess I know my purpose in life now."

They drove to the restaurant in silence, and after they parked across the street, Poppie opened her door and got out before Jasper could come around and open it for her. She then walked ahead of him and opened the door to the restaurant, and held it for him.

He nodded and went inside.

The dining room was almost full, and they made their way to a table near the kitchen. Jasper pulled a chair out for Poppie, who looked at it and then went around the table and sat in the other chair.

Jasper shook his head and sat in the chair he'd pulled out. "Okay. Duly noted. You don't want to be taken care of."

She slid her chair in and leaned toward him. "I don't want to be coddled."

"Having respect for a woman isn't coddling her."

She leaned back and took a breath. "So, now you respect me?"

He took a moment, then smiled. "I respect the fact that you're a woman."

Poppie started to respond but stopped when Peg came to the table. She had a pot of coffee and two cups in her hand.

She set one in front of Jasper and filled it, then looked at Poppie. "Coffee for you?"

"No, thank you. I'll just take water and an orange juice."

"Coming right up." Peg looked at Jasper. "What's going on with your shoulder?"

"I've been a little too active. Just giving it a rest."

She squinted at him. "I'm not sure I believe you, but okay. Do you know what you want to order?"

"We'll have…" He glanced at Poppie. "*I'll* have French toast and bacon, please. And a couple of scrambled eggs."

Peg smiled at Poppie. "For you, dear?"

"The same. Minus the eggs."

"It'll be just a few minutes."

Jasper took the pill bottle out of his pocket and removed a single capsule. He swallowed it with a gulp of coffee, then leaned back in his chair and rubbed his right arm. "I'm sorry."

"For what?"

"For being grumpy."

Peg delivered her water and orange juice, and Poppie took a sip of juice. "I'm sorry, too."

"For?"

She took a moment. "For being a pain in the…butt."

He shook his head. "*Ass*. A pain in the ass. Just say it."

Kat came to their table. "You made it." She dragged a chair over from another table and sat down, then reached to tousle Jasper's hair. Something Poppie figured she'd been doing for his whole life.

He dodged her hand and picked up his coffee cup.

Kat turned her attention to Poppie. "So, how long are you here for?"

Poppie glanced at Jasper, then smiled at Kat. "I think I've about worn out my welcome. I'm leaving on Saturday."

"Aw. But you'll be back to see us? Soon I hope."

"Yes, I will. I've missed my brother, so I'll be visiting again."

"Good." She looked at Jasper. "Don't think I don't know that you hurt yourself again."

He gave her a small smile. "I just overdid it yesterday."

"Chasing down the suspected killer?" She patted his hand. "Dr. Hannigan came in this morning."

"What happened to patient confidentiality?"

"I'm listed on your paperwork, dear. Besides, he thought you'd told me."

"It's fine. Really."

Kat looked at Poppie. "Is it fine?"

Poppie glanced at Jasper, then shook her head. "No. It's not fine. Your son is being stubborn but also trying to protect you."

Kat stood and kissed Jasper on the temple. "It's my job to protect you. Not the other way around." She put the borrowed chair back and headed for the kitchen.

Jasper took a sip of coffee. "Thanks for having my back."

"You should've told her."

"I know." He fiddled with the napkin and silverware for a moment, then drank some more coffee. "So, you're leaving Saturday?"

"Yeah."

"To start your new job?"

"Yes."

"Well, I wish you all the best."

She tilted her head. "Thanks, Jasper. I think."

"I mean it. And I hope you meant what you said about coming back to visit."

"I did." She drank some more orange juice. "Probably in the spring. Not sure I'm ready for your winter weather."

He smiled. "It can be rough."

"Why do you love it here so much?"

He thought about the question. "It's home. It's my family. It's the place I want to be happy in again, someday."

She reached across the table and put her hand over his. "You will be."

"You think?"

"I know."

Chapter Nineteen

Lilac and Jasmine.

After breakfast, Poppie offered to walk Jasper to the station. As they got near, she asked, "Do you have to go right to work?"

"I don't need to go to work at all if I don't want to. But that guy's out there."

"Yeah. And he has your Jeep."

"Why do you ask?"

She shrugged. "I thought maybe we could go to the gazebo for a few minutes."

"Why the gazebo?"

She smiled. "We got along at the gazebo. Well, mostly."

"Do you think it's a magic gazebo?"

"Could be. You never know."

"Let's go find out."

They passed the station and headed for the park. When they arrived, there were four boys playing on the structure.

Poppie watched them for a moment. "I guess it wasn't magic after all."

"I'll take care of this." Jasper walked across the grass toward the boys. When they saw him, they stopped playing and watched him approach. "Hey, guys."

A boy who appeared to be the oldest said, "We weren't doing anything."

"Oh, I know. I thought you guys might be thirsty."

The boy eyed Jasper warily. "I guess."

Jasper took out his wallet and handed the boy a five-dollar bill. "Take this to The Sailor's Loft and tell Peg that Jasper said to get you whatever you want to drink."

The boy took the money and stuffed it in his pocket. "Cool. Thanks, Deputy."

"Go on now."

The boys ran off, and Poppie went to Jasper. "Smooth."

They went up the steps and to the bench, then Jasper sat on Poppie's right side. "Just to be safe."

"As long as you behave yourself, you'll be fine."

"So what does life in Boston look like for Poppie Jensen?"

"Pretty uneventful. I have a small apartment in a quiet part of town. I don't go out much. With school and all, I mostly studied and watched movies."

"So, I'm supposed to believe you never go out?"

"You mean on a date?"

"Yeah."

"Occasionally." She glanced at him. "I tend to scare guys off."

Jasper grinned. "No way."

"At least I can admit it."

Jasper watched a pair of Canadian geese land a few yards in front of the gazebo. "I'm sure in all of Boston, there must be one guy willing to put up with you."

"You'd think." She stood and went to the rail to watch the geese. "I guess I'm just not that interested in finding him at the moment."

He got to his feet and walked to her, then turned and leaned against the railing. "When you're ready, you'll find him."

She was quiet for a few minutes while she watched the geese. "So, I have a question for you."

"Okay."

"Why do you smell like lilac and jasmine?"

He smiled. "My mother's shampoo."

"Oh. That makes sense."

Jasper ran a hand through his hair. "It does make it really soft."

Poppie laughed. "Well, as a macho deputy, you can totally pull it off."

"Yeah? Hmm. Maybe I'll keep using it." He returned to the bench and sat down. "Macho, huh?"

She walked over and sat next to him. "Don't let it go to your head."

When the boy he'd given the money to came running up to the gazebo, Jasper stood.

"Are you okay?"

The boy took a moment to catch his breath. "I have a note from your mom." He dug into his pocket and pulled out a folded piece of paper. Jasper took it from him and read it.

"Shit." He looked at the boy. "Thanks."

The boy nodded and ran off as Poppie went to Jasper.

"Is everything okay?"

He glanced at her. "I need to go."

"What's wrong?"

"Nothing I can't handle. I'll see you later."

Poppie watched him jog across the grass, then head down the street.

"Does he remember he has the keys to the truck in his pocket?" She sat on the bench. "To honestly answer your question, Deputy, compared to here, life in Boston is boring. Which is really weird because there's nothing to do here. If you don't count hanging out with you."

She sighed. "And I'd rather hang out with you than do anything else."

James lived in an apartment above the movie theater. It was once two small apartments, but when the theater closed and went into foreclosure, James bought the building and knocked down the wall between the apartments, then remodeled it into one large one.

The building was now used by the community theater group, which put on one or two plays a year. The school also used it for concerts and award ceremonies. The rest of the time, it sat empty.

Jasper went up the stairs in the back of the building, then knocked on the door.

"Chief?"

He waited a few moments but got no response. He knocked again, then checked the door. It was locked. He took the key ring with the lighthouse key and used the other one to unlock the door.

He opened it and peered into the dim room. "Chief. It's Jasper."

The large living room was cluttered, but it was neater than his house had been. Jasper had been to the apartment several times but never socially. This wasn't a social call, either.

He went through the living room and looked into the kitchen. Other than a fish in a bowl on the counter, the room was empty. He sighed and headed for the bedroom.

James was sprawled on the bed, face down. There was an empty bottle of whiskey on the floor and a half-empty one on the table next to the bed.

"Oh shit." Jasper went to the bed and studied James for a moment. He was breathing.

Jasper took off James' shoes and pulled a blanket over him. Then he picked up the two bottles and left the room. He took them into the kitchen, poured the remaining whiskey down the sink, then put the bottles in the trash. The kitchen was messier than the living room, with a sink full of dirty dishes and several used pots sitting on the stove.

Jasper took his arm out of his sling, rolled up his sleeves, and started washing the dishes. When he finished, he searched the cupboards for more alcohol. He found two more bottles and poured the contents into the sink. He knew it was fruitless. James would just buy more. But at least he was doing something.

During his search, he noticed there wasn't much food. James ate at the café most days, steering clear of The Sailor's Loft. He'd go to the deli at the grocery store for sandwiches and chicken, so he never had much in the way of groceries. But today, he didn't even have the bare essentials, such as coffee, sugar, bread, or milk.

Jasper checked on James again, then left the apartment and went to the grocery store. He was on foot and could only carry one bag, so he just bought the bare necessities before heading back to the apartment.

He put the groceries away, then started a pot of coffee. When he heard James grumbling from the bedroom, Jasper went to the door and stood in the doorway.

James was sitting on the edge of the bed, and he glanced at Jasper.

Jasper stayed in the doorway. "Take a shower. I started a pot of coffee." When he got no response from James, he backed up a few steps, then turned and headed for the door. He'd done what he had to do. The old man was awake and functioning. Or would be soon. It was all he could do for him.

He left the apartment, knowing they'd never talk about it. They never did. James would show up at the station later today or in the morning, and both of them would act as though nothing had happened.

Jasper went down the stairs and around the building, then went into the Rusty Pelican. They weren't open yet, but Mellie was there setting up. She smiled at him.

"What the hell happened to you?"

Jasper glanced at his sling. "A minor mishap."

"Hmm. I've heard some rumors."

"All lies." He reached the bar. "I think I owe you some money from last week."

She nodded, then went to the cash register and took out a receipt. "Twenty-five dollars."

"Is that all?" He took his wallet out.

"You got interrupted pretty early on."

He handed her two twenties. "You're not charging me for that concoction you gave me, are you?"

She laughed. "No, that was on the house." She put the twenties in the till and took out the change. When she held it out to him, he shook his head. "Thank you." She put it in her apron pocket.

He nodded. "You always take good care of me."

"Well, maybe so. But I look forward to the day when I don't have to."

He knocked on the bar. "Me too, Mellie. Me too."

His next stop was The Sailor's Loft. Kat would be anxious to hear from him. She stopped loving James a long time ago, but that didn't mean she stopped caring about him. Jasper found her in the kitchen kneading bread. When Kat was upset or worried, she baked bread.

When she saw Jasper, she wiped her hands on her apron and went to him.

Jasper nodded. "He's okay."

Kat put her arms around him. "Thank you." She stepped away and went back to her dough. "Every time Maisy calls to tell me he didn't show up for work—"

"I know."

She shook her head. "One of these days...he's not going to be okay." She started kneading the dough. "What do you think brought it on?"

As Jasper had told Poppie, James was a high-functioning alcoholic. He drank all day, every day, but he only lost control of it when he was upset about something.

"I guess it was probably losing Roger yesterday."

"Roger?"

"The criminal running around our island." He sighed. "Currently in my Jeep."

She shaped the dough into a round loaf, then put a towel over it. "He's been worried about you, too."

"Me? Since when?"

"Since you got hurt. Lost your house. Now your Jeep."

Jasper sat on a stool in front of the wooden counter she was working on. "The man's a frickin' robot. He doesn't care about anything or anybody. Least of all, me. He let the alcohol get to him today because of his pride, nothing more."

She reached across the table and took his hand. "You know that's not true. Your father loves you."

"Hmm."

She let go of his hand and went to the large stainless steel sink to wash hers, then returned to the counter while drying them.

"Are you taking the day off?"

"The chief is out of commission. Someone has to man the boat."

"Please take it easy." She studied him for a moment. "And don't go looking for that man by yourself."

"He has my Jeep, Mom. He's dislocated my shoulder twice, burned my house down, and damn near broke the chief's nose. If I get the opportunity to go after him, I'm going to do it."

She picked up a measuring cup and put two cups of flour into a bowl.

"Mom."

"You go do what you have to do. But you better come back for dinner and help me eat some of this bread."

He got up and went around the counter to kiss her on the cheek. "I'll be back." He put his hand in his pocket and pulled out Lewis' truck keys. "Oh damn."

"Whose keys are those?"

"Someone who's going to be royally pissed I left her at the park."

Kat smiled. "You better go find her."

"Yes, ma'am."

Chapter Twenty

"Oh look. A unicorn."

Poppie stayed at the park for almost an hour before walking to the marina to find Lewis, where she'd dropped him off for work before going to Jasper's. She went into the Harbormaster's Office to find out where she might find her brother.

Duke O'Conner gave her a smile when she walked in.

"You must be Lewis' sister."

"Guilty."

Poppie guessed Duke was in his mid-forties but, having spent most of his life as a fisherman, may have aged him prematurely. He acted like a younger man, right down to his flirtatious attitude.

"He never said how pretty you were."

"Well, you know brothers. They never notice."

Duke laughed. "You going to be at the Loft on Friday to listen to the music?"

"Yes, I am."

"Maybe I could buy you a drink."

"I'll see you there, and we'll talk about it then. Do you know where Lewis is?"

"Oh, sure. He's down the far left pier working on the Empty Nester."

"Okay. Thanks." She headed for the door.

"I'll see you Friday."

She waved and went outside, then mumbled to herself, "Not if I see you first."

She walked down the wooden walkway to the last pier on the left, then went down to the only boat tied to it. She found Lewis sanding the teak deck.

"That looks like fun."

He held up a block with sandpaper on it. "Want to join in?"

"No, I'm good. Thanks."

He stopped sanding and sat on the freshly sanded teak seat. "Did you bring me some breakfast?"

"Um. No." She gave him a smile. "Sorry. I can go get you something."

"It's okay. I'm about to call it a day."

"It's not even noon yet."

"This guy's in no hurry. But I've got another customer who is, so after I get something to eat, I'll be painting his bottom." He smirked. "Or his boat's bottom."

"Sounds like fun. Do you want some company? Eating, not painting some guy's bottom."

"Sure." He tossed some things into a wooden tote, then stepped off the boat. "Did you get your breakfast with Jasper this morning?"

"Yeah. After some dueling at his house. I think I got the upper hand, but I'm not sure. It was a close call, either way."

Lewis shook his head as he headed down the pier. She stepped up beside him, and he glanced at her. "You had an advantage, seeing as he was wasted last night."

"That was weird. And pretty darn cute."

"You're right. He's adorable." He stopped walking for a moment to avoid the arm swing he knew was coming.

She swung and missed, then waited for Lewis to catch up again. "He was fine this morning. Grumpy as ever. I got to see his room, though." *And a bit more.*

"What were you doing in his room?"

"Snooping. Did you know he was a Boy Scout?"

"Yes."

"Did you know he's a pilot?"

"Yes."

"Is there anything you don't know about him?"

"I don't know why he puts up with you."

"Tell me something I don't know. Something he wouldn't want me to know."

They got to the parking lot, and Lewis stopped walking. "Where's the truck?"

"Oh, yeah. Jasper has the keys."

"Why?"

"Because he insisted on driving, seeing as he's the man and all. Then he left me at the park to go on some mystery mission for his mother."

"It's probably the chief." He set his toolbox outside of the marina office, then turned to Poppie. "The chief goes on a bender every once in a while. Kat always calls Jasper to go check on him and make sure he's alright."

"Well, that's kind of sad."

"He's been doing it for years."

They started walking toward town. "So, about that thing you were going to tell me about Jasper."

"No way. He's my friend."

"And I'm your sister. I won't use it against him. It'll be like hidden inside information that he doesn't know, I know."

"What's the point of that?"

"Come on."

He stopped walking and folded his arms across his chest. "Okay. But if he finds out you know, I'll deny to the death it came from me."

"Okay. Tell me. Tell me."

"He gets seasick."

She thought for a moment. "He seemed fine on the motor boat on Saturday. Although, he wasn't really on it long enough to get sick."

"Little boats are fine. It's the big boats. In the big water. That rolling motion. He gets sick taking the ferry to the mainland."

"So, even before—"

"Yeah, even before Ivy. Since he was a kid."

"Well, good thing the family business wasn't fishing."

He started walking again. "So, there. Now you know something about him."

"It seems like that's something everyone knows."

"Not everyone. But you only asked for something *you* didn't know."

"You're a cheater."

Lewis shrugged. "Like I said, he's my friend. And I wouldn't want him telling my girlfriend—if I had one—all my secrets."

"I'm not his girlfriend. Not even close."

"Well, whatever you are." He glanced at her. "You wish you were his girlfriend."

"I do not. Yes, he's tall and handsome and really buff."

"Can we change the subject, please?"

"And pretty darn sweet when he's not being grumpy."

Lewis pointed across the street. "Oh, look, a unicorn."

"He also loves animals, which is adorable. Except for horses for some unexplained reason."

"If I tell you why he doesn't like horses, will you stop talking about him?"

She turned toward him and smiled. "Yes."

Lewis sighed. "You're a brat."

"His hair is—"

"Fine. Stop. When he was a kid, he rode all over the island. He had his own horse that he kept at his grandparent's house. But one day, he went out after a storm, and the horse got bogged down in the mud. The more it struggled to get out, the deeper it sunk in."

"Please don't tell me the horse died."

"No. It didn't. But he messed up his front leg, which left him lame and riding him out in the wilds was too much for him."

"So Jasper stopped riding?"

"And felt guilty for hurting the horse. He keeps it out on the chief's property."

"So, the chief takes care of the horse?"

"No. He doesn't live out there. He lives in town above the movie theater. Jasper takes care of the horse."

"Of course he does." She was quiet until they stopped in front of the grocery store. "Why are we stopping here?"

"Best chicken nuggets in town."

"Are they the only chicken nuggets in town?"

"Yep." He opened the door and held it for Poppie, then they went to the back of the store to the deli.

It had more to offer than any grocery store deli she'd visited in Boston, with a wide variety of meats and cheeses, plus fried chicken, chicken strips, and chicken nuggets. There was also a taco bar offering soft tacos with a choice of fillings.

"This is amazing."

"I know." Lewis smiled at the woman behind the counter. "Hi, Tonya. I'll take a dozen nuggets and some BBQ sauce."

"The Jo Jo's are fresh. Just came out of the fryer."

"I'll take some of those, too." He looked at Poppie. "You want anything?"

"I'll take a Pepsi."

Lewis added to the order. "Two large Pepsis, please."

They took the food to one of three picnic tables in front of the store and sat down.

Lewis handed her a nugget. "You have to try one."

She took it from him, dipped it into the BBQ sauce, and took a bite. "Oh my gosh."

"Told you."

"How does everywhere in town have good food?'

"Well, in a town this size, if you don't have good food, you're not going to last very long."

She reached for another, and he pushed her hand away. "Hey. Go get your own."

"Just one more."

He sighed, then handed her another. "That's all. I've got to paint a bottom this afternoon."

Poppie studied the enlarged black-and-white photo on the wall behind the picnic area. "Why is there a picture of a bunch of naked guys running toward the ocean?"

Lewis glanced over his shoulder at it. "The original Polar Bear Club members."

"You mean the guys who jump into the freezing water in the middle of winter?"

"Yeah. Only we do it on the first day of spring."

"We?"

"Yeah. There are fifteen to twenty of us every year. Me, Jasper, the guys in the fire department. And a few more."

"You and Jasper run into the cold ocean, March twenty-first every year, buck naked?"

"We don't do it naked anymore." He motioned over his shoulder. "We wear trunks now."

"Bummer."

Lewis raised an eyebrow.

"Well, or not... I didn't mean... Anyway. No women?"

"There's no rule against it. A few have tried. None have made it." He stopped chewing and looked at her. "Uh-oh."

"What?"

"You want to be the first." He shrugged and finished his bite of chicken. "Come back in March." He squinted at her. "I dare you."

She took a sip of her soda. "I just might do that."

He grinned at her. "You might want to put on thirty pounds or so. The fat will keep you warmer."

"You don't have any extra fat. Neither does Jasper."

He slurped some of his Pepsi. "How do you know Jasper doesn't have any fat? He could have a pot belly under that uniform of his."

She shook her head. "No. He doesn't."

He set his empty cup down. "What else happened in the bedroom this morning?"

"Nothing. God. Gross. I swear."

"Gross, my ass. Pretty sure you'd jump on that the minute you had a chance."

"Shut up. Time for a change of subject." She cocked her head. "So, did you know Ivy very well?"

Lewis shook his head. "Nope. Not going there."

"I just want to know what she was like. I saw her picture in Kat's house. She was gorgeous."

"Yes, she was. And she was a great person. They were happy and in love. And that's why Jasper is still mourning her almost two years later."

"Well, if he's ready to move on someday, I don't stand a chance against someone like her. Tall, beautiful…great. I might as well give up now."

"You're all those things and more. Except for maybe the tall part."

She moaned. "Why does everyone think I'm so short? You're not nearly as tall as Jasper."

"Yeah. But I'm taller than you."

She took a sip of her drink, then rested her head on her hand. "He is really tall, isn't he?"

"Jasper is…a specimen."

"He is, isn't he?"

Lewis laughed. "I don't know. I was… I don't size guys up the same way you do. To me, Jasper is a good friend. Someone I can trust and rely on. He's… Jasper is the kind of guy you can call in the middle of the night with a problem, and he'll come help you solve it. He'll give you the shirt off his back or fifty dollars if you're down and out. And never expect to get it back. He's a good guy."

"And I'm not nearly good enough for him."

Lewis smiled at her. "You're a good guy, too."

"Thanks."

"Can you loan me fifty bucks?"

"No. But I have a shirt you can have."

Chapter Twenty-One

Game Night

Jasper tracked down Poppie and Lewis as they were finishing their lunch.

Poppie smiled at him as he came up, dangling the keys from his finger. "I wondered how long it'd take you to remember you had them."

"Sorry." He sat next to Lewis and smiled across the table at her. "Did I not feed you enough for breakfast?"

"I'm not eating, just watching Lewis eat."

Lewis wiped his hands on a napkin, then finished his drink. "Everything okay with the chief?"

"Yeah. Still breathing. Semi-functional. What are you doing tomorrow?"

"Nothing. My day's clear. What do you need?"

"Could you tow the chief's trailer to my property for me?"

"Sure. I heard we're going to get some of that storm headed north. Do you want to wait until it passes?"

"I need to get out of my mom's house."

Poppie laughed. "You've been there two nights."

"I like having my own space."

"From what I saw this morning, you have a perfectly nice bedroom to hang out in."

Jasper frowned at her, then turned his attention back to Lewis. "Early afternoon?"

"I'll be there."

When Duke O'Conner came out the door with a to-go bag in his hand, he spotted them and walked over to the table. "I got some updated information on the storm. They're calling it a hurricane now, and it's going to hit further south than they originally thought."

Lewis looked up at him. "Are we going to get hit?"

"Not full-on. It's still aiming for Nova Scotia, but we'll get the south end of it. Rain, wind, the usual."

Lewis looked at Jasper. "Maybe you don't want to be in the trailer during that."

"I can always go back to Mom's if it gets too bad."

Duke took a step back from the table. "I'll keep you updated on any changes."

"Thanks, Duke."

"Oh, and I heard they're doing game night tonight since tomorrow night will be nasty." He gave the men a wave and Poppie a wink, then headed down the street.

Poppie shivered. "He's a little creepy."

Jasper laughed. "He's got a thing for pretty women."

She tilted her head. "Did you just compliment me?"

Jasper thought about it. "Um. Hmm. I guess I did."

Lewis stood. "Totally unintentional, I'm sure." He gathered the trash from the meal. "So, game night tonight? You going?"

"Of course. I have a Monopoly championship to defend."

Poppie shook her head. "Game night?"

Lewis dropped the trash in a nearby can and returned to the table. "Every Thursday night. Or Wednesday if there's a hurricane bearing down on us. And once a month, this week, it's potluck game night. A lot of good food."

Jasper got to his feet. "And some not-so-good food."

Poppie stood, too. "So, we need to bring food?"

Lewis took her arm. "Which means we need groceries." They headed for the entrance to the store. "See you tonight."

"Later."

Jasper was standing inside the door of the Ice House, talking to Duke about the impending storm, when Poppie and Lewis came in with Lewis carrying a large pot in his hands.

Jasper excused himself from Duke and went to them.

"What did you bring?"

Lewis held up the pot. "Jensen family chili."

"Mmm. Sounds good. Is it spicy?"

Poppie smiled. "It's perfect."

"Right. Okay."

Lewis took the pot to the table, already filled with an array of food. It was mostly casserole-type dishes, with some desserts, a few salads, and a nice assortment of bread.

Poppie checked out the bread. "This has to be from your mom."

"She bakes when she's upset. If they hadn't moved game night, I'd be expected to eat all that."

"Why was she upset?"

Jasper sighed. "Despite their history, she worries whenever the chief goes on a bender."

"I'm sorry."

He shrugged. "It's an every six to eight-week occurrence." He lifted the lid on the pot of chili. "I guess I need to try this. Did you make it? Or Lewis?"

"Me. Lewis can't cook. Or won't cook."

"He's managed to get along just fine for the last six years, so I'm guessing it's more he won't cook when you're here to do it for him."

She gave Lewis a shove. "I knew it."

Lewis laughed, then when he spotted Sarah, he left them to go talk to her.

Jasper picked up a bowl and filled it with chili, then took two slices of Kat's bread.

Poppie surveyed the choices. "What's good?"

"I'll help you out. Steer clear of the enchilada casserole, whatever that is in the blue bowl, and the brownies."

"How can you mess up brownies?"

"Trust me. It's possible. Eunice brings them to every potluck."

While Poppie helped herself to a slice of lasagna and some of Kat's bread, Jasper balanced his bread on top of his bowl and got a bottle of beer from an ice chest at the end of the table. "You want one?"

"No, thanks."

He shook his head. "No coffee and no beer. There's definitely something wrong with you."

She picked up a bottle of water, and they headed for a table with a Monopoly game in the middle of it.

"Can I watch you play?"

"Watch? No. You can play. It's called game night. Not watch other people play games night."

"I'm not a fan of Monopoly."

"You're seriously messed up." He studied her for a moment. "It's because you always lose, isn't it?"

"No. Well, yes."

"Maybe you'll get lucky." He set his food down and pulled out a chair. "Take a seat."

She sat next to him. "Who else is playing?"

"Duke, Willis, Lewis, and you and me."

"And who usually wins?"

He smiled. "Me, of course."

"I should've known."

"Sometimes Duke wins. And occasionally Willis does."

"Not my brother?"

"I think he's won once or twice. But he's a good sport."

"Unlike me?"

He turned in his seat and looked at her. "Are you going to pout when you lose?"

"Are you?"

He laughed. "Oh. A challenge. You're on, Penelope."

Forty-five minutes later, Poppie regretted playing the game. As usual, she was way behind, with only two partial sets of properties and a dismal amount of money in her bank. Jasper was, of course, ahead and taking every opportunity to remind her of it. The only good thing that had happened was he was on his second bowl of her chili.

Lewis had left after his turn to get some dessert, and when he came back, he set a brownie in front of Poppie.

"Is that for me?" She glanced at Jasper, who gave her a wink.

Lewis smiled. "Yeah. I know how much you love brownies."

She turned in her seat. "Did Eunice make this?"

Lewis sighed and leaned back in his seat, then looked at Jasper. "You bastard. You told her?"

Poppie nudged Lewis' shoulder. "Unlike my brother." She pushed the brownie aside. "Alright, let's get the torture over and let me lose this game."

Jasper picked up a property card she needed to complete a set. "Tell you what. If you eat the brownie, I'll give you this card. With a complete set, you might be able to hang in there a few more turns."

"Thanks. But no. I'll leave with my dignity if it's all the same to you."

He picked up two fifties from his bank. "How much is your dignity worth? I'll throw in a hundred dollars."

She studied him for a moment. "Fine. How bad can it be?" When Willis and Duke both mumbled something under their breath, she thought about withdrawing from the deal. But instead, she reached for the plate and tore off a small bite of brownie. She put it in her mouth as the four men watched her.

It was worse than she had feared. So bad she couldn't even figure out why it tasted the way it did. "Hmm. Not bad." She took another bite and bit down on something hard and unidentifiable. "Oh my gosh. Gross."

She spit it into her napkin and drank the last couple swallows of her water. "I need more water." She nudged Lewis again. "Go. Get me some water."

As Lewis got to his feet, Jasper offered Poppie his beer.

She shook her head. "No. Beer is gross, too."

"More gross than the brownie?"

She grumbled and took the beer bottle from him, then took a swallow. "Eww." She wiped her mouth and handed him the bottle as Lewis returned with water for her. She took the bottle and handed him the plate with the brownie. "I hate you." She glared at Jasper, who was grinning. "And I hate you, too." She looked at the other two men. "You two? I dislike very strongly." She stood. "I think I'm finished here." She left the table, taking her water with her.

Duke shook his head and smiled at Lewis. "Man, that is one feisty woman."

Lewis frowned at him. "Shut up, Duke."

Willis started stacking his cards. "I think we should concede this game to Jasper. No sense dragging it out to the inevitable end."

Duke nodded, then stood. "I think there's a game of checkers with my name on it."

Willis left, as well, leaving Lewis and Jasper to put the game away. When Jasper got distracted watching Poppie across the room talking with some people she probably didn't know, Lewis cleared his throat.

"It's okay, you know."

Jasper looked at him. "What?"

"To feel something for someone, again."

He shook his head. "I don't. I'm not going there. Never again."

"Never is a long time."

"I know. And I've made my peace with it."

Lewis squinted at Jasper. "Have you?"

Jasper sighed, then nodded toward Poppy. "Maybe you should stop trying to analyze me and go apologize to your sister for trying to poison her."

Lewis got to his feet. "Okay, friend. But lying to yourself is only going to make you feel worse."

Jasper watched Lewis walk away as he leaned back and took a drink of his beer. "Everyone thinks they know me better than I know me." *I don't need a woman in my life to feel whole again. I have a giant piece of my heart missing. No woman is going to heal that.* "Especially not, Penelope Jensen."

She laughed at something Lewis said to her, and Jasper grumbled. "I don't care how infectious your smile is."

Mellie appeared at the table and sat next to Jasper. "Talking to yourself, Deputy?"

"Everyone left me. I had no one else to talk to."

She patted his arm. "What do you want to talk about? I'm a bartender, thus a great listener."

"Nothing. All talked out, I guess."

"Why don't we talk about…Lewis' sister."

"No. Let's not."

"She's quite pretty. Independent—"

"Stubborn, annoying…"

"So you do like her."

Jasper finished his beer. "No. Isn't it time for the final game?"

She smiled, then got to her feet. "I'll go get things started."

Poppie and Lewis joined the crowd assembling around Mellie, who was standing with three other women on a Twister game board.

"Okay, we need one more player. Any volunteers?"

Jasper stepped up next to Poppie and raised his hand. "Right here."

Poppie glanced at him. "You're going to play Twister?"

"No. You are." He gave her a nudge.

"I certainly am not."

Lewis laughed. "We'll even put our money on you."

"There's money involved?"

Jasper leaned toward her. "It's our PG equivalent of Jell-O wrestling. We place bets on who'll win."

Poppie was skeptical since Jasper seemed to enjoy embarrassing her.

Lewis took her arm. "Come on. It'll be fun." He glanced at Duke, who was grinning at Poppie from across the crowd. "Duke will probably put five bucks on you, too."

"Well, in that case…" She pulled her arm away from Lewis, then sighed. "Fine. Whatever." She went to the group of women.

Mellie smiled at her. "Okay. Let's get this game started."

It was as embarrassing as Poppie thought it would be, and when she caught a glimpse of Jasper grinning at her behind once she had both hands on the board, she lost her focus and fell over.

Duke helped her to her feet. "Aw, better luck next time."

"Don't hold your breath." She gave him a polite smile, then headed for Lewis and Jasper.

Jasper shook his head at her. "Wow. First one out. That must be embarrassing."

"Shut up. You're just mad because you lost your money."

"Oh, we didn't actually bet on you."

Lewis laughed. "We bet on Mellie. She's been on a winning streak."

Poppie glared at Jasper. "I'm never speaking to you again."

"Fine by me."

Chapter Twenty-Two

The Storm

After spending another fruitless morning looking for Roger, Jasper ordered lunch from the deli and sat outside to eat. The wind was already picking up, and the clouds were dark and heavy to the north. The storm pattern had continued to be unpredictable, and it was now projected to give them more than a glancing blow, with wind gusts expected to be in the fifty-mile-per-hour range and heavy rain for most of the night. Unless things changed again, it was all supposed to start right after sunset.

Everyone in town was busy preparing for the weather, and Kat expected Jasper at The Sailor's Loft to help them board up the windows. He'd already shored up her house. She tried to convince him to stay another night and move the trailer tomorrow, but he wanted to get it done. Even if he didn't stay in it tonight.

The storm hit right at dusk, an hour after Jasper and Lewis finished setting the trailer up on the tree line of his property. It'd be somewhat protected from the wind, and Jasper was relatively confident it'd still be standing in the morning.

Poppie seemed to be avoiding him, as he hadn't seen her all day. Lewis told him she stayed home to prepare for the storm.

As the storm raged outside, Jasper was having trouble getting comfortable in the small bed in the trailer. He missed his couch. Pepper was still on the mend and staying with Kat. But Penny seemed to accept their new home and the noise outside as she settled down next to Jasper.

The power went out around eight, and since he had no candles, there was nothing else to do but go to bed. He read for a while using a flashlight, but the sound of the wind rattling the aluminum siding, shaking the windows, and rocking the trailer was unnerving. He was half-afraid the whole thing would blow right over, and had the rain not been blowing sideways, he would've considered returning to his mother's and his childhood bedroom. But without his vehicle, he'd need to call for a ride. So, he was where he'd put himself for the duration.

When he heard a bang on the door, he realized he'd finally dozed off. He sat up and listened. It was probably something blowing by. No one would be outside knocking on his door in this weather.

He heard it again, followed by a yell he couldn't quite make out. He got out of bed and moved the curtain over the window to peek out into the stormy weather.

"What the hell?" Jasper opened the door, and Lewis blew in, along with enough rain to soak the floor a few feet in front of the entrance. Jasper pushed it closed behind Lewis.

"What are you doing? What's going on?"

Lewis glanced at the puddle inside the door, growing even bigger from his slicker and his rubber boots, then looked at Jasper. "It's Poppie."

"What about her?"

"She was making us dinner. I got home. She wasn't there."

"She wasn't at the house?"

Lewis shook his head and wiped some rain from his face. "I got home, and she was gone."

"She didn't go somewhere?"

Lewis frowned. "Where would she go? I had the truck." He waved toward the door. "There's a hurricane out there."

"Sorry, you're right. How long ago did you go home?"

"Forty-five minutes ago. I tried calling, but the phones are down. Then the power went out. I secured the windows and doors against the wind, then came over here. What are we going to do?"

Jasper thought for a moment. "We're going to go to your house and see if we can figure this out."

Lewis seemed relieved to have some sort of a plan. "Okay. Okay, yeah. Let's do that."

"Just give me a minute to get dressed."

Jasper was wearing long johns, so he pulled jeans and a shirt over them, then covered it all with a wool sweater and coat. He took his gun and a slicker from the small closet by the door. Put the gun on his belt, pulled on the slicker, and slipped into his wellies. He then picked up Penny and tucked her into his coat.

"I don't want to leave her here by herself."

"Of course. She can bunk with Hank."

Before going outside, Jasper put on a ball cap and pulled up the hood of his raincoat. He was as protected as he was going to get.

The two men took a moment to prepare themselves, then went out the door and ran to Lewis' truck. Jasper got completely soaked in the ten feet between his door and the truck. He got in, fought the wind for a moment to close the door, then glanced at Lewis.

"This weather is going to slow us down."

Lewis started the motor. "How long is it supposed to last?"

"The worst of it should blow over by sunrise or soon after."

"I thought we weren't going to get hit this bad."

"I guess hurricane Emilio had other plans. It was supposed to bounce off Nova Scotia and head back out to sea. Instead, it decided to settle down and stay awhile."

It took them twenty minutes to make the five-minute drive to Lewis' house because the wipers couldn't keep up with the rain, and visibility was barely beyond the front of the truck. He parked as close as he could, then they dashed to the porch, then went inside and left their slickers and boots inside the door. Lewis picked up two flashlights from a table inside the door and handed one to Jasper.

Jasper turned it on, then went to the woodstove and set Penny next to Hank in a large pet bed. He put his back to the heat as he removed his hat and dropped it onto the floor next to the stove, then hung his coat on a chair to dry out. Using a sleeve of his sweater, he wiped the rain off his face.

"Okay, tell me everything."

"We all expected a bit of weather, so I was helping Duke secure the boats in the marina. I told Poppie I'd be home by eight, and she said she'd make dinner. I didn't get home until about eight-thirty."

He went to the kitchen, which was separated from the living room by a breakfast bar with two stools. He picked up a pot from the stove. "She started. There's spaghetti sauce here and a pot of water. Seems she had time to turn the burners off." He looked at Jasper. "It's him, isn't it?"

Jasper took a deep breath. "I don't know who else it'd be."

Lewis sat on one of the stools. "Shit."

"I want to run out there and look for them as much as you do, but the weather makes that impossible."

"We can't just sit here."

"We need to wait it out, Lewis. We can't track him in this."

Lewis ran his hands through his hair, then got to his feet. "I need a drink." He went to a cupboard and took out a bottle of whiskey and two glasses. He set the glasses on the counter and poured a healthy shot into each one, then looked at Jasper. "Join me?"

Jasper went to him and picked up a glass. "On one condition. We stop after this shot."

Lewis glanced at the other glass and then the bottle next to it. He nodded. "You're right. Just one."

They both drank their shots, then Lewis returned the bottle to the cupboard.

Jasper looked around the kitchen and living room. "I don't see any signs of a struggle. Seems like she went without too much of a fight."

"Doesn't sound like my sister."

"No. It doesn't."

Lewis pointed a finger at Jasper. "But if he drove up in your Jeep, she might've thought it was you."

Jasper stuck his hands in his pockets. "This is my fault."

"No, man. Of course, it's not."

Jasper nodded. "Everything that's happened since Saturday is my fault. Including losing my house. If I'd just—"

"You were hurt. You swam through frigid water with a dislocated shoulder, dragging an unconscious man with you. You did your best, man."

"No. I screwed up. I got too close to him. I was so…stupid."

Lewis stood and took a turn around the room. "Okay. Let's say you screwed up. Jasper, you screwed up. You let the bastard get away from you." He stopped a few feet in front of Jasper. "It doesn't matter anymore. The how. The why. It doesn't matter. He's got my sister."

Jasper nodded. "And we're going to get her back."

With little else to do in the dark house, lit only by candles, Lewis finished making the spaghetti, and they ate it along with a few slices of garlic bread from Buns of Steele. While they ate, they discussed the possible scenarios they might face once the weather cleared enough to venture out.

After clearing his plate of a second serving of spaghetti, Jasper pushed it aside and leaned back in his chair. "That was damn good."

"Yeah. Poppie's a pretty good cook."

"She made the sauce?"

"Yeah. I sure as hell didn't. All from scratch, too. She actually loves to cook."

"Really. Didn't expect that."

Lewis smiled. "I don't know why you two are at odds all the time. But she thrives on it. She's always up for a good fight."

"She doesn't listen. She thinks she's right all the time. She's...stubborn as hell."

"Yep. That's my sis." He lost his smile. "We've got to find her, Jasper."

Jasper nodded. "We will. Hell, by the time we do, Roger will probably be glad to hand her over. 'Please. Take her. I surrender.'"

"Are you sure we can't have one more drink?"

"One more should be okay."

It took another six hours for the rain to die down enough to even think about going out. Then another hour before the sun came up. When it did come up, it was hidden by a heavy layer of clouds. Between that and the fog, visibility was still down to about twenty feet.

They spent the six hours trying to sleep, but neither of them was successful. Lewis went to his bed, and Jasper took the couch. But Jasper couldn't shut his mind off. He couldn't help thinking about all the things that could be happening to Poppie at the hands of Roger. Then he'd tried to convince himself Roger had no reason to hurt her. He just took her as leverage—a hostage to give himself something to barter with.

He tried reading but couldn't concentrate on the words and had to keep rereading passages. So he gave that up. He considered taking another shot or two of Lewis' whiskey, but he knew that wasn't the answer. That'd put him at a disadvantage when it came time to go out. He didn't need to be drunk or hungover while tracking Roger.

Lewis came out of the bedroom when the windows turned from black to gray, and he looked as bad as Jasper felt.

Jasper sat and rubbed his eyes. "Did you get any sleep?"

"No. You?"

"No."

"Breakfast?"

Jasper shook his head. "Don't think I could eat. Let's get out there and track the bastard."

"Sounds good. I can't eat, either."

They dressed for the cold and mud, leaving behind only their slickers, then went outside. The driveway was thick with mud, and any tracks Roger might've left were long gone. They walked along the road, searching for any sign that might help them.

They were headed toward the ocean when Lewis stopped and looked behind them. "He could've gone either way."

"Yeah. But, for some reason, this feels right." Jasper walked another fifty yards to two oak trees on either side of the road. The hanging moss in their branches created a canopy over the road. He knelt and examined a two-foot section of tire tread that wasn't washed away by the rain.

He looked up at Lewis. "This is my tread." Jasper stood. "He's in my Jeep like you suggested."

"He couldn't have gone too far in the weather last night. Maybe we'll get lucky."

Jasper nodded. "Let's hope so. I'm going to keep walking the road. Go get your truck and follow me."

Lewis turned and jogged back toward the truck as Jasper continued down the road. He found two more partial tracks, which encouraged him to keep going. The road they were on led to Half Moon Bay. It was the site of the original Gracie home. Henry and Alma built there, thinking the small bay would offer them some protection from the weather coming off the ocean. But they soon discovered the winds would circle around the bay, gain momentum, and then head inland with more force than if they'd blown straight in.

They stuck it out for fifteen years but finally gave up and moved to the current site of the town of Gracie. All that remained now was the stone foundation and half of the chimney. But the pier they built, going out into the bay, had been restored several years ago, and you could still bring a good-sized boat into the bay and tie it up at the dock.

Roger was definitely headed to the bay, but Jasper wasn't sure why. The road ended at the house. With any luck, they'd catch him coming back out.

Jasper continued up a small rise, which he knew would give him a clear view of the bay a quarter mile away.

When he got to the top of the rise, he stopped. The fog had lifted, and he saw his Jeep parked next to the remains of the house. He turned back to Lewis and motioned for him to pull over and stop. Then he joined Lewis as he got out of the truck.

"My Jeep is parked down by the Gracie house."

"Did you see Poppie?"

"I didn't see anyone. They could be in the Jeep, but it's too far away to know for sure."

"So, how do we approach it?"

Jasper looked at the trees on the south side of the road. They went all the way to the house and beyond for another quarter acre.

"We'll stick to the trees until we can see into the Jeep."

Using the trees for cover, they crested the hill, then went down the other side until they were even with the house and the Jeep.

When they could see through the window of the vehicle, Jasper sighed. "It's empty."

Lewis leaned against a tree. "Where the hell are they?" He suddenly straightened and moved to where he could see the pier. "Shit."

"What?"

"Burt's boat."

"What about it? It's been at the marina for a few years now."

"Until three months ago." He looked at Jasper. "O'Conner caught Burt trying to take off in it, so he asked me to help him move it here."

"You're kidding."

"I wish I was."

"What kind of shape is it in?"

"O'Conner and I checked it all out before we moved it. It's sound. The motor's good."

"Sound enough to ride out a hurricane?"

Lewis shrugged. "I hope so."

They left the trees and went to the Jeep. It appeared to be undamaged. A search of it revealed the shotgun had been left behind but didn't give them any clues as to Roger's plans. They continued to the pier and walked to the end of it.

Jasper felt the need to give Lewis some sort of hope to hold on to. "I'm sure he didn't go out until the wind and rain stopped. So, they're only an hour ahead of us, at most."

Lewis looked at the water. "Yeah. But an hour in what direction?"

Jasper adjusted his cap. "North. Canada. It's his only chance of avoiding arrest." He turned to Lewis. "Until we tell them he's coming, of course."

Jasper and Lewis drove to town and arrived at the station just as the chief was unlocking the door.

He turned toward Jasper. "Glad you're here. We've got a lot of cleaning up to do. That damn storm did a lot of damage."

"I'm not here to clean up, Chief. Roger took Poppie last night."

"When?"

"Right before the weather got too bad, we think. Sometime before eight-thirty. We tracked him to Half Moon Bay. Seems he took off in Burt's boat."

"The Dragonfly? How much of a head start does he have?"

"Hopefully, only an hour or two. If he's not a complete idiot."

James opened the door, and the men went inside. "Do you know which way he went? I suppose he's headed to Canada." He sat behind his desk.

"That's what we figured. I want to go after him."

"The water isn't our jurisdiction. We need to turn this over to the Coast Guard."

Jasper sat on a chair in front of the chief's desk. "They can bring him in. But I need to get Poppie off that boat."

"Son. The Guard is more than capable of protecting Poppie."

Jasper stood and shook his head. "I need to do it."

"So, what's your plan? Take off in a boat and hope you run into him. We don't have the resources or the men to back you up."

"I don't need backup. When I get on the boat, you can send them in."

"You're not thinking clearly, Jasper. This is an impossible task you're trying to pull off. And I think I know why."

"This has nothing to do with Ivy. You do what you need to do. Call the Coast Guard. Call the authorities in Canada." He headed for the door.

"Jasper. I can't let you go rogue on this. You need to stand down."

Jasper took his badge out of his pocket and set it on the chief's desk. "Consider me on that vacation you've been bugging me to take."

He stalked out of the office, with Lewis following behind. When they got to the sidewalk, Lewis put a hand on Jasper's arm.

"Are you sure about this?"

"Between us, the chief, and the Coast Guard, we're going to nail Roger and bring Poppie home."

"You sure this isn't a little bit about Ivy?"

Jasper sighed. "Lewis, I don't know. All I *do* know is I can't lose someone else to the damn ocean. If that puts me out of line or makes me reckless or irresponsible, then so be it. You're welcome to stay here and help out the chief." He started hurrying down the sidewalk.

Lewis caught up to him. "What's the plan?"

"We need to go wake up Mellie."

Chapter Twenty-Three

"That's not part of the plan."

There were three pilots on Gracie Island, Jasper, Dr. Hannigan, and Mellie. Lewis and Jasper drove to her house, parked on the street, and jogged onto the porch.

Lewis checked his watch. "She probably didn't get to bed until after two. They kept the Rusty Pelican open for anyone who felt safer there than at home."

"Well, then she got more sleep than you and me." Jasper knocked on the door. When she didn't answer after a few moments, he knocked again. "Mellie?"

Mellie cracked open the door. "What the hell, Jasper? Are you drunk?"

"At eight in the morning?"

"What do you want?" She noticed Lewis behind Jasper. "Hey, Lewis. What's going on, guys?"

"We need your help. Can we come in?"

She hesitated, then opened the door and let them in. She was wearing a short silk robe with not much else under it, and Jasper tried not to notice. He glanced at Lewis, who appeared to be doing the same. Mellie pulled it closed and tied the belt, then took an oversized sweater off a hook by the door and slipped it on.

She headed for the kitchen, and the men followed her. "This better be really good." She started a pot of coffee and set three cups on the table. "Sit."

They sat, and Jasper said, "We don't really have a lot of time."

"If you want me to help you, I need coffee."

"Fine."

She tapped her nails on the counter as she watched the coffee slowly percolate. "So, what's the big emergency?"

Lewis cleared his throat. "Poppie's missing."

Mellie turned to face him. "Oh, my God. You guys could've led with that."

Jasper frowned. "You didn't give us much choice."

She sat at the table. "Tell me what I can do."

Jasper explained the situation as succinctly as he could, then told her his plan. "I'm going to borrow Jake's boat and head in the general direction I believe they're traveling. I need you to take the plane up and find them for me."

"I thought once a suspect left solid ground, the Coast Guard takes over."

"They do."

"And the chief's backing you on this?"

"Not exactly."

Lewis put a hand on Jasper's arm. "Jasper's on vacation as of about ten minutes ago."

"I see. But the plane belongs to the sheriff's department. And I'm not exactly cleared to fly it."

Jasper gave her a little smile. "We're going to borrow the plane."

"Jasper."

"I know. I'll take the hit if shit rains down on us. It won't be the first time. And it probably won't be the last. But this guy dislocated my shoulder twice, burned my house down, stole my Jeep, and now he's taken Poppie. I'm not too concerned with protocol at this point."

Lewis added, "Not to mention the guys wanted for murder."

Mellie smiled. "Well, I always was a sucker for a little foul play."

Jasper nodded. "So, you'll help?"

"You've got yourself a pilot."

Jasper stood. "Okay. Get dressed. Put your coffee in a to-go cup, and get your ass up in the air." He headed for the door. "Take Lewis with you. Keep in touch. Let me know the minute you spot him."

Lewis stood as well. "Why am I going on the plane instead of on the boat with you?"

"Because you know what the Dragonfly looks like. Keep in touch on channel four."

Jasper left Mellie's house and hurried to the marina. The streets were still quiet, and he didn't run into anyone. He was afraid someone might spot him when he passed The Sailor's Loft, but he made it by without interruption and continued to the marina office. He knew Duke O'Conner would be there. He got to work at four every morning to see the fishing boats off. This morning, though, they would've waited for the torrential rain to stop and the wind to die down.

The Harbormaster's Office was painted a bright yellow with white trim around the door and the pane windows. There was a flag pole in front, flying the American flag and Maine's state flag. It was tall enough to see from most of the town. Duke was ex-military and respected the flag. He took it down every night at dusk and put it up every morning at dawn. If it was raining or too windy, he'd bring it in. The flags were flying this morning, so Jasper assumed Duke put them up as soon as the wind died down.

Jasper went inside the office and found Duke at a table studying a topographic map. He looked at Jasper when he heard the bell on the door ring.

"Morning, Deputy. Looks like you survived Emilio."

"Yeah. I need to borrow your boat."

"Which one?"

"The fast one. Your runabout."

"It's still pretty rough out there. She doesn't have much of a keel on her."

"I won't be going out too far."

"Is this sheriff business?"

"Not exactly."

Duke turned to lean against the table and folded his arms across his chest. "What's going on, Jasper?"

"Lewis' sister is missing, and the guy who took her is out there on the Dragonfly with her. He's got an hour or two lead. Most likely headed for Canada."

"The hell you say. What guy? That guy you've been looking for? That the whole town's been looking for?"

"Yeah. I need to get a location on him so the Coast Guard can bring him in."

He gave Jasper a skeptical tilt of the head. "You sweet on this girl?"

"What? No. I don't trust the bastard to not do something stupid when they surround him."

"Hmm. Does your father know about this?"

"The chief is going through official channels."

"While you play rogue cop?"

"Can I use your boat or not?"

Duke walked to his desk, opened the top drawer, and took out a set of keys. He handed them to Jasper. "Who am I to stand in the way of true love?"

"Dammit, Duke, that's not what this is."

"Sorry, kid. Guess I'm just an old romantic at heart. Watch your back. This guy seems like he's a slippery one."

"His slippery days are over."

"You're going to bring her back in one piece, right?"

"Of course. That's why I'm going alone."

"I meant my boat."

"Right. Of course. You'll get her back in perfect condition."

Jasper took the keys and left the office. The boat was moored at the end of the middle dock. It was a fifteen-foot sport fishing boat with two, two-hundred and fifty horsepower engines. It was built for speed and stability in relatively calm water but had enough of a keel to run in the ocean if the waves weren't too rough. It was certainly capable of catching the Dragonfly with its less powerful inboard motor and a wide hull that dragged through the water.

Assuming they were both going the same direction, and Roger had the hour or so lead Jasper assumed he had, it wouldn't take long to catch up to him.

Having Mellie in the sky would certainly help too. He picked up the radio and tried to reach her. Just when he was about to give up, she answered.

"Mellie here. I finished my pre-flight. We'll be in the air in five."

"Okay. I'm taking off now. I'll head due north as soon as I round the point. Keep an eye on the weather. If it gets too rough, take her back down."

"You too, Deputy. Don't be a hero and get yourself killed."

"That's not part of the plan."

"Being a hero or getting yourself killed?"

"Neither one. Take care and stay in touch."

"Will do."

Jasper checked his gas levels, then left the marina and headed for the open water. He decided to head northwest until he got a little closer to the coastline, then go due north. He could only guess what Roger might do. Hopefully, Mellie would spot the Dragonfly soon.

It was cold in the open boat, and Jasper pulled his coat tight around him and buttoned it. He wished he'd brought his slicker. It would've been a better barrier against the wind. He turned his cap around backward and powered up.

After he'd been out nearly an hour, his radio crackled, and he picked it up. "Mellie?"

"No, Jasper."

"Chief?"

"Did you really think I wouldn't try all the channels until I got you?"

"I'm not coming back in."

"I know. The Coast Guard has dispatched two search and rescue boats with security officers onboard. They shouldn't be too far behind you. When you get eyes on the Dragonfly, please relay the information."

Jasper sighed. "I will."

"You know I could have Mellie arrested for flying the department's plane."

"Please don't. She's helping with the search. She's a damn good pilot."

"As long as the plane ends up back on the ground and in one piece, I'll forget who was piloting it."

"Thank you."

"Be safe out there, Son."

"Yes, sir."

Jasper signed off, then took in the open water surrounding him. His resolve to find the boat was beginning to slip a little. It was a big ocean.

When the radio went off again, he answered, "Jasper here."

"Hey, it's Mellie. We spotted him."

"What are the coordinates?" Mellie gave them to him, and a quick check with his location put the Dragonfly ten miles ahead, northeast of him. "Thank you. You're the best."

"You owe me a drink. Or several drinks."

"Anything you want. Get back to Gracie Island."

"One more thing, Jasper. From up here, we can see the hurricane. It's not that far ahead. Maybe fifty miles or so. Don't get too close."

"I won't. Thanks for the heads up."

Jasper signed off, then called the chief back and gave him the location of the Dragonfly. They came up with a plan, which James wasn't completely happy with but agreed to. Then Jasper upped his speed and headed for the boat and Poppie.

Chapter Twenty-Four

The Dragonfly

When Jasper saw the Dragonfly ahead of him, he radioed the chief.

"I've got him. He's about a quarter-mile ahead of me."

"Are you sure you want to do this? You can just stay on his tail, and we can send in the coast guard now."

"I don't trust this guy. I'm going to move in. Give me time to get aboard, then have them track me to the location."

"Okay. Watch your back."

"Yes, sir."

Jasper increased his speed until he was within a hundred yards of the Dragonfly. When he saw Roger come out of the cabin with his arm around Poppie's neck and a gun to her side, he powered down and raised his hands as he drifted closer to the bigger boat.

"I just want to talk, Roger. I'm alone, and I'm unarmed."

"I've got nothing to say to you."

"I assume you're headed to Canada. We've already contacted them. They'll be looking for you and the boat."

Roger took a moment as he seemed to be assessing the news. "It's a long coastline. I can bypass customs, no problem."

"Then why don't you let me have Poppie, and you go sneak into Canada? I really don't care about stopping you anymore. I just want my friend back." He'd drifted within twenty feet of the Dragonfly now, and he could see the fear in Poppie's eyes.

"Come on, Roger. Give her up and be on your way."

"Right. So you can radio my position as soon as I hand her over." He walked to the rear of his boat. "Tie your boat off and come aboard." When Jasper didn't respond right away, Roger tightened his grip on Poppie. "Now, Deputy."

Jasper piloted the boat to the rear of the Dragonfly and then maneuvered so he could grab the aluminum ladder hanging off the deck. He shut down the motor, then tied off the boat to a cleat.

Roger had moved to the back of the boat, still holding Poppie. "Open your coat."

Jasper held the sides of his coat open and then turned and raised the back of it and his sweater to show he had nothing in his belt. He turned back around. "Like I said, I'm unarmed."

"Okay, climb up the ladder. Slowly."

Jasper climbed the ladder and stepped aboard the boat. He looked at Poppie. "Are you okay?"

She nodded.

Roger motioned toward the wooden bench seat on the side of the rear deck. "Sit down."

Jasper sat. "Let her go, Roger. You're in control here."

Roger removed his arm around Poppie, then gave her a small push toward Jasper. "Go sit next to him."

Poppie sat and took Jasper's hand. He squeezed it and looked closely at her. "You sure you're okay? He didn't—"

"I'm fine. Really."

Jasper looked back at Roger. "What now?"

He again took some time before answering. "Down below."

Jasper nodded, and he and Poppie stood, then went to the hatch and down the three steps into the cabin. It was a barebones boat used for recreational fishing. The main cabin had a galley on one side, and on the other, a built-in table with a bench on either side of it, which folded into a bed. Other than a few storage cabinets, that was it.

The boat could handle some blue water, but it wasn't built to go too far offshore. They were already pushing it in the rough water caused by the hurricane. Lewis had told Jasper the Dragonfly was still in good condition and the motor checked out, even though Burt hadn't used it in several years.

Roger followed them into the cabin. "Straight ahead to the captain's berth.

The headroom in the main cabin was an inch over Jasper's head, but when he ducked into the sleeping berth, it went down several inches. The compartment contained only an oddly shaped bed that followed the form of the bow of the boat and had a twelve-inch porthole on each side. The bedding, three pillows and two wool blankets were arranged to accommodate sleeping across the bow rather than parallel with it. No matter how one slept, it wasn't made for someone as tall as Jasper.

He needed to hunch over when he stepped into the berth. And he sat on the end of the bed, which was two feet from the door. Poppie, who had plenty of headroom, sat next to him. Roger studied the small space before he closed the door and locked it.

Poppie turned to Jasper. "What were you thinking?"

"When?"

"Coming here, unarmed? Coming right up to the boat? Letting him take you?"

"Poppie."

"What?"

"Calm down. It's alright. I didn't trust the bastard on this boat alone with you."

"You came to rescue me?"

"I came to protect you—" he lowered his voice, "—while we're being rescued."

She turned away from him, and he put a hand on her shoulder.

"Poppie."

She waved over her shoulder.

"Okay. Take your time."

He removed his hand and gave her some time while she took a few deep breaths and swiped at the tears she didn't want him to see.

When she turned back around, she said, "Thank you. What do you mean, 'while we're being rescued?'"

He put a finger to his lips, then spoke into her ear. "I left the radio open on the runabout. The coast guard has our location and is tracking us."

She whispered, "Thank goodness."

Jasper felt the motor rumble, and the boat started bouncing over the waves with an increase in speed instead of cutting through them. Jasper peered through one of the two portholes in the forward compartment.

"This boat wasn't made for this water. The bastard needs to slow down." He felt the familiar feeling of seasickness starting to wash over him. He sat back down next to Poppie and tried to shake it off.

She gave him a small smile. "I can't believe you're here."

"Like I said, I don't trust him."

"But you could've come blazing in with the Coast Guard. Or just let the Coast Guard take care of it. You didn't have to risk getting hurt or worse for me."

"Of course I did. I told Lewis I'd bring you home safe, and this was the best way I knew how. If the Coast Guard had shown up with me, I don't know what Roger would've done. If he panicked and... I couldn't leave it up to chance. At least with me here, I might be able to keep you safe."

She smiled again. "So, does this mean you care about me? Dare I say we're friends?"

He took a moment. "Well, I care about your safety. And it's kind of my job to protect you. But friends?" He shook his head. "I don't know. I'm not sure I can get past the annoying, 'I'm always right,' 'don't coddle me,' parts of you."

"Shut up. You care. You just don't want to admit it."

"Whatever."

The boat lurched as it rolled over a big wave, and she reached for his hand. "You can call it what you want. I'm glad you're here."

When the boat hit another wave, he groaned. "I need to lie down." He removed his hat, dropped back onto the bed, and closed his eyes.

"You're not going to throw up, are you?"

He glanced at her. "No. Why?"

"Lewis told me you get seasick."

"Is there anything Lewis hasn't told you about me?"

"I'm sure there's quite a bit I don't know."

He rubbed his face. "I don't throw up. I just feel like I need to. Along with my head feeling like I'm in a whirlpool."

She peered through one of the portholes again. "Oh, is that all? You should have no trouble fighting off the bad guy when the time comes, then."

"I can do what I need to do. Don't you worry about that."

She laid on her side next to him and rested on an elbow. "Tell me about Penny. How long have you had her?"

"Why do you want to know about Penny?"

"I'm distracting you. And I need you to distract me."

He opened his eyes and put his good arm behind his head. "Okay. We… Ivy and I were doing our monthly shopping trip to the mainland, and the humane society was holding an adoption event at the park next to Costco."

Poppie smiled. "You shop at Costco?"

"Why wouldn't I?"

"It seems so…un-Gracie Island."

"*Building* a Costco there would be un-Gracie Island. Do you want to hear about Penny or not?"

"Yes. Go on."

"So, there were a lot of big dogs, Pit Bulls, Labs, Shepherds…"

"Hold on. I can see this scenario. You're checking out all the big manly dogs—"

"Poppie."

"Sorry. Continue."

He stared at the ceiling of the cabin three feet above him. "Penny was in a crate with three other pups from her litter. The other three were wrestling around, but Penny was sitting in the corner, watching the people go by. Anytime anyone would look at her or try to interact with her, she'd just look back but not respond in any way. But when we went over to her, she put her front paws on the crate and started wagging her tail. Then she barked at us." He turned his head toward Poppie.

She smiled. "So, you didn't pick her. She picked you."

"Exactly. You can't walk away from that."

"And that's why I know under your tough-guy, stubborn, grumpy, borderline mean exterior is a heart of gold."

Jasper frowned. "I'm not stubborn." He sat up and glanced around the small space. "I also never thought I was claustrophobic, but now, I'm not so sure."

"It is pretty stifling in here." She looked through the porthole again. "Maybe it'll help you to look out the window."

"And watch the waves hit the boat? No thanks." He ran his hands through his hair and closed his eyes again.

"So, shouldn't that hurricane be somewhere over Canada by now?"

"Why?"

"Seems pretty ominous up ahead."

He moved next to her, then she leaned back so he could look through the porthole. "Emilio slowed down again."

"Which means?"

"Which means we're in for some rough weather." He crawled off the berth and pounded on the door. "Roger!"

It took two more rounds of knocking on the door before Roger yelled at Jasper through it. "Shut the hell up."

"Have you noticed the weather you're headed into?"

"It's just some rain."

"No, Roger. It's the tail end of Emilio. It must've slowed down again. You need to turn back south. Or, at the very least, go west until you hit land."

"I'm not falling for that."

"Roger?" When he got no response, Jasper turned back to Poppie. "Idiot."

Poppie sat on the edge of the bed. "Are we going to be okay?"

Jasper sat next to her. "Yes."

"You can tell me. I can take it."

He patted her knee. "It's much too soon to give up." He felt the motor power up again. "I guess we're racing toward the hurricane now. Good plan."

"How soon are we expecting the Coast Guard?"

"Well, if he doesn't slow down, not soon enough."

When they felt the motor slow, they both went to the porthole again.

Jasper watched the waves for a moment. "He's turning around. Maybe he's not as big of an idiot as I thought." A wave broadsided them and rocked the boat violently. Jasper put a hand on the ceiling for support as Poppie lost her balance and fell into him. He dropped his hand and took her arm as she was about to hit the floor.

"You're turning too tight, Roger."

"Are we going to flip over?"

The boat rocked again, then settled a bit as it came around and headed due south, and started hitting the waves head-on.

"No. He's got it." He let go of Poppie's arm, and they sat on the end of the bed again.

She glanced at him. "How's your stomach?"

"I'm trying to ignore it."

"You look a little green."

"That's not helping me ignore it."

She peered out the porthole. "We turned around, right?"

Jasper closed his eyes as a wave of nausea washed over him. "Yeah. We're headed south. Right toward the coast guard." He glanced at her. "Why?"

"Because the sky is just as bad."

He returned to the porthole. "Looks like Emilio changed course again. Damn storm can't make up his mind." He heard the rain start to fall and the wind pick up. "Shit." He banged on the door again but got no response. He knew he wouldn't. Roger was out there trying to navigate the boat through the outer edges of a hurricane.

Chapter Twenty-Five

"What do we do now?"

The seas continued to get rougher, and Jasper wondered how much longer his "I don't throw up" statement would be true. He tried to get Roger's attention two more times, then gave up. Poppie seemed to sense he was concentrating on keeping down what little food he had in his stomach, and she left him alone as he laid back and tried to think of anything else besides the rocking boat.

When Roger threw open the door, Jasper sat up.

Roger seemed to be in a state of panic. He was soaked from the rain and shivering, though Jasper wasn't sure if it was from the cold or fear. Probably a little of both.

Roger took a breath. "I need help."

Jasper got to his feet, being careful not to hit his head on the top of the berth. "Let's go."

Roger hesitated a moment. "No funny business."

"I don't want to go down with the boat. That's all, Roger."

Roger turned and walked away from the open door. Jasper picked up his hat, then glanced at Poppie.

"Please listen to me. Stay down below. It's nasty out there."

She nodded. "I'll stay below until you tell me otherwise."

"Thank you." He went into the main cabin, then climbed the steps to the deck. The weather was worse than he thought. The waves were high enough to almost break over the side of the boat. And the wind and rain were coming in so hard it stung his face and hands.

He went to the controls and leaned close to Roger. "You're going too fast." He put his hand on the throttle, and Roger backed away from the wheel. Jasper powered the boat down to a more manageable speed, then took stock of their position. They were farther from the coast than they should be, but the waves were coming from the north and would hit them broadside if he turned too sharply west. He took an angled approach and hoped it'd be enough.

Jasper hadn't spent a lot of time on the water, but he knew enough to get them home as long as it didn't get worse. They were headed away from Emilio, but it seemed to be moving with them. The hurricane had changed its mind once again and had turned south. They just needed to stay ahead of it. As bad as the weather was, Jasper knew they were still only on the edge of the hurricane.

He tried to search the horizon for the Coast Guard, but seeing much farther than the bow of the boat in the rain was nearly impossible. Hopefully, they'd just suddenly appear. He looked toward the rear of the boat.

"Roger? Where's my boat?"

"I cut it loose. It was dragging us down. Filling up with water. Messing with the steering."

"When? How long ago?"

Roger shrugged. "Been kind of busy. Don't know."

If the coast guard hadn't been called back because of the weather, they were following the wrong boat. The boat that belonged to Duke O'Conner, who was going to be royally pissed when he found out what happened to it. There was no way it would survive this weather. If it hadn't sunk already, it would soon.

When the wind gust grew stronger, and the waves started coming in over the right side of the boat, Jasper adjusted their position a little more south. Emilio was gaining on them.

He studied Roger, who seemed terrified. Jasper needed to distract him if he was going to be of any use. He yelled over the howling wind. "Why'd you kill your brother?"

Roger leaned closer. "What?"

"You heard me."

Roger wiped the rain from his face. "I didn't mean to. It was an accident."

"You accidentally shot your brother in the head?"

Roger nodded as he crouched next to Jasper to get out of the wind. "He went to your island to check it out. He was planning on moving there."

Jasper glanced down at him. "How does that lead to you shooting him?"

"He was planning on moving there with my wife."

"That sucks, Roger." Jasper adjusted his course again. "But a death sentence?"

"I didn't mean to kill him. I just wanted to scare him."

"So why not tell me that at the lighthouse? Why not come in peacefully instead of burning my house down, stealing my Jeep and this boat, and taking Poppie hostage?"

"The fire was an accident, too."

Jasper shook his head. "So you're just an accident-prone bastard? None of it's your fault?"

Roger nodded again.

"Why take Poppie? Was that an accident, too?"

"No. I took her for insurance. A bargaining tool so I could get away." Another gust of wind brought a wave crashing over the bow, and Roger stood and held onto the cabin door frame.

Jasper had heard enough. "Go down below and check the fuel. See if there's a spare tank."

"Are we getting low?"

"Just go check."

Roger nodded and headed into the cabin. He took way longer than he should've, and Jasper figured it was because the man had no idea what he was supposed to be looking for.

Jasper wiped the water from the gas gauge. They had a third of a tank. He didn't know what the range was on the forty-foot boat, but he knew a third of a tank wouldn't get them all the way home. He hoped it'd get them past the edge of the storm. Emilio had to lose steam at some point.

When Roger appeared at the cabin door, Jasper yelled, "Is there a spare?"

Roger shook his head.

"Okay. I need you to send a mayday."

Roger didn't move from his spot.

"We're going to run out of gas. We need help."

Roger came through the door and made his way to Jasper. "I destroyed it. The radio is no good."

"Well, shit, Roger." Jasper wiped the salt water from his eyes. "Take the wheel."

Roger shook his head.

"I'll be right back. I need to talk to Poppie for a moment."

Roger stepped near and took the steering wheel. "Don't leave me out here."

"I'll be right back."

Jasper made his way to the cabin hatch and went down the steps. Poppie was sitting at the table and seemed almost as frightened as Roger. He sat down across from her and took her hands.

She leaned toward him. "It's bad, isn't it?"

"It's not good. But it's not over."

She squeezed his hand. "What was he looking for in the engine compartment?"

"To see if there was a reserve gas tank."

"Are we going to run out of gas?"

"It's highly likely."

"Oh my God."

"Poppie. The Coast Guard is still out there. They'll find us. I just need to keep us headed south until we get out from under the storm."

She tried to smile but didn't quite make it. "Simple, right?"

"Hell, yeah." He stood. "I need to get back out there. Sit tight. It's going to be rough a little longer."

She nodded, and he gave her a wink. "I've got this. Don't you worry." He turned away, then, and went back on deck.

As he stepped into the weather, a gust of wind, followed by a huge wave, washed over the boat. Roger was torn away from the steering wheel, lost his balance, and was headed for the right side of the boat. Jasper ran, then leaped toward Roger and grabbed his arm as he was headed overboard.

Roger looked into Jasper's eyes. "Don't let go, man."

"I got you."

Roger's legs and stomach were over the side of the boat, and he was resting on his chest. Jasper had instinctively grabbed Roger with his right hand, and the pain in his shoulder was severe. Roger was holding onto Jasper's wrist with his other hand, so all his weight was pulling on Jasper's injured shoulder. The metal support under the bench seat running along the side of the boat was the only thing keeping them both from going into the water, as Jasper clung to it with his left hand.

When another wave rocked the boat, he felt his grip on Roger's forearm slipping.

"Roger. Let go of my wrist and grab the boat."

Roger shook his head. "I can't. If I let go, I'll go over."

"You're going to go over if you don't. I can't hold you."

Roger shook his head. "No. I can't. Don't let go. Pull me in."

Jasper tugged with all of his strength and tried to ignore the pain. But the injured arm wasn't going to be enough. He couldn't let go of the support beam, though. It was the only thing keeping him in the boat.

When another wave hit them and rocked the boat low enough for Roger to go under, Jasper felt his arm being pulled from the socket. By now, it was a familiar sensation. When the boat bounced back up, he felt Roger being sucked from his grasp.

When the wave crested and the boat righted itself, Roger was gone.

Jasper remained where he was, leaning over the side of the boat, with only the metal support rod keeping him from following Roger into the water.

After a few moments, he rolled onto the deck, still clinging to the lifesaving metal bar. Another wave broke over him, then dissipated. He needed to get back to the steering wheel and straighten the boat, but he couldn't make himself let go of the bar.

When he saw Poppie crawling toward him on her hands and knees, he didn't know whether he should be relieved or pissed that she'd come out of the cabin. One thing he did know, though, he was damn glad to see her.

She made it to him and put a hand on his bent knee. "Are you okay?"

"Not sure yet." He glanced at the metal bar. "I can't seem to let go."

She reached for his hand and gently pulled it away from the support. "Where's Roger?"

He could tell by the way she asked that she already knew the answer. "I tried to hold on, but the second wave was too much."

"It's not your fault."

"Yeah. I know. It doesn't make me feel any better about it, though." A wave hit the side of the boat but didn't make it over the side. "I need to get back to the steering wheel." He tried to get up, but the pain in his shoulder was worse than it'd ever been, and his arm was useless. "Might need a little help."

Poppie took his left arm and helped him onto his knees. From there, he was able to get to his feet. They made it to the steering console, and he took hold of the wheel with his left hand.

Poppie put her hands on the other side of it. "I can help."

He didn't argue with her. He needed her help. He couldn't keep the boat going in the right direction without it. "We need to bring it to port." When she looked at him, he added, "To the left."

They got the Dragonfly back on course. When the wind died down a little and the waves started decreasing in size, Jasper sped up a little.

Poppie glanced at him. "This is like being in the Jeep all over again."

"How so?"

"Going as far as we can before the gas runs out."

"It seems to be a recurring theme." He noticed the light jacket she wore over a sweater, then took his coat off and handed it to her. "Put this on before you freeze to death. I know it's wet, but the wool will help keep you warm.

She slipped it on and buttoned it. It was huge on her, and she rolled up the sleeves.

She looked at him. "What about you?"

"I'm fine."

They continued on, mostly in silence, maintaining their course and speed. The weather slowly started to improve, and the sky in front of them was clearing.

Poppie glanced at Jasper. "That looks promising."

"Yeah. We might be outrunning it, finally."

After thirty minutes, the rain had almost stopped, and the winds had lessened to something more manageable.

"How's the gas?"

"Just about out." Jasper glanced behind them. "It lasted long enough, though. Looks like the weather is heading east now."

Twenty minutes later, they were in a calm sea with a light breeze and had they not just lived through it, it would've been hard to imagine they were fighting for their lives an hour ago. The gas lasted another ten minutes before the engine coughed and sputtered before stopping. The Dragonfly coasted another five hundred feet, bounced around in its wake for a few moments, then stopped.

Jasper looked at Poppie. "And that's that."

"What do we do now?"

"We wait."

"Can we wait down below?"

Jasper let go of the wheel. "No sense sitting out here."

Chapter Twenty-Six

"Maybe I need a little help."

Poppie helped Jasper down the steps, and he dropped onto the bench by the table. She sat across from him. "You're exhausted."

"A little bit, yeah."

"And in pain."

"A lot, yeah."

She got up, went to the galley, and started opening cabinets. "Are you hungry?"

"I guess."

"When did you eat last?" She dug through some cans of soup, then turned around and leaned against the counter. "My spaghetti. Did you guys eat it last night?"

"Um…yes. We had to wait until the storm passed before we could go looking for you."

"What did you think of it?"

He took a moment. "It was...good."

She folded her arms across her chest. "Just good? You're such a liar. I know my spaghetti is excellent. How many servings did you have?"

"Two, I think." He pushed back some damp hair from his forehead. "Fine. It was *really* good."

Poppie smiled. "Thank you." She returned to the cupboard. "So, there's good news and bad news. The good is, there's quite a bit of food in here. The bad is..." She held up a can. "It's all vegetable soup. Generic. Not even the good stuff."

"Burt does like his soup."

"This is Burt's boat?"

"Yeah. It was moored at Half Moon Bay because he kept trying to take it out." He took a moment. "So, really, we can blame this whole adventure on Lewis. He and Duke moved the boat there. If they hadn't, Roger wouldn't have had anywhere to go."

"No. I blame Roger." She set two cans of soup on the counter, then went to the table. "Before we eat, we need to get you out of those wet clothes."

He squinted at her. "Are you trying to get me to undress, Penelope?"

She shook her head. "Been there. Seen that."

Jasper laughed. "Yeah. I guess you have."

"Sweater first."

"No. It's going to hurt."

"Come on, you big baby. I'll help you."

He moved to the edge of the seat. "I have a fun fact for you. Each time you dislocate your shoulder, it hurts more than the last."

"I'll remember that next time I dislocate my shoulder." She helped him out of his sweater without causing too much pain. "Okay. Shirt next."

He started unbuttoning his shirt but stopped and let her finish doing it. Then she slid it off gently and looked at his thermal top.

He glanced at it. "No."

"Fine. Pants, then."

He sighed, stood and unbuckled his belt, then unzipped his pants and stepped out of them. "The long John's stay."

"Definitely. By all means."

He sat back down. "You're just as soaked as I am."

She took off the coat he gave her and the jacket and sweater she had on underneath it. "That's as far as I go."

Jasper glanced at his long johns. "So unfair."

"I don't have anything under this. Well, I do... You know what I mean."

"Yes. I do." He watched her return to the galley. Somehow, despite having spent hours in the wind and rain, she still looked good. He wondered if he should tell her he could see exactly what she had on under her wet blouse. *Probably not.*

She ran her hands through her wet hair and scrunched it a few times. "I must look like a drowned rat."

Jasper shook his head. "Nah. Just one who went for a swim in the ocean, then took a shower in the rain."

"Hmm. Was that a compliment?"

He shrugged. "Possibly."

Poppie dug through a drawer for a can opener and two spoons. "Do we have to eat it cold?"

He rubbed his shoulder. It hurt like hell. "Use the stove. It's propane."

"Do I need a pot?"

"If you use a pot, then you need to use bowls. Which means you have dishes to wash. My God. Have you never gone camping? How'd you eat at that horse camp of yours?"

"In the cafeteria. We were there to ride horses, not survive in the wilderness."

"Open the can, take off the label, and set it over the flame."

"Easy enough."

She prepared the cans, then lit the stove. After setting the cans on the burner, she returned to the table. "Did you sleep while you were waiting for the weather to clear?"

The question made her realize how tired he was. "No. Tried. But no luck."

She smiled. "Good."

"Why is that good?"

"It means you were worried about me."

He covered a yawn as he tried to get comfortable in the seat. "I think me showing up pretty much gave that away."

She reached across the table and patted his hand. "Thank you."

"You're welcome."

She got up again. "Maybe Burt has some painkillers. Or alcohol."

"Either one would be appreciated. Or both, preferably."

"You'll get silly again."

"Don't care." Silly would be okay. Passing out would be better.

Poppie checked the cupboards above the stove, then started going through the drawers.

When she found a bottle of prescription pain medication, she turned and showed it to Jasper.

"Will this work?"

She handed him the bottle, and he read the label. "Don't know what it is, but it says, 'take for pain.' That works for me. And it's only slightly out of date."

She continued her search through the cabinets. "Score number two." She held up a bottle of whiskey. "Looks like you'll be getting some sleep tonight." She brought it to the table and set it in front of him.

"Is there a glass over there?"

"You just said you didn't want to make dirty dishes."

"Yes. But I'm not a barbarian. I'll take a glass, please."

She found a glass and brought it to him.

He poured a double shot into the bottom of the tumbler. "You going to join me?"

"I don't like whiskey."

"Right. Rum."

"And tequila if it's in a margarita."

"Well, sure." He took a swallow of whiskey, then put a pill in his mouth and took another. He glanced behind her. "Your can's on fire."

She turned and then squealed as she picked up the can with a pair of tongs and set it in the sink. "Oh my gosh." She blew on the small flame until it went out.

"You need to take *all* the paper off."

She turned to him. "Thanks. I'll remember that next time." She brought the can to the table and set it down hard in front of him.

He pushed it away. "I want the one that didn't catch fire."

She put her hands on her hips. "Why? The soup didn't burn."

"My house just burned down." He looked up at her and saw her hold back the sarcastic remark she wanted to make.

She shook her head. "Do you have PTSD now?"

"Possibly."

"Whatever." She went to the stove and retrieved the other can, then set it down on the table hard enough to splash a little soup onto the table. "There you go, Deputy Goodspeed."

He stirred the soup in his can, then licked the spoon before pointing it at her. "You call me that when you're mad at me."

"Not true. If it was, that's all I'd ever call you."

"Wow. Okay."

She used a napkin to wipe up the spill, then sat and took a bite of her soup. "Mmm."

"Really?"

"No, it's terrible."

Jasper laughed, which hurt, but he couldn't help it. Poppie Jensen always seemed to make him laugh even in the worst of situations. "Eat it anyway."

She took another bite. "So, since we have lots of time on our hands and nothing to do, why don't you tell me what the deal is with you and your dad?"

"No."

"Come on."

"There's nothing to tell. He never wanted to be a dad. He told Mom that when they first met. I was an oops, and it didn't change his mind." That was the simplified version and it was all he was prepared to tell her.

"I'm sorry."

Jasper shrugged. "I had my mom. That's all I needed. She's always said I was the best mistake she ever made." He finished the whiskey in his glass and poured another shot. "This isn't really working, but I'm feeling kind of fuzzy, so that's something."

She finished her soup and then peered into his can. "Eat up. Then let's get you to bed."

He raised an eyebrow.

She smiled at him. "Before you get too sleepy. I really don't think I could carry you. Nor would I want to."

He grinned. "I'd like to see you try."

She stood. "Eat."

Jasper finished his soup, then picked up the pill bottle. "I'm going to take another one of these—" he put a hand on the whiskey bottle "—with a swallow of this. Then I think I'll be able to sleep. I've been up for…" He shook his head. "I have no idea what time it is, so I don't know how long it's been."

Poppie looked out the door. "The sun's about to go down. So, over twenty-four hours."

"That sounds about right." He took the pill. "You too, right? I assume you didn't sleep last night after Roger took you."

She shook her head. "No."

Jasper stared at the whiskey bottle for a moment. "He was a bastard, but he didn't deserve… Well, no one does, I guess." He looked at Poppie. "My wife certainly didn't." He gave Poppie a small smile. "And no, I'm not going to talk about it."

Poppie took his empty can and picked up his glass. "Are you done with this?"

He nodded and screwed the lid onto the bottle. "Yep. Time for bed."

She put the can and the glass in the sink, then took the bottle and put it away in a cabinet. She then went to Jasper. "Okay, big guy, let me help you up."

"I don't need help." He stood, then leaned on the table for support. "Maybe I need a little help."

Poppie took his left arm. "Come on." She started to pull him up, then stopped and the neckline of his thermal top above his right shoulder. She pulled it back. "Oh wow. You're really bruised this time."

He pulled away from her. "That doesn't help make it feel better."

"Sorry. I think you really messed it up this time."

"That doesn't help, either."

She got him to his feet and they headed for the berth. Jasper ducked before going in, then sat on the end of the bed. "This bed wasn't made for a normal-sized human being."

"I'm pretty sure I'd fit on it just fine."

He shook his head, then laid on his back with a groan. He had to bend his knees to fit. He struggle back up to a sitting position. "This isn't going to work." He took one of the pillows and tossed it into the pointed end of the bed at the bow of the boat. He laid down again, and this time, just his feet hung over the edge.

Poppie took one of the wool blankets and put it over him. "Cozy?"

"No."

"Okay. Well, I'm going to go figure out how to fold the table into a bed."

She went into the main cabin, and Jasper listened to her mumble for a few moments before calling out to her. "Poppie?"

"What?"

"Just come sleep here with me. I promise you, I don't have the desire or the strength to mess with you."

She returned to the berth. "Are you sure? I mean that I won't bother you? Not the other thing."

"Just get your ass to bed."

"Although it's a little insulting that you have no desire to—"

"Penelope. It has nothing to do with you or your…desirability. I've been up for two days, just spent hours fighting to stay afloat in a hurricane, and I'm in a lot of pain. Another day. Another situation. It might be a different story."

"Well… Okay then." She blew out the propane lantern, and came into the cabin with a flashlight, then crawled up next to him and wrapped the other blanket around her, then laid on a pillow. "Hmm. Yeah. I fit just fine."

"Like I said, it wasn't made for normal people."

"Go to sleep Deputy Goodspeed."

Despite the pain and the uncomfortable bed, Jasper fell asleep almost instantly. Poppie watched him for a few moments. There was enough light coming in through the portholes to be able to see his face.

She sighed, then whispered, "Finally at peace. For at least a few hours, anyway." She wouldn't define him as a tortured soul, but he'd certainly had his share of heartbreak during his thirty or so years. She wasn't quite sure how old he was. He hadn't said. But she figured he was a year or so older than Lewis.

Poor Lewis. He must think... I hope he doesn't think I'm dead. The whole town might think we've drowned. She sighed. *I'm still here, brother. We're both still here. Keep looking for us.*

She looked at Jasper again. *What a wonderfully handsome face you have.* She started to reach for his hair. She just wanted to... *No. He'd wake up. Then he'd either be mad or make fun of you.* She rolled onto her side, putting her back to him. *Deputy Jasper Goodspeed. What am I going to do about you?*

Jasper woke with a start and it took him a moment to remember where he was. He could feel the boat bobbing lightly in the water and it was still dark. He could see the moon through the porthole above Poppie. *Why did I wake up?* Pain, or the lack of it. He rubbed his upper arm. It was numb. His whole arm was numb, all the way down to his hand.

He reached over and patted Poppie's arm. "Hey."

She stirred and mumbled in her sleep.

"Poppie." He felt her turn toward him.

"Are you okay?"

"I think I'm in trouble."

She sat up and he could see her face reflected in the moonlight. "What's wrong?"

"I can't feel my arm."

Poppie groped for the flashlight, then turned it on and shone it on his shoulder. "It's really swollen. I think your sleeve is cutting off the circulation."

Jasper glanced at it. "Shit. You need to cut it."

She went to the edge of the bed. "I'll see if I can find something."

"There's a knife in my pants' pocket."

She went into the main cabin, then returned in a few moments and handed him the flashlight. "Hold this." She pulled out the blade and he pulled back from her.

"Be careful."

"I will." She put the blade at the end of his sleeve above his hand.

"Hold on."

"I'm not going to cut you. Relax."

"It's kind of hard when you're about to slice right next to my skin."

"Jasper, I've seen you do some pretty heroic things today. But now, you're being a baby. I'm not going to cut you."

"I'm just a little freaked out at the possibility of bleeding."

She laughed. "Does the sight of blood bother you? How did you take pictures of Roger's brother. There had to be quite a bit of blood inside that car."

"Other people's blood isn't so bad. It's just mine. I'd rather keep it inside where it belongs."

She put the knife at his wrist, again. "I promise you, I won't make you bleed."

He took a deep breath. "Okay. Just do it."

She started slicing his shirt sleeve. "Besides, I imagine your arm falling off from lack of circulation will cause a lot more blood loss than if I nick you with this knife."

"Stop. Jesus."

She made it to his elbow, then stopped for a moment and glanced at him. "What else makes the deputy queasy?"

Jasper sighed. "Shots."

Poppie started up his bicep toward his shoulder. "So, I'm guessing no tattoos?"

"You've seen most of my body. You already know the answer to that."

She reached his shoulder and continued to cut to the neckband. "This looks really bad, Jasper."

He opened and closed his hand a couple of times, then groaned. "And now it's waking up."

She took his hand and rubbed it between hers, then rubbed his lower arm.

The pain was bad and getting worse as the numbness wore off. He wanted to curse long and loud, but he held it in.

She patted his hand. "Go ahead."

"No. I'm good. I got this." He gave her a small smile, which was all he could manage. "What would Poppie say in this situation?"

"I wouldn't say anything. I'd just cry."

"Somehow, I don't think that's going to help."

Chapter Twenty-Seven

"I spy a party-pooper."

At the sound of a moan and a whispered curse, Poppie rolled over to face Jasper. The cabin was light. Apparently, they'd slept the whole night.

"Good morning."

He closed his eyes for a moment. "Not so sure about that."

She sat and peered out the porthole. "The sky's clear ahead of us. No waves. No wind."

"That's something, I guess."

She sat cross-legged and looked at him. "Are you in a lot of pain?"

He nodded, then winced with the movement.

"On a scale of one to ten?"

"Fifteen. Twenty."

She moved to the end of the bed. "I'll go get the pain pills." She stood. "Do you want the whiskey, too?"

"No. Just pills and water. Hopefully, the water in the tank is fresh."

Poppie left the berth and went up the steps to the deck. The sea was completely calm. She searched for any sign of another boat or land. But there were only miles of ocean around them.

She went into the cabin and rinsed his whiskey glass out before filling it with water. Then took two pills from the bottle before returning to Jasper.

He held his left hand out to her. "Pull me up."

She took his hand and tugged until he was in a sitting position.

He took a moment to get past the pain it caused, then said, "Thank you."

She handed him the pills and the water. "You should eat again with those."

"More soup?"

"Yeah."

"I don't suppose you found any coffee with the soup."

"No. There was a box of teabags, though."

He took the pills and handed her the glass. "Not the same."

"What's the first thing you're going to do when we get rescued?"

"Eat breakfast at the Loft. Ham, eggs, hashbrowns, sourdough toast with marmalade. And a giant cup of coffee.

"Sounds wonderful. Except for the coffee."

"I'll drink yours."

"They're going to find us, right?"

"Of course. Mellie's probably up in the air right now."

"Mellie? The bartender?"

"Yes. She's a pilot."

"Wow. Interesting. Did she and you go to pilot school together?"

He smiled. "No. Her father taught her when she was in high school. She got her license when she turned eighteen. I went to flight school after I graduated from the… From sheriff school."

"Well, it makes me feel better that someone's up in the sky searching for us. Seems like that'd be the easiest way to spot us. Even if the pilot is a bartender."

"They'll be looking from land, sea, and air. And she's a damn good pilot, along with being a damn good bartender."

"I suppose the whole town is involved in rescuing their favorite deputy sheriff?"

"And their favorite boat guy's sister."

She patted his knee. "I'm very glad you're here because if I was out here alone, I'd be freaking out right about now."

"Nothing to freak out about. We'll be on land before the day's over."

"Promise?"

"Well, no. But I'll be pretty damn surprised if we're not."

"Okay. I guess that'll have to do." She took the glass to the galley, then returned to Jasper. "It's pretty beautiful out on the deck. The fresh air might make you feel better."

He stood up slowly. "Sounds good." He glanced at his long johns. "I guess I should get dressed first."

She brought him his pants and shirt, then left him to get dressed. When he came out into the main cabin, he had on his pants, but only his left arm was through the sleeve of his shirt. The other side hung over his right shoulder.

He continued past the galley, and Poppie followed him to the hatch. She could tell by the way he was moving, he was in more pain than he'd been with the first and second injuries. He went up the steps, took a deep breath of fresh air, then sat on the wooden bench next to the spot where Roger had gone overboard. The whole thing was surreal. The difference between last night and this morning was unbelievable.

Poppie sat next to Jasper. "Why aren't you seasick anymore?"

He thought about the question. "Huh. Weird. I haven't even thought about it. I guess I got over it last night in the storm."

"Do you get over seasickness?"

"Apparently."

"Maybe God wanted to give you a break."

"That's probably not it." He rubbed the right side of his chest.

"Why do you think it hurts more this time?"

"I probably tore something. Or strained something. Or maybe I broke it this time. I don't know."

"Are you hung over?"

"No. I only had two shots of whiskey."

Poppie shrugged. "I don't know how much it takes. I hardly drink."

"You've never been drunk?"

"No. I never felt the need."

He smiled. "I need to get you drunk."

"No thanks."

His smile turned into a grin. "Like right now."

"What? Right now? On this boat? At whatever time it is in the morning?"

"What else do we have to do?"

"Talk. Play cards. I Spy. Anything else but that. I'd even play Monopoly with you if there was a game onboard."

"Go get the whiskey."

"You're crazy. No."

He leaned back on the bench. "Fine. We'll just sit here and do nothing."

"What happened to playing cards, or I Spy, or anything else?"

"I Spy a party-pooper."

"So, this is a party now?"

He nodded toward the cabin. "Just go get the whiskey."

With an exaggerated sigh, Poppie got to her feet, rolled her eyes, then went into the cabin. She returned a few minutes later with two bottles, a can, and two cups.

She set them next to Jasper. "This gin was in the cabinet with the whiskey."

"What's in the can?"

She picked it up and read the label. "Grapefruit flavored carbonated beverage."

"Sounds yummy." He looked at the alcohol bottles. "So you prefer gin over whiskey?"

"I've never had gin. But if I'm being forced to drink, then I'll drink gin with this grapefruit stuff. That's a known drink, right? Some kind of dog?"

"A Greyhound. But it's made with vodka and actual grapefruit juice."

She shrugged. "Close enough." She sat on the other side of the beverages. "So, we're just going to sit here and get drunk?"

He laughed. "No. We're going to make a game of it. For every drink, you need to answer a question. You have to answer truthfully. Anything goes."

"I'm not going to do that."

"Nothing too personal or intrusive. And the chief and Ivy are off limits." He opened the whiskey and poured a shot into a cup. "How about you? Any taboo subjects?"

She thought for a moment. "I reserve the right to decline to answer should a taboo question come up."

"Fair enough." He poured a shot of gin into the other cup, then opened the can and added a shot's worth into the gin. He handed her the glass. "Drink."

She took a breath, then drank the gin and grapefruit soda. "Yuck."

"First question." Jasper took a moment. "What's with the bottle of rum in your purse?"

She laughed. "That's what you want to know?" She set her glass down. "It was a gift from a guy I dated briefly. I had some lip balm shaped like a tiny bottle of Coke. So he gave me the rum to go with it."

"And you carried it around for…how long?"

"Two years."

"Hmm." He drank his shot and looked at her expectantly.

"This might fall under the 'no questions about the chief rule,' but why'd you become a deputy under Chief Goodspeed?"

"I'm not really sure, but I think it was because it was better to have a working relationship with him than no relationship at all." Poppie stuck out her lower lip, and he pointed at her. "No sympathy pouts allowed. Drink up."

She poured gin and grapefruit drink into her glass and drank it in two swallows. "When does it start tasting better?"

"Never. What are you afraid of? What scares the holy shit out of you?"

"Flying."

"Seriously? Have you ever been on a plane?"

"No. And I don't intend to. So don't think you're going to get me up in your little plane."

"So, you've never left Boston?"

"Flying isn't the only form of transportation. And I'm here, aren't I?"

"Right." He poured himself another shot and drank it.

Poppie pulled her feet up onto the seat and hugged her knees. "How old are you? When's your birthday?"

"Twenty-nine. October fifteenth. And that's two questions." A breeze blew by, and he ran a hand through his hair. "I lost my damn hat in the storm last night."

Poppie leaned forward and looked under the bench across the deck from them. With a smile, she got up and knelt by the bench, then pulled out his hat, still wet but mostly undamaged.

"You mean this hat?" She brought it to him.

"Yes. My hat. Thank you." He adjusted the brim as well as he could with one hand, then put it on. "Drink."

She took her drink. "Are you going to ask me when my birthday is?"

"I already know. March seventeenth. St. Patrick's Day."

"How do you know that?"

"On your last birthday, we had a storm, and Lewis was in a panic because the phone lines were down, and he was afraid he wouldn't be able to call you."

"Aww. I have the best brother."

"You do. Don't forget it."

"He thinks we're dead, doesn't he? He's probably already called our parents."

"Poppie. They haven't given up on us."

She wiped a tear from her cheek, then looked at her glass. "How many more of these do I need to drink before I'm drunk?"

"Pretty sure you're about there."

"I don't feel anything."

"Stand up."

She hesitated a moment, then got to her feet and held out her arms. "See." A slight breeze blew by and moved the boat, causing her to lose her balance. She fell toward Jasper, and he caught her with his left hand. She sat next to him and closed her eyes. "That wasn't the gin. It was the wind."

He smiled at her. "I think it was a little of both." She looked at him, and he held her gaze for a long moment, then started to lean in toward her.

When she saw the realization of what he was about to do hit him, she backed away, and he got to his feet. "I...can't." He walked away and went around the edge of the boat to the bow and knelt with his back to her.

He stayed there for several minutes, but when he stood, Poppie tried to figure out what she was going to say to him. Instead of coming back, though, he took off his hat and looked at the water in the distance.

He glanced back at her. "There's a boat."

"Really?"

"Yeah. Come here."

She walked carefully around the edge of the boat and joined him. He took hold of her arm. "Straight ahead."

It took a moment, but she finally saw a boat in the distance. "Are they going to see us?"

"Of course. They're headed right for us." He let go of her and headed for the rear of the boat. "Come on." He glanced at her. "Don't fall in now that help's on the way."

"I won't."

They returned to the rear deck, and Poppie picked up the bottles and returned them to the cabinet in the galley. When she came back out, she said, "I don't want them to think we've been partying out here."

He smiled. "Not sure you're going to be able to hide the fact you've had a few."

"Of course I can." She straightened her jacket and ran a hand through her hair. "How do I look?"

"Like you've been through a hurricane."

"Thanks a lot."

Chapter Twenty-Eight

"They don't just pop out."

When the Coast Guard ship got to within a thousand yards of them, the captain honked the horn and flashed the lights. Jasper honked back at them, then waved a greeting.

When the ship seemed to stop, Poppie looked worried. "Why are they stopping?"

"They're going to send a smaller boat."

They watched the men lower an inflatable runabout into the water, and three of them climbed aboard. The motor started, and the boat headed toward the Dragonfly.

When they got closer, Poppie peered at the men aboard. "Is that Lewis?" She looked at Jasper. "It's Lewis. He knows I'm alive."

Jasper smiled at her excitement, then watched the inflatable pull up beside the Dragonfly. Lewis was aboard along with two men from the

Coast Guard. They went to the end of the boat and tied off, then asked permission to come aboard.

"By all means. Get the hell up here."

Lewis came up first and went directly to Poppie. He hugged her. Stepped back and checked her out, then hugged her again. Then he went to Jasper and held out his hand.

Jasper took Lewis' hand with his left. "Sorry. My shoulder's out of commission again."

"Thank you for taking care of her." He glanced around the boat. "Is he in custody?"

Jasper took a step back. "He went over in the storm last night."

"Shit. It must've been bad."

Jasper nodded. "It was."

Lewis went back to Poppie and put his arm around her. "You're okay?"

"I'm fine."

He studied her for a moment, then leaned in close. "Are you drunk?"

She laughed. "No. Of course not."

Lewis looked at Jasper, who shrugged. "I'm going to need a full accounting of what happened on this boat."

The two Coast Guard men came up, and Lewis introduced them to Jasper and Poppie. The older one, Lieutenant Evans, took Jasper's hand for a moment. "We'll get you to the ship and get you home. What's the condition of the Dragonfly?"

"Just out of gas. She's sound. Got us...well, most of us, through the hurricane last night."

"You can give our captain a full report. We'll get her back to Gracie Island for you."

They helped Poppie and Jasper into the inflatable, then headed for the Coast Guard ship.

When Jasper saw Poppie glancing back at the Dragonfly, he leaned toward her. "You look a little sad."

"Well, she did keep us safe."

"That she did."

When they got to the ship, there was a medic alongside the captain, waiting for them as they came aboard.

Lewis made the introductions, then nodded toward Jasper. "He's going to need some medical attention, Dr. Howard."

Poppie smiled at the captain. "We also haven't eaten for two days."

The captain took her hand. "We'll get you to the mess hall, then."

When Jasper tried to follow, Dr. Howard stopped him. "Let's get that arm checked out. I'll have some food sent to the infirmary for you."

Jasper nodded as he watched Poppie and Lewis leave with the captain.

The doctor tapped him on the shoulder. "She'll be fine."

"Yeah. I know." He sighed, then followed the man down below decks to the infirmary.

The examination room in the infirmary was clean and shiny and filled with the latest medical technology, which made Jasper think of Poppie's comment about Dr. Hannigan's clinic. She was right. It was a bit outdated. He looked at all the machines. He'd take outdated over all this any day.

Dr. Howard nodded toward the stainless steel table with a thin black cushion. "Take a seat. What's going on here?" He took off Jasper's shirt, then began probing his shoulder.

"I dislocated it a week or so again. Then again a few days ago. Pretty sure it popped out again during the storm."

"They don't just pop out."

"Mine seems to."

"What were you doing?"

"Trying to keep Roger from going overboard."

"Am I to assume you weren't successful?"

"Yes, you can assume that. I couldn't hold him."

"Let's get an x-ray and see what's going on in there."

"An x-ray? Doc Hannigan just popped it back in."

"That could be why it keeps popping out." He helped Jasper off the table and led him into another room.

Jasper was once more impressed by the equipment. "Are all Coast Guard ships this well-equipped?"

"We're search and rescue. We never know what we might find, so we like to be prepared."

"So, will you go search for Roger?"

"If we're ordered to do so."

"Right."

Dr. Howard helped Jasper out of his thermal, then took several x-rays of his shoulder. When he finished, they returned to the examination room.

Jasper stopped walking when he saw James standing next to the examination table.

"Chief? What are you doing here?"

"How're you doing, Son?"

"I'm fine."

James looked at Dr. Howard. "Is he?"

"We'll know soon enough. The shoulder's in pretty bad shape. Honestly, I'm not sure how you're still on your feet."

James nodded. "My deputy is very good at compartmentalizing. Especially when it comes to pain."

Jasper sat on the table. "I lost Roger."

"I heard. I'm sure you tried your best to save him."

Dr. Howard seemed to pick up on the unease between Jasper and James, and he cleared his throat. "I'm going to go see about some food for you and check those x-rays."

The doctor left, and Jasper glanced at James. "I didn't think you'd be here. Who's minding the island?"

"The island will be fine until we get back." James stared at the white tile floor for a moment, then tucked in his shirt that didn't need tucking before glancing back at Jasper. "Your mother…we both… Dammit, we thought we lost you."

Jasper had never seen his father show emotion. Certainly not on his behalf. "You didn't. I'm fine."

"Yes, you are." He seemed to have gotten his control back. "You messed your shoulder up again?"

"When Roger got washed over, I grabbed him." He opened and closed his right hand. "He wouldn't let go of me and grab the boat. I told him… The next wave took him."

"I don't guess he's going to be missed by anyone."

"He had a wife. Apparently, his brother was planning to run off with the wife. Roger claims he didn't mean to kill him."

"Do you believe him?"

Jasper shrugged. "Doesn't really matter now whether I do or not."

"True." He glanced toward the door. "Seems like Poppie made it through okay."

"Yeah. She's a tough one."

The doctor returned with a tray of food in his hands and some x-ray film under his arm. He set the tray next to Jasper. It had a two-inch thick ham and cheese sandwich, along with a cup of coffee.

Jasper picked up the coffee and took a drink. "Thank you."

"The young lady insisted I include it with your lunch."

Jasper smiled, then glanced at James, who at least pretended like he didn't see Jasper's reaction to the mention of Poppie.

Dr. Howard looked at Jasper. "So, I took a look at your x-rays." He glanced at James.

Jasper swallowed a bite of sandwich, then nodded. "It's okay. Go ahead."

He put the four x-rays on a lighted board. "You've got quite a bit of damage here."

The doctor pointed at something in one of the films, but Jasper was more interested in his sandwich and coffee.

James, however, showed more curiosity. "So, what are we looking at?"

Jasper tried not to listen. He didn't want to hear it. He knew it'd only make it hurt more if he knew how much damage there was.

When the doctor finished talking, Jasper asked, "So, how do we fix it?"

"You're going to need surgery, Son."

Jasper set down the sandwich. "Surgery?"

"Afraid so. There won't be any popping it back in this time."

Jasper looked at James. "Guess I'm going to need to extend my vacation."

James smiled and shook his head. "We'll call it extended sick leave. You're not to come back to work until you're cleared by a doctor."

Jasper looked at Dr. Howard. "How long will that be?"

"Depends on how the surgery goes and how fast you recover. But I'd say you're looking at six weeks or so."

"Six weeks?"

"Or so." He took down the x-rays. "When we get closer to shore, we'll call in a chopper and have you flown to Augusta."

Jasper looked at James. "Augusta?"

"You'll get the best care there. Don't want to half-ass it."

Jasper sighed and pushed the last quarter of his sandwich aside, no longer hungry. "When will the chopper be here?"

The doctor checked his watch. "About an hour." He handed Jasper a hospital gown. "I'll see you before you go. You want some pain medication?"

"No. I'm fine."

The doctor left, and James approached the table. "Sorry, Son. But you'll be back in no time." He picked up the gown and held it open. Jasper put his left arm through it, and then James tied it in the back. "Can I do anything for you?"

"Will you track down Poppie? I'd like to see her before I go."

"Of course." He hesitated a moment before turning and heading for the door.

Jasper watched him, then sighed. "Dad?"

James turned back.

"Thanks for being here."

"Of course. You're welcome, Son." He opened the door. "I'll send Poppie in."

Jasper was second-guessing his decision to turn down the pain meds when the door opened, and Poppie walked in.

"Hey, big guy. How's it going?"

"It's not."

"I heard about your shoulder. Surgery?"

"Yeah. No big deal."

Poppie crossed the room and stood in front of him with her arms folded across her chest. "Of course it's a big deal."

He smiled at her. "You sobered up."

"I was never drunk. Just a little tipsy."

"We'll have to try harder next time."

She shook her head. "There's not going to be a next time."

"Sure there is. When you come back to visit Lewis. We'll play another round."

She smiled. "Fine. Maybe. But I get the first question."

"Okay."

She moved to the table and sat on Jasper's left side, then took his hand. "I'm going to miss you, Jasper Goodspeed."

"And I you." He was quiet for a few moments. "I want to apologize for—"

"No. You don't need to apologize for anything."

He hesitated again. "I seriously considered kissing you."

"I know."

"I'm not ready."

"I know that, too." She laid her head on his shoulder. "You saved my life. What more could I ask of you?"

"I guess that is a pretty big deal."

"It's huge." She straightened back up, then slipped off the table. "I want you to let me know how you're doing. Not through Lewis. I want direct contact. Call me. Write me a letter. Put an ad in the paper. Something."

"Okay."

"Okay." She walked around the room and started checking out the equipment.

"You probably shouldn't touch that stuff."

"I won't hurt it." When something she touched beeped at her, she jumped back.

Jasper laughed. "I told you not to mess with it."

She returned to the table and put a hand on Jasper's cheek. "You take care, Deputy Goodspeed."

"You too, Penelope."

Jasper watched Poppie leave and was surprised by how much he didn't want her to. When the door closed behind her, he got off the table and went to a reclining chair. He sat and adjusted it to a forty-five-degree angle, then closed his eyes.

When he heard the door, he opened his eyes, hoping Poppie had come back. But it wasn't her. It was Lewis who crossed the room and perched on the examination table.

"I heard they're flying you to Augusta for surgery."

"Yeah. That's the plan."

"I wanted to talk to you before you go." He studied the floor for a moment. "I wanted to thank you for going after Poppie."

"You don't need to thank me for that. I was just doing my job."

"Bullshit. It was so much more than that. So, thank you."

Jasper nodded. "I had to make sure she was safe."

Lewis gave him a little smile. "I know you're not ready to admit it yet, but I want you to know I approve." He got to his feet. "Not that you need or want my approval. I just wanted you to know."

"Lewis."

He held up his hands. "You don't need to say anything. I know you're not in a place to see it yet, but you and Poppie... Well, someday. *You* and Poppie."

Jasper leaned forward in the chair. "I do see it, Lewis."

Lewis grinned. "Good." He headed for the door. "Take it easy, Jasper. I'll see you when you get back home."

Chapter Twenty-Nine

"I'll be sure to bring my boxing gloves."

Jasper took Kat's hand. "Mom, stop. I'm fine. Quit fussing."

Kat stepped back from the hospital bed. "I just want you to be comfortable."

"I am. They're pumping me full of high-quality drugs. If I was any more comfortable, I'd be unconscious."

Kat smiled. "Okay." She sat in a chair next to the bed. "The doctor said you're doing well and should be able to come home by Wednesday."

"I'm shooting for tomorrow."

"Jasper."

"I miss home. I miss Penny and Pepper. Most of all, I miss your and Aunt Peg's cooking."

"Well, you'll be staying with me for a while. I'll fatten you right up."

Jasper frowned at her. "I'm not staying with you, Mom. And I don't want to get fat. I just want to be home."

"Your father's old camp trailer isn't home."

"It's home for now. And that's good enough." He looked at her for a moment. "I'll stay with you for a couple of days."

She smiled. "Thank you." She got to her feet. "Now. I'm going to let you get some rest." She kissed him on the cheek. "I'll see you in a bit."

Jasper watched her leave the room, then sighed. He was glad she was there, especially the first couple of days. But now? He was feeling better, and she was beginning to get on his nerves.

When the door opened again, Jasper said, "You really need to go take a walk or something."

"Okay, if you insist." Poppie stuck her head in the door. "But I kind of wanted to say hi, first."

Jasper grinned. "What the hell are you doing here?"

Poppie came into the room and stood at the end of the bed. "I've been waiting three days for some communication from you."

"Right. I was just composing the ad for the Globe. Deputy Goodspeed will make a full recovery."

"Good news for a change." She nodded toward the chair. "May I sit?"

"Of course. Why aren't you at your new job? You were supposed to start on Monday."

"Well, I told them about the traumatic trip I had to Maine, and they gave me a week to recover."

"You told them everything?"

"I may have left a few things out. It wasn't all traumatic." She leaned back in the chair and crossed her legs. "So, what's the prognosis?"

"I'll be good as new in six to eight weeks."

"If you follow doctor's orders and don't go back to work too soon?"

"Yeah."

"Which, of course, you're going to do."

"Of course."

"Who's here with you?"

"My mother." He pushed the button to raise the head of the bed a little and lowered his voice. "She's driving me crazy."

"She loves her son."

"I suppose." He adjusted his blanket. "So, when are you coming back to Gracie Island?"

"In the spring. Lewis said the winters are rainy, windy, and cold. I've kind of had enough of that for now. Besides, I should probably work for a few months before I ask for time off."

"Probably be a good idea. I bet you're glad to be back in Boston."

Poppie shrugged. "I guess. It feels different now. Crowded. Noisy."

"Wow. It only took you a week to fall in love with my island."

"I don't love your island."

"Whatever." He picked up a pink plastic cup filled with water and took a drink. "I want to talk to you about something."

She looked at him warily. "Okay."

"It's not a bad thing. At least, I don't think it is." He took another moment. "I want to clarify something. That day on the boat—"

"I know you're not ready, Jasper."

"Right. For now. What I want to clarify is, I will be. You've opened up the possibility of someone else, and I'm okay with that."

She gave him a little smile. "So, what are you saying?"

"I'm not asking you to wait for me. I mean, if Mr. Tiny Bottle of Rum is still in the picture…"

"He's not. He's married and expecting a child soon. He's very much out of the picture. There's no one in the picture."

"Good to know." He straightened his blankets again. "So, when you come back in the spring, maybe we could spend some more time sparring."

She laughed. "I'll be sure to bring my boxing gloves." She uncrossed her legs and leaned forward in the chair. "Just a couple of things, though. I'm not flying in your plane. No more boats. And no driving your stupid manual shift Jeep. And at the first sign of a hurricane. I'm out of there."

"You jinxed us. There hasn't been a murder on Gracie Island for seventy-five years. And we haven't had a hurricane in thirty. Also, you wouldn't have had to drive the *stupid* Jeep if you'd macraméd Roger better."

She opened her mouth, apparently unable to speak. She took a breath and glared at him. "Roger getting away had nothing to do with me having to drive your damaged self to town. And I certainly had nothing to do with him shooting his cheating brother." She pointed at him. "Why are you grinning at me?"

"I love making you mad."

She folded her arms across her chest. "You're such an—"

"Asshole? Just say it, Penelope. For me, just once. Say it."

"I'm not going to compromise my morals for you."

"Come on. You know you want to. Repeat after me. Deputy Jasper Goodspeed is an asshole."

More Books By Leigh Fenty

The Three Oaks Ranch Series

Memories Of You

The Good Son

The Wayward Son

Little Sis

The Carmichael Series

Deacon

Tobias

Abligale

Tanner

The Christmas Wedding

Faith's Journal

The Gracie Island Series

The Deputy
The Best Woman
The Chief
The Family Man
The Visitor

About the Author

Leigh spends her days with cute, sexy guys. Unfortunately, they're on paper. But still, not a bad way to spend your day. She also writes about strong, independent women, who can hold their own against these irresistible guys. She's not a pure romance writer, because she breaks the rules a bit. But that's the fun part. Leigh's stories have adventure, family relationships, and the struggles life throws at you sometimes. But boy always meets girl. They tussle a bit while they figure out what they really want. Then find their happily ever after. Even if it's not what they thought it was going to be.

Made in United States
Orlando, FL
16 October 2024